Forge Books by Juilene Osborne-McKnight

Daughter of Ireland
I Am of Irelaunde
Bright Sword of Ireland

Bright Sword
of Ireland

JUILENE OSBORNE-McKNIGHT

A TOM DOHERTY ASSOCIATES BOOK
NEW YORK

This is a work of fiction. All the characters and events portrayed in this book are either products of the author's imagination or are used fictitiously.

BRIGHT SWORD OF IRELAND

A Forge Book
Published by Tom Doherty Associates, LLC
175 Fifth Avenue
New York, NY 10010

www.tor.com

Forge® is a registered trademark of Tom Doherty Associates, LLC.

ISBN 0-765-35004-1
EAN 975-0765-35004-6

First edition: January 2004
First mass market edition: February 2005

Printed in the United States of America

0 9 8 7 6 5 4 3 2 1

For Aunt Vivvy,
our Niniane

ACKNOWLEDGMENTS

I would like to thank the following people for their invaluable assistance with this work: Randy Lee Eickhoff, who so delighted my mythology students and whose work on the Tain is comprehensive; De Sales University, where I teach Celtic Mythology and Irish Culture, for understanding that every act of teaching and learning is a sacred act, and particularly poet Stephen Myers, my department chair, who arranged my schedule so that I could write; Neville Gardner of Donegal Square in Bethlehem, Pennsylvania, my favorite Ulsterman, for his help with my geography; Cynthia Gibby for her assistance with my Latin; Deirdre MacFarland, my Irish teacher; Maddie, Mike, and the staff of my local Barnes & Noble for their hospitality and their help (and the coffee and toffee bars!); Bucks County Community College for their stunning collection of Celtic literature; Curtis Brown and especially Maureen Walters and Dave Barbor for all their work on my behalf; Claire Eddy for her superb and careful editorial eye; and Hoodster and Ubie, because you have been my friends since we were fifteen. Anybody who can put up with me (and with those nicknames) for that long deserves thanks. Most of all, I would like to thank my family, who sustain me through every sorrow and share with me every joy. To every reader who told me that they "could not put it down," I say a heartfelt thank you. This book, as every book, is for you, and I truly hope it keeps you up nights.

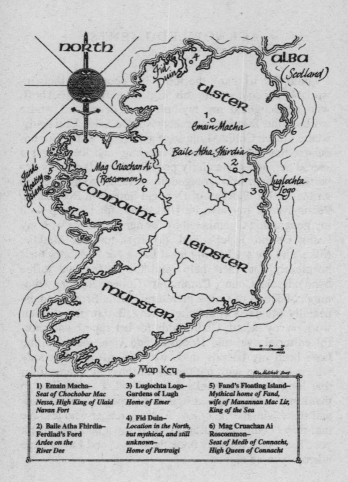

Map Key

1) **Emain Macha—**
*Seat of Chochobar Mac
Nessa, High King of Ulaid
Navan Fort*

2) **Baile Atha Fhirdia—**
Ferdiad's Ford
*Ardee on the
River Dee*

3) **Luglochta Logo—**
Gardens of Lugh
Home of Emer

4) **Fid Duin—**
*Location in the North,
but mythical, and still
unknown—
Home of Partraigi*

5) **Fand's Floating Island—**
*Mythical home of Fand,
wife of Manannan Mac Lir,
King of the Sea*

6) **Mag Cruachan Ai
Roscommon—**
*Seat of Medb of Connacht,
High Queen of Connacht*

GLOSSARY OF CHARACTERS,
PLACE NAMES, AND VOCABULARY

CHARACTERS

Ailill	As spelled
Aoife	Eefa
Cathbad	Caffa
Conall Cearnach	Conal Keernach
Conchobar	Conor
Conlaech	Conlach
Cuchulainn	Coo Hullen
Dechtine	Dektina
Deirdre	As spelled
Emer	Ayver
Fand	As spelled
Finnchad	Fincad
Froech	Frake
Jigahnsa	As spelled
Laeg mac Riangabra	Loyg mac Reeangavra
Levarcham	Levorsham
Maine Mathramail	Mahnee Mahravil
Medb	Mave
Morrigu	Mooreehoo
Badb	Bive
Macha	Maha
Nemain	Nevin
Nessa	As spelled
Niniane	Nineean
Naoise mac Uisliu	Noyshe mac Ishloo
Rochad	Rock'ed
Scathach	Skawha

Setanta   Shaydonda
Sualdem   Sooeldev

PLACE NAMES

Alba   Scotland, Wales,
                             England
Baile Cinn Trachta   Bawlya Kin Trawkta
Craebderg   Crayverg
Craobh Rioga   Crave Reeohga
Cruachan Ai   Crooahawneee
Cymri   Kimree (Wales or
                             Welsh)
Emain Macha   Evin Mawha
Eriu/Eire   Aireeoo/Aireh
Fid Duin   Fee Doon
Glen na Bodhar   Glen na Bawver
Muirthemne   Myoorheevna
Tete Brec   As spelled
Tir Inna m'Beo   Teer ne mo
Tir Nàn Og   Teer ne nog

VOCABULARY

Aither (a her)   father
Ard Ri (as spelled)   high king
Atrebates (ahtrebaytees) Eastern Briton Celtic
                             tribe
Bainfennid (banfenid)   outlaw woman
Bain sidhe (ban shee)   woman of the Other
Bodhran (baur an)   goatskin drum
Cnoc (knock)   hill
Curragh (cur ah)   small skin boat
Draiocht (dray oct)   magic
Fidchell (fid kell)   game similar to chess

Filidh (fee lee)	master poet or story-teller
Gae bolga (gay bowlga)	Cuchulainn's fishhook spear
In Cadabolg (as spelled)	the prototype for Ex Calibur
Lughnasa (loonasa)	August 14
Maither (ma her)	mother
Mo ghra (mow gra)	my beloved
Na caoine (na keeny)	keening or wailing, esp. at death
Ogham (om)	ancient Irish stick language
Partraigi (partraygee)	forest tribe of the stag
Riastradh (ri es tre)	Cuchulainn's war transformation
Rosc (rosk)	poem of high praise
Samhain (sau win)	October 31
Sidhe (shee)	the Others
Slan abhaile (slan awoya)	safe home; a farewell greeting
Suantraighe (soo en tra ee)	sleeping music, played on a harp
Welisc (wellish)	Roman name for the Welsh

BOOK ONE

The Rosc of Medb

THE ROSC OF MEDB

Autumn-haired is our Medb
  glorious our red queen
see her skin of milk
  her lissome, fearless form
battle-eager, fire warrior
  with speed her chariot comes
her blown tresses caught by wind,
  her many-colored cloak a banner
how sweet the fire of our Medb,
  who calls for battle as for mead
who rewards her soldiers with sweetness
  milky thighs of our generous queen
deep in every warrior's desire
  one night in firelight with Medb
many shields will be reddened
  great forests of slaughter
the boy Cuchulainn wearied
  for the war of our great queen
for her heart's most deep desire
  the brown bull of Cuailnge
fitting treasure for our hungry queen
  none will stay from battle
in the hope of one night's succor
  we brave the boy Cuchulainn
we will not fear his magic
  protectors from the sidhe
for Connacht's great queen
  we dare the men of Ulster
arise you warriors of Ulster
  arise and come
heed the call of the Connachtsmen.

1

I waded into the water carefully, placing my feet between the stones that lined the riverbed. Moonlight streamed over me like snow; my cloak spread behind me on the water like a tipped sail. When the water reached almost to my chin, I did as my mother had taught me in childhood.

"Let your head carry you," she admonished as I struggled against the current. "Don't fight the water. Your body is the *curragh* of Eriu; let it skim on the surface of the water." But I, naked and skinny, her mouse-brown, desperate child, had never been able to achieve that floating calm. Daughter of Medb of Connacht, afraid of a little water, clinging and thrashing.

Eventually, exasperated by my flailing arms and frightened mewlings, Medb would abandon me midriver, wading naked to the shore, shaking her head in disgust as my father hurried forward with her cloak. Sodden and terrified, I would paw my way to the riverbank and collapse weeping in the mud.

I remembered this now in utter calm. The overblown moon beckoned with its wide white path across the water. I leaned back beneath it in the silvery light, let my head lift the weight of my body, just as she had taught me to do.

Then I had been five; now I boasted twenty summers. Then I had been naked and shivering. Now I was swathed in my heaviest woolen gown, in my cloak lined with ermine, in my sandals weighted with gold and silver trim. Then my heart had ached for her love and approval. Now I had no heart. And now I was fearless, as clear and cold as this river in moonlight. Medb would be proud of me now. I shook my head. Not so. Neither Medb nor my father would even know that I had gone. They would think only that I had ridden off with my new husband. Perhaps they were feeling triumphant delight that their little daughter was now the perfect spy in Ulster. It would be weeks before they realized that I was gone. Even Rochad Mac Faitheman, he to whom they had sold me, did not know.

Well enough. I had always been the one alone. It was fitting to depart in this way. The clouds shifted, silver white across the disc of moon.

"This is what I will remember," I said aloud to the night gods. "This wind, this moonlight, these scudding clouds. I thank you for the gift of beauty at my dying."

I felt the water begin to tug me down from below and I imagined the Others, waiting beneath the surface to take me in, to bear me on the current out to sea, on to Tir Nàn Og. Would Froech be among them there, my lost beloved?

I drew in one last breath of air. My face slid beneath the surface and the water closed above me like ice-cold silk. From beneath the water, I kept my eyes open, fixed on the moon, prepared to draw in the breath of water that would carry me to the deep river bottom.

I felt the horse before I saw it, felt the thud of hooves on the river bottom, the churning when the water grew too deep.

Terror overtook me. I could not let him take me!

I sucked in a mouthful of water, drew it into my lungs.

The horse was above me then, snorting and tossing, a black water dragon. I saw the hand descend from the saddle, saw the leather arm shield. The hand closed around

my hair. Darkness came up from the sides of my eyes
then, closing me in a tunnel, narrowing my sight. I welcomed it. Just before it enclosed me entirely, I felt a swell
of pride. I had defeated him, had defeated them both. My
loathed enemy—Rochad—my husband. And my mother.

My eyes opened to a room lit by warm fire, redolent with
a wondrous smell. Over a hanging cauldron, a tiny woman
stirred a brewing mash. Her door hanging parted for a second and a man ducked beneath the lintel, then stood. His
skin was black as Rochad's horse, beautiful and gleaming.
His hair curled around his head in tightly wound springs
of grey, stitched with gleaming black. His upper arms
were tattooed with symbols I had not seen among my people. Around his neck he wore a scarf of the finest silk, pat-
terned in turquoise and gold; it was wound several times
around his throat. He murmured to the little woman in a
tongue I had never heard before. In response, she turned in
my direction.

She was as tiny as he was massive, her motions quick
and precise. Her hair was a close-cropped cap of dark
auburn curls, shorter than my own shorn locks. Her eyes
were a deep brown.

They were not of my people, not of the tribes of Eriu.

Joy surged through me.

So I had succeeded! I had robbed him of his prize!
Robbed my mother of her war booty. The river had borne
me down and I had awakened in Tír Nàn Og. Surely these
two were of the Other. I watched them wide-eyed.

The dark man spoke again, ducked beneath the door
hanging and disappeared into the night.

The little woman approached me, placed her palm
against my forehead. She lowered her face toward mine. I
lay perfectly still, though I could feel my eyes widen further at her approach. The Other are known for their surprising and dangerous ways.

When her face was almost next to mine, she did something I had never experienced in my life. She pressed her lips, warm and gentle, against my forehead. Tears sprang unbidden to my eyes at so welcoming a gesture. She drew back slightly.

"*Bain Sidhe*," I addressed her respectfully. "Woman of the Other, I am Finnabair, daughter of Medb. I have crossed the river of death and request residence here in Tir Nàn Og among the Other Ones."

"Ah, child," she said softly. She sat down beside me and I edged my naked body beneath the warm furs to give her room. She lifted my hand and pressed the back of it gently against her cheek.

"So that's the way of it, then?"

"Will you give me shelter?"

She sighed, a huge gusting of wind.

"Child, you are not dead. You remain in Tir Inna m'Beo, the Land of the Living."

"No! Oh no." I clutched at her hand. "But you. You are not of my people. What are you if not a woman of the Other?"

"I am Niniane. I am of the people the Romans call Welisc. We dwell in the hills and mountains across the water from Eriu. Many years ago, I was sold here as a slave."

"So you are not of the Other."

"Only an Outsider. Only that."

"And the dark one?"

For a moment her eyes looked confused and then she smiled.

"That is Flavius. Flavi."

"He is Other?"

"He is a Nubian, brought from Egypt. Once he, too, was a slave of the Romans. Once he was my rescuer; now he is my friend."

"Where am I? How did I come here?"

I led my gaze around the spare room with its sleeping platform and fire. Countless bundles of herbs and flowers hung upended from the ceiling and bowls with heavy crushing stones covered every bench and table. The woman stood and began to stir the mash.

"This is Flavi's dwelling. You were brought here to me by Rochad, warrior of Ulster. He fished you from the river near the war camp of Medb of Connacht where you were drowning. You would have remembered all of this, but he threw you over his saddle, the great lout." She made a motion of disgust, waved her tiny hand in the air. "Still, I suppose it was that which caused you to throw up the river water and so return to the living."

"I did not wish to return."

She did not question me, came instead and sat beside me again, regarding me steadily. Finally she spoke.

"Twice in my life I have wished to die. Now I look back on each time with the certain knowledge of all that I would have missed had I gone over the water at those times."

I shook my head. "You cannot understand. I will never wish to live again. Because of me, seven hundred men have died. Seven hundred!"

"And your death would return them to life?" Her tone was arch, almost chiding.

"No. I am neither fool nor child. They are gone. I am the cause of their dying. Someone must make sacrifice for that loss!"

Understanding flooded her eyes.

What she did next was most strange. She stood, walked to the door of the hut, peered out into the darkness, listening. Then she came back and sat beside me. When she spoke again, it was in a whisper.

"Someone will bear this for you. It need not be you, Finnabair, daughter of Medb."

"I do not understand. Someone stood in for me? Was it my mother?"

"Your mother? No, certainly. Medb of Connacht lives and is well." Her tone turned wry. "As always and ever, she is Medb."

Hoofbeats thundered into the clearing outside the hut. I knew who it would be before he swept into the room. Rochad. Rochad the Beautiful, the women called him. Rochad the Warrior. For one day, I had thought of him that way. Now I knew better. Rochad the Deceiver, the Liar. My husband. The one to whom I had been sold.

"Protect me," I whispered in terror to the little woman. "Please do not give me to him."

I closed my eyes, feigned unconsciousness, wished for it fervently.

He swept into the chamber on a cold draft of wind.

"How does the daughter of Medb?"

This he shouted at tiny Niniane. Blessings upon her, the little woman protected me.

"Hush," she said. "Her spirit has not returned to her body. Your great loudness will scare it further away. Step out into the night."

I risked peering through slitted eyes as she pushed him before her through the door. He loomed nearly twice her height, but she seemed unafraid, pushing at him with her birdlike hands. Outside, I could hear a softly whispered conference.

"Who stands at the ford?"

"Cuchulainn. He is tireless at the river."

It was at that moment that I knew where I would go and what I must do next. What sorrows more would arise from this decision I could not know. Nor did I care. I am familiar with sorrow; it is my trusted companion. Though they continued to whisper beyond the door, I closed my eyes and sighed, calm again.

The little woman returned alone, the smell of her wonderful spice wafting before her through the doorway. I remained still until I heard his hoofbeats retreating into the distance. I opened my eyes.

"He is gone."

"He is."

"Thank you for keeping me from him."

"Do you fear him?"

Her eyes were soft, sympathetic. I knew suddenly that with this woman, it was not necessary to pretend at bravery as I must do with my mother.

"Yes," I said simply. "But I loathe him more than I fear him."

"Why?"

"He played for me by trickery and deceit. He purchased me to marriage, and he a warrior of the enemy army, an Ulsterman." I made a rude sign for the enemy armies. "He made a dark bargain with my mother, this Rochad. And by that trickery, seven hundred men have died. He repulses me! Overlarge and overloud and a dishonest great brute. I will never be wife to such a one as that!"

"Ah," she nodded. "I, too, was forced into marriage with one of his kinsmen. I, too, was sore afraid."

"Who forced you?" I asked her.

"The one who sold me as a slave." She shrugged. "He sold me for a good price."

She stirred the bubbling mash again, then brought me a bowlful. She spooned it gently into my mouth.

It burned a little at the back of my river-raw throat, but the smell and taste of it was delicious. I reached up for a second bite like a starveling bird, surprised and a little ashamed at my appetite, for one who would have chosen a watery death short hours earlier.

"What is the spice? I have never tasted such a thing."

She smiled with delight.

"It is called cinnamon."

"It is not a spice of our people. Did you bring it from among the Welisc?"

"No, sweeting, I brought it all the way from Egypt."

I shook my head in confusion at the strange name.

"Egypt is—an outpost of the Roman Empire. A desert place of sand and of beautiful cities."

"Rome I have at least heard of, in bardic tales. How is it that you were in Rome?"

"My father was Roman. My mother was Welisc." Her eyes filled suddenly with remembered sorrow.

I regarded her with curiosity and respect.

"It would seem that your life has been both broad and wide."

She laughed.

"Ah, Finnabair, it has been both of those, surely."

"I, too, was sold into marriage, Niniane. Like a horse. Like a gold neck ring. Would you know who sold me?"

"All have heard," she said softly, but I told her anyway.

"My mother, Queen Medb of Connacht."

"So I was told," she said softly. She cradled my hand.

"And this great Rochad. The beast they call my husband. How is it that you know him?"

She fed me another spoonful of the cinnamon porridge, her eyes regarding me above the spoon. When my mouth was full of the mash, she spoke.

"Finnabair," she said, "Rochad is my son."

2

Perched on a rock in the middle of the river sat the boy warrior of Ulster. All night, in the quiet hours after I had slipped away from the hut of Niniane, I had watched this boy from my position behind a thick copse of underbrush and trees. Even in the wide moonlight, even having heard Niniane and Rochad whisper of his place here in the river, it had been difficult in darkness to tell where the rock ended and the warrior began, so still was he in the moonlight, so fused with the giant boulder. I admired his stillness; my mother had been always restless, always moving, always driving those around her to action. My childhood had been filled with her admonitions to move, to run, to waste no more hours in silent contemplation. But this boy had contained himself in absolute stillness until dawn.

What would he choose for me now that the sun had risen, for soon, soon, I would gather my courage, make myself known. Surely his war rage would be unleashed then, that I, the daughter of Medb, would accost him once again. And when he was in his rage, then would I pay the price I had come to offer. The light had pearled up around us while I thought. The boy shifted on his rock. I watched him closely.

When last I had encountered him, my terror had been so great that nothing had registered but watery fear. But now I could see him clear in morning light. I shook my head in disbelief. This was the warrior all of my kinsmen feared, the one they called the Hound, the name that sent shivers through the men of Connacht? The man for whose death I had been sold into marriage . . .

Cuchulainn.

He seemed too young to carry upon his shoulders all the warriors of Ulster. And yet, that was what he did, for all of the Ulstermen suffered under a curse that rendered them unable to fight or even to rise up at certain times of the year. Momentarily, I wondered how such a curse had come upon them and by whom. I had never asked my mother, having no interest in the life of a warrior. And yet, she had based her whole war strategy around this curse somehow, sending warrior after warrior against this boy on the rock. I shook my head in incomprehension. How foolish it had all seemed to me. Until I was made a pawn in the war game. Now I wished that I knew all. I looked again at the boy on the rock.

Much upon my own years, he was still at least a head shorter than I. How had I not noticed that before? His body was dense and compact, as though a man's height had been crumpled down into a boy's frame. This made him bulky. Thick bands of muscle rippled across his abdomen and flexed in his legs when he stood, which he now did periodically, to throw what looked like bones toward the riverbank. His arms were thick and heavy and no bone missed its mark.

When he lowered himself to a sitting position again, he seemed to simply fold down, as fog curls around the base of a mountain. He resumed picking at whatever bird or game he was eating with obvious delight, chewing and chuckling aloud. Where had he come by food? Surely he had not left the rock in all the hours I had watched him.

How strange he was to look upon. His red-gold hair curled around his head in springy tight whorls. Evidently no artifice was needed to achieve this bizarre effect, for periodically the wind would pick up the hair, move it about, realign it in some wild new pattern. It looked like so much sprung milkweed, and I doubted that a comb had ever passed through it.

And then his face. It was broad and heavy, with double chins and a bulbous nose. I had heard stories that the women of Ulster admired him, vied for his attentions, offered him their services. Did they do so with their eyes closed?

My hand strayed to my own shorn locks and I felt a hot blush of shame creep up my face. What was I doing, after all? Would he remember me?

He started to whistle. The sound was captivating; perfect birdcalls issued from his mouth. Perhaps that was his appeal, then. Sound and not sight.

He stopped.

"Do you like what you see or what you hear?" He called this aloud to the open air.

I looked around, wondering whom he addressed.

"You, girl with the brown hair, there in the ermine cloak."

Gods, the man had seen me!

My heart hammered in my chest and blackness began at the sides of my eyes as it always did when I was afraid. I took a deep breath and steadied my hand on the trunk of a tree. I stood, but still kept out of his line of vision.

"How did you know I was here?"

"I smelled you; your cloak smells like dried river water and horse."

I lifted the folds of my once-beautiful ermine cloak, not completely dried by the fire of Niniane. I sniffed at it.

"So it does."

Cuchulainn thought this was funny; he began to laugh, tumbling backwards on the rock, kicking his feet in the air.

"You stink, girl," he said. "Now that is a thing that women love to hear."

Something about it caught at me, I can't say why. I began to laugh, and the laughter, so many years imprisoned, refused to stop. I laughed until my breath left my body, until I dropped to the ground, undone by laughter, the smelly cloak swallowing me up. Suddenly, the laughter folded down into tears and the two rolled over each other like wind and water. At last it wound down. Hiccuping, breathing deeply, I stopped. Cuchulainn was no longer laughing. Legs crossed, head cocked, he sat watching me from the rock.

I sat up, keeping my face concealed behind the trunk of a tree.

He smiled pleasantly.

"Well, now. We shall converse. Have we met before? Beautiful but foul smelling. Can I overlook one for the other? Ah, well, some seem to do that for me."

He stood and made a flourishing bow.

"I am Setanta, called Cuchulainn. Have you come to seduce me? Most women do."

Again I burst into laughter.

"Do they? Why?" I realized how rude the question was, made a deprecating motion with my hand. "I mean no offense."

"None taken. They come for three reasons. Some have heard that I am a hero. Some wish to win me from my beloved. Some wish my death."

Had he recognized me then? I hung my head in shame.

"Girl, which are you?"

"Well, which of them wins you?"

He shouted aloud with laughter. "A good answer. A good question. You are more clever by half than most. I will tell you which one wins me. Only the one who can be

my friend. For I am no hero, except in story, none could
win me from my beloved, and those who wish my death
have failed. But she who could be my friend would soon
learn that I truly like women; few do, girl."

"Truly, that has been my experience," I called from
behind my tree. "But what is it that you like about
women?"

"I like that their laughter sounds like bells. I like that
when they walk, it looks like water. I like how they look
and how they smell. Or at least how most of them smell."
He grinned in my direction from the rock. "I like that they
puzzle and puzzle at language until language yields them
an answer. Wisdom from words. Wordplay. I like that so
few of them wield weapons to make war. Though of
course they do make war. With words. And that I like as
well. I cannot win against the words of women; the
strangeness of that losing delights my heart.

"And now, Stinkweed." He smiled in my direction.
"Who are you and why have you come?"

I stepped from behind my tree, dragging up cloak and
brown grasses that clung to it. I had pictured all of this as
much more dignified, certainly not so smelly. I swatted at
the weeds clinging to my hair.

"I am Finnabair. Last night I tried to cross to Tir Nàn
Og in the river, but I failed. So I bring myself to you. We
have met before, Cuchulainn."

He shook his head, perplexed. "Do I know you?"

I sighed. So he, too, had forgotten.

"I am Finnabair, sold in marriage to Rochad, warrior of
Ulster. By that transaction seven hundred men have died."

"By the gods! You are the daughter of Medb. I remember you now!"

What happened next was terrifying. He stood on the
rock; he seemed to gain in size and strength. He looked toward me, one eye bulging, and then he leaped! The rock
was in the middle of the river, as far from me as ten chariots length, but the great leap carried him to me.

I turned to run; his hand caught in the cloak. His voice was soft.

"Have we not played this game before, Finnabair? Do not run from me again. Do not fear me."

I clasped both of my hands to the sides of my head, caught as much hair as I could in my fists.

Behind me Cuchulainn began to chuckle.

"Turn around; let me see your shorn locks."

I turned slowly and regarded him. His eyes were intense blue; one seemed larger than the other. His mouth was wide and sensual; his arms were tree trunks. All of his energy was concentrated in the stillness of that body, in its great muscularity, the smell of it like sage and peat fires. In that instant I knew why the women came to him.

He whispered softly, "Do not fear me, Finnabair."

"I fear everything," I said.

Tears welled in my eyes and I began to shake. My limbs grew watery. He held me up with one arm, unpinned the cloak. He lifted my curls, which had grown to shoulder length, let them spill along his hand.

"I am a fine barber," he said, and he grinned at me.

Anger rose in me, or perhaps weariness with all of it. "I liked it long, Hound. It came almost to my knees."

"I kept the braids," he said cheerfully. "Do not worry; I will return them to you."

"What? Will you pin them to my head with your brooch?"

He hooted with laughter, called out to the field around him. "She is a witty one, no?" But he did not remove his huge hand from my upper arm.

I looked around, perplexed again by his odd behavior.

Out of the reeds by the river a man arose. Where Cuchulainn was squat and muscular, this one was himself a reed, tall and too thin, all angles and bones, from his nose to his elbows to his knees. His brown hair was knotted back in a braid and he wore a white tunic, brown cloak, and sandals. On his forehead was the deep red-gold circlet of the charioteer.

Cuchulainn turned to me, as if he were making a formal introduction in the Hall.

"This water-reed is my charioteer, Laeg mac Riangabra. Laeg, may I present Finnabair, daughter of Medb."

He turned to Laeg.

"Did you hear all?"

"I did. When did you meet this one before? Where was I?"

"It was one of those times when I sent you to fetch Emer to me. This one came—or perhaps was sent—with a man who was dressed as her father, King Ailill."

Cuchulainn turned to me suddenly, his face shifting into anger, the blue eyes sparking. So this was it then, the beginnings of his famous war rage. I braced myself to accept it. Had I not come here to die? He shouted at me.

"Do they think me stupid, your father and Medb, that they could fool me with that character? Even standing at the edge of the river, I could see that he was no king."

I hung my head.

"He was the camp fool. We called him Tamun the Stump."

"More fools they to send me such a one. Two words from his mouth and I could hear that he was no king."

A little anger moved in me for poor old Tamun, who, like me, had been nothing more than a pawn.

"You killed him with a stone from your slingshot. A poor old man who had never done you harm," I lashed out angrily, shaking myself against the bond of his hand.

"Finnabair, I did not know that he was the camp fool. I thought he had been sent to kill me. Do you know how many your mother has sent against me? And what was I supposed to believe? That she had in all honesty sent her only daughter to bed me?"

I lowered my eyes.

"I was to be your distraction, to keep you from this rock, from fighting the warriors of my mother's army." My face flamed. My father refusing to accompany me, sending the poor fool in his stead, my mother calling her last words to me, jocular and sure of her newest plan, "Bed him often and well. Keep him distracted enough that we can cross the river into Ulster." And then the further shame of Cuchulainn's utter rejection.

He chucked my chin up with his hand. The anger seemed to have gone out of him. How changeable he was. Now his blue eyes were dancing with mischief.

"Oh, I did like the dress you wore that day," he said. "I remember it well." He turned to Laeg. "You should have seen it, friend Laeg. Thin as a fog, gossamer and white. Through that dress, I could see everything, the round apples of this fertile plain." His hand brushed at my neck. "And the golden triangle below."

"I miss all the good events," grumbled the charioteer. "For me, it's just battles and driving."

Cuchulainn laughed aloud. "And that so tedious and dull."

He moved his face close to mine, spoke softly.

"So tell me, Finnabair. Why has she sent you now? Is it not enough for her that I cut off your hair? How will she have me return you now?"

"Medb did not send me." I spoke the words clearly, but my legs had turned to porridge beneath me. Only Cuchulainn's strong arm kept me standing.

"No, truly? Then who did?"

"I came here of my own will."

"Ah, then, let us see. The last time you came before me, I killed your fool, cut off your braids, and tied you to a pillar stone."

Again a little puff of anger moved in me.

"Why did you do that? Was it not enough that you cut off all my hair?"

Cuchulainn actually looked wounded.

"Finnabair, you passed out. Right here in the field, with me holding your braids in my hand. I could not very well carry you back among your people, could I? Should I have left you lying in the grass so that the carrion birds and wolves could find you? I tied you to the stone so that your people would find you safely."

"Then why did you cut off my hair?"

"It was a message. I could have killed you. And it is growing back nicely." Again he lifted his hands through my brown curls.

"So, your mother still quests after her bull. Tell me truly now. We think her mad in Ulster. No one wages war for a bull, Finnabair."

"It is not the bull, it is the power of the bull."

He watched me intently, his whole body cocked for listening. Something about the fullness of that attention, its completeness, gave my tongue courage.

"My mother is a woman and a queen. Her power must be equal to that of my father, superior to that of her warriors. To own the bull is to match my father, who owns the white bull Finnbennach. To send her warriors to fight you is to wield the power to win the bull. Thus, Medb rules over all. Do you see?"

"You have made me see as she sees, yes. And you, Finnabair? You are her willing tool, come to offer yourself to me again, to make of me a little doorway so that your mother can pass through?" His eyes were insolent, burning, but his mouth quirked. I met his eyes directly.

"I have come to offer you my life."

Cuchulainn was so startled that he dropped my arm. My legs began to crumple underneath me, and he reached out and steadied me against him.

"I do not understand. Has Medb put you up to this? She would have you die by my hand? And for what? Passage into Ulster? This is repugnant, mother, warrior, or queen."

"No. You mistake me. Medb does not know that I have

come. My death would not serve her well. None knows that I have come." I thought briefly of Rochad. I shook my head. I sounded as though I were defending Medb, the mother who had betrayed me. I drew a deep breath. Best to tell it to him clear and unvarnished.

"Medb sold me in marriage to Rochad Mac Faitheman, a warrior of Ulster. While he was captive among my people, that marriage was . . . sealed." I blinked against the shame of it, my stupidity. "But Rochad returned to his people. In his wake, the chiefs of my own country discovered that they had been cheated of their bargains. Many of them had been promised my favors if only they could . . . well, if only they could assist my mother with her goals."

"Kill me, you mean."

"Yes, I do."

"And so what of their disappointment? Men have lost women to their rivals since time began."

"In their anger at my mother, at the breaking of the bargain, they fell to war with her and with each other. Seven hundred of my kinsmen died in that war among the clans. And I am the cause. I must make sacrifice. I offer you my life, Cuchulainn of Muirthemne."

Abruptly, then, he did drop me; I crumpled to the ground at his feet.

"I will not take it."

I looked up at him from my seat on the ground. "I must make sacrifice."

"What sacrifice? Sacrifice for the lust of a group of old men who hunger after your sweet, white thighs? Sacrifice for your mother who started this foolish war over her selfish desire to own the Brown Bull of Ulster? Tell me something, Finnabair. Would you have bedded me on that day they sent you to me in your thin, white tunic?"

"Of course."

"Why?"

"Because someone has to end this foolish war. I would bed with whomever she sent to me, bed all of both armies, if it would stop this fighting, cease the death of all my kinsmen."

Now he knelt beside me, lifted my chin.

"I see that you are a person of honor, Finnabair, not so much the daughter of Medb. So I will tell you what I know. Seven hundred did not die."

"What say you?"

"Propaganda, Finnabair. They wish me to think seven hundred of the forces of Connacht were depleted by this foolishness over Finnabair. They think that I may become too confident. Or careless. And they wish me to think that you are a prize worth seven hundred men. So I will hunger to have you. But I have spies." He shrugged.

"How many died?"

He looked away, looked back. He seemed to be gauging my ability to hear it. Or perhaps his wisdom in telling it to me, the daughter of Medb. He sighed, spread his arms wide.

"Seventy died."

Giddy relief and sorrow warred inside me.

"This is true? Absolute truth?"

"Seventy men and their minions fighting each other for the sake of their lust, for the promise of your thighs. None of this is upon you, Finnabair. I see now that you are no more than a pawn on Medb's *fidchell* board. Your guilt was heavier than that cloak, Stinkweed. Perhaps the truth will lighten it."

"It is seventy more than my soul wishes to bear, but it is better, Hound."

"A warrior bears what he or she must."

I swam up from my sorrow then, remembered that he was Cuchulainn, that he had killed dozens of Connachtsmen, most of them my kinsmen.

"Oh, gods, why am I here? This seemed like such a good and just idea in the dark by Niniane's fire."

"Perhaps it was."

"No, I am, as always, a fool."

"A fool does not seek justice, does not understand that the soul must cleanse itself of darkness." He lifted my chin. "Perhaps you are a true human being, Finnabair, daughter of Medb."

"I came to die."

"Do you wish that still?"

"I do not know what I wish."

"Perhaps you wish not death, but freedom. Perhaps there we can help you after all."

He turned to Laeg.

"What say you, old friend? Shall we take on a pupil?"

Laeg replied, his voice caustic.

"The daughter of your enemy, she who started this great war, most envious and grasping of all the chiefs of Eriu, her daughter will be our pupil."

"Only that such service will expiate the deaths she caused."

"Oh, yes, only that."

"No other motivation."

Laeg nodded. His voice, when he spoke, was heavy with sarcasm.

"Well, on the strength of so obvious and simple a reason, I say why not? If we cannot find enough trouble in all the armies of Connacht, then it must come looking for us. And we should welcome it in; after all, that's what we do."

They fell to laughing, clapped each other on the upper arms. Cuchulainn held out his hand to me.

"Come then, Stinkweed. Let's get you to camp and start by doing something about that foul-smelling cloak."

3

They scrubbed my cloak, the two of them, rubbing it on rocks by the river, clucking over soaps and herbs and stink like two washerwomen. I sat by their fire, chewing the meat from a rabbit the two of them had cooked, throwing the bones like a dog-hunter. At the edge of the forest, a grey wolf skulked along the tree line. Cuchulainn deliberately threw every bone in its direction. The wolf skittered away and returned. This made both Cuchulainn and Laeg laugh aloud. What a strange pair they were. I began to memorize the evening as a story, to take with me, but where? I belonged nowhere, pawn of Medb and Ailill, castoff of Rochad mac Faitheman. Perhaps still I belonged in Tir Nàn Og, the country of the dead. There, at least, I would find Froech, my one beloved, who had loved me because I was Finnabair.

The twosome finished their work, came to sit at flanks with me. So companionable a pair, jesting at each other and laughing over old, remembered stories while they tore at rabbit and gorged themselves on mead. Envy of them flowed through me like water. Oh, to belong somewhere like this.

At last Cuchulainn wiped the back of his hand across

his mouth. He rubbed his hands together, grinning at me, a little stain of grease at the base of his chin. I pointed at it, ducked my head. He brought up the corner of his cloak, rubbed his entire face.

"Ah, well," he said, evidently abandoning the task.

Beside him Laeg shrugged. "There are other things you do well," he said. "Sartorial splendor is not one of them."

"True enough." The boy warrior gave a great windy sigh.

"Is the wolf your companion?" I asked.

"What wolf?"

"The dark one by the woods line. You have a very long throw; once or twice you have winged her with your rabbit bones."

"You have very long sight." He regarded me intensely for a moment; his countenance brightened.

"Girl," he said. "Your coming here must be fortuitous. We have no enemies to fight tonight."

"Your mother keeps him busy," Laeg said, as he added a log to the fire.

"That she does," said Cuchulainn. "That she does. One warrior after another. But this evening we have time for stories. Finnabair, you begin."

"Me? I am no *filidh,* trained for the fireside tale." My heart began to beat rapidly. "My tongue will tie. I will not be able to finish the tale. Medb has told me so often. 'Mushmouth,' she calls me."

"Mushmouth," said Cuchulainn. "I do not like it as well as Stinkweed. But perhaps I will. Tell me the Mushmouth story."

I laughed aloud. "You have no courtesies, Hound of Chulainn."

"None," he answered cheerfully. "So tell."

"It happened first when I was young. We were riding across the plain in my mother's chariot. I was standing before her, as I always did, holding tight to the wickerwork and quivering with terror at her wild style of driving.

Above us winged a flock of birds, silver in the sunlight. Far to the west they flew and landed at the crest of a distant hill."

I paused looking into the fire, looking back.

"Even now I do not know if I can make you see. I followed their flight with my eyes and gazed at the hill where they had landed. It was as if the hill were made of water and I could see within. Beneath its surface there were Others dwelling and they were . . . so beautiful . . . so completely strange. I pointed at the hill and Medb, thinking I wished to reach it, laughed aloud in delight and whipped at her horses' backs. We thundered toward it. I screamed over the horses' hooves, 'No, no, the ones inside,' but with the rush of the wind and the speed of the chariot, she could not hear me. At last we stopped before the hill and I flung myself against it, screaming, 'Let me come in, let me come in.' Medb yanked me up and demanded to know what I was screaming about. I tried to tell her. I tried to say, 'They are in there,' but all that would come out in my frenzy to tell her was, 'Tey nere, tey nere.' And so I became 'Mushmouth' and got a cuff for my trouble. But all the while I could see them watching me, reaching out their hands toward me with gentle, fluttering motions, singing something that I could feel, the sound issuing from beneath the hill. And I could not still my mouth to tell her."

Cuchulainn regarded me in open-mouthed astonishment. "You have the Bird-Sight."

"I do not understand."

"But you saw the Others. Saw them as a child. From far away. That is rare indeed, Finnabair. A rare and priceless gift. Did none among your people recognize the gift? Your druids should have honed it."

I shook my head. "Medb kept me from the druids. She wished for me to be a warrior, and it was her belief that nothing could faster ruin a good warrior than druids."

"A shame, then, and a waste." He shook his head. "All

my childhood I wished to see the Others, to know them, for to go among them is to dwell in light and wisdom."

Now it was my turn to stare at him in surprise.

"But they say that you are of them, that your father is Lugh of the Long Arm, he of the Light."

Laeg and Cuchulainn exchanged a veiled look. The boy shrugged, "Do I look like one you saw?"

I regarded him again, the wild spring of red-and-gold hair, the face that could only be described as ugly.

"No. I must admit that you do not."

"Describe them to me."

"They look as we look, human, small and slender, but they incandesce, as if a candle burns within. They are most beautiful. They seem always to be singing, and even when they are in repose, they give off a sound, like soft wind or like the slow waves that curl against the strand. Their movements are stately and light, as if they do not touch the ground."

From the far side of the fire, Laeg spoke.

"It is said that one of them was your lover."

Grief burned my cheeks, and I lowered my eyes.

So even the Ulstermen knew of Froech, *mo ghra,* my beloved. He who dwelled now in Tir Nàn Og. But I would not speak of him to them or to any. His love was mine to keep alone. And his leaving my sorrow only. Aloud, I said simply, "Look at me. I am a mouse, a vole, a skittering, terrified creature. The Others are all fire, all light, all wind. How could one such as I be expected to hold the wind?"

A long silence played out among us, and then Cuchulainn stretched out against the ground, his head on a log.

"I am thinking that we are perfect, we three, for I am a dog, and Laeg is a reed in the wind, and you, Finnabair, are a field mouse. But now I am thinking that will change. For soon we will teach the field mouse a new way. We will teach her the way of the wolf."

"Of that wolf?" I gestured toward the woods line where

she sat still, watching us, the wind ruffling her fur in the dusky light.

Cuchulainn sighed. "You also have long memory, Finnabair."

"I am a woman. All women have long memory. Surely this is something you are wise enough to know."

"I am. She has long memory, too."

"Who?"

"The wolf." He pointed in her direction; she saw the gesture, shifting her position toward us.

"You talk as if she is a woman."

"She is. You are looking at the Morrigu."

I looked away from her immediately, clasped my hands together in my lap. Terror ran through me like ice water. The Morrigu! I did not want her to see the knowledge in my face, in my movements.

I could feel fear, palpable and cold, drawing the color from my face. Perhaps her sisters were at work on me already, filling me with panic, turning me to carrion.

"Where are her sisters?" I whispered. I did not want to look up into the trees where they might shift their shape as crows.

The Hound patted my hand.

"She is one more thing for you to fear, Finnabair. That is why I did not wish to speak of her."

"She is the War God, Cuchulainn. Who does not fear her, she and her sisters? That threesome weaves the darkness in the world, war and carrion, death and confusion, panic and grief. Why does she shift as this shape? Why does she follow you?"

Cuchulainn sighed. "This will be my story. But while I tell it you must put your fear aside."

"I will put my fear aside when she is gone."

"She will not harm us. I have done her some service."

"You are in the service of the Morrigu." I began to move away from him. He closed his hand over my arm.

"Finnabair, all warriors are in the service of the Morrigu, after all. Warriors are agents of death; it is the work we train to do. But that is not what I meant.

"A few years ago, when I was on my way to Scathach to train in the warrior arts, I met a young and beautiful woman on the road. She had long, black hair that gleamed in the moonlight. Her skin was pale, and her eyes were grey and smoky. With no preamble, she stepped before me and offered me her milky thighs. I did not think such women existed!"

"My mother is such a one," I said.

"So she is; she too made offer to me," he said, nodding at me and smiling, as if this made the behavior more normal somehow. "At any rate, I rejected her offer. I had come from courting Emer, and it hurt my heart to be apart from her. She filled my thoughts as I traveled." He shook his head.

"But the woman persisted; she said that she had watched me, that she had fallen in love with my warrior skills. She stood naked before me, like shimmering milk in the moonlight. Three times I turned her away. On that last rejection, she changed. Before my eyes, her hair sparked fire; her hands brought chaos to the wind. I knew then that she was the Morrigu, that I had rejected the goddess of war."

He shook his head ruefully.

"'Foolish human,' she called me. And that was true enough. 'For spurning me,' she said, 'I will come against you in battle as a heifer, as an eel, as a wolf.'

"I replied, 'And each time I will wound you, warwoman. Nor will I heal you; you will carry my wounds upon you forever.'

"She did as she had said she would. Once when I was fighting in the river—one of your mother's warriors, of course—she wound herself around my leg, an eel, and tried to drag me down. I crushed her underfoot until she slithered away. Once, as a red heifer, she stampeded the cattle against me, until I broke her leg. And again, as that grey wolf," he gestured toward the woods line, "she drove the beasts into the water until I could not see my enemy."

"And how did rid yourself of her that time?"

"I used my slingshot to put out her eye."

"She has been sore wounded by you; why do you not fear her?"

"Because I have also healed her."

"But you said that you would not."

"She is clever, that one. One day when I was weary from this warring, hungry and thirsty to the bone, I came upon an ancient hag who was milking a cow. The woman had a broken leg, a single eye, and she held her ribs most gingerly, but humans only see what they expect to see. 'May I have to drink?' I asked her. Without a word, she gave me milk. 'Blessings on the giver,' I said.

"She smiled. 'Are you thirsty still?' she asked me. Again she gave me milk.

" 'May the gods give health to the giver,' I answered her and drank.

"The third time when she offered it I could not drink it all, but blessed her still. Before my very eyes she changed, not broken-ribbed or one-eyed, strong on both her legs, the woman of the night road. I do not know why my blessings healed her; they must have had in them the power of forgiveness, for do not our Druids say that forgiveness is a healer of great power?

" 'You said you would not heal me,' said the Morrigu, and she was laughing.

" 'You have tricked me, Morrigu. I did not know that it was you. But I will let the blessings stand; the milk was fresh and sweet.'

"This made her laugh aloud. 'I will declare a truce with you, Dog-Boy. You are a true warrior; you wounded me well when none other could do so. I will not hinder you further; when I can, I will protect you. But at death, you will be mine.' "

He gestured toward the woods line.

"And so she shadows me now, one day as a wolf, one day as a raven. I do not know if she protects me, or if she waits for me to die that she may feed on carrion. But you are safer from her here with me than anywhere in Eriu."

I shivered. "I like it not; better a pack of actual wolves than her."

From the forest, she began a high keening wail.

"You will sleep between us," Cuchulainn said, and he spread the blankets so that I was wedged between his bulky form and the skinny pole of Laeg. Strangely, I slept safe and warm, like a fearless, dreamless child.

Niniane, the mother of Rochad, arrived at the first pearling grey of the light. She came bearing warm bread and pots of pure honey, a tankard of mead and another of water. She walked in among us like a woman serving tables at a feast, and Cuchulainn leapt to his feet and bowed low before her.

"Niniane, mother of Rochad, we thank you for your kindness to our welfare."

She bent down to me, holding out a loaf of bread and a pot of honey.

"Flavi said that you would come here, but I did not believe it. I suppose I should have known, for the river is the closest thing to his hut. I could have found you yesterday with but a little hour's walk."

"Why would you do so?"

"You are my daughter-in-law."

"Not by my choosing," I snapped. Sadness chased the shock from her face. But no anger. "Does your treacherous son follow you to me?"

"He does not. I stayed him, thinking that you would not welcome him."

The simple dignity of her speech made my face grow hot with shame.

"Woman of the Welisc," I said formally, "I am sorry. I

do not mean to hurt you for you have been most kind to me, but your son bargained for me like I was a horse or a cow."

"Have you asked him why he did so?"

"I care not. For surely it was the usual two reasons—to get between my mother's thighs or to garner my mother's favor. And he was not the first. I was promised again and again. Warrior after warrior was promised my maidenly favors if only they could defeat this Dog-Boy."

She gasped at my characterization of Chuchulainn, pressed her hand across her mouth, watched him with dismay.

But he calmly tore his bread and chewed.

"And none of them could," he said. "So you could say that I saved your maidenhood."

Thoughts of Froech drifted across my mind, his hands, gentle as feather willows, his warm mouth and sinewed arms. I dropped my head forward and let my hair cover my face. At least I had given my maidenhood where I willed and to none other. I said nothing.

Niniane spoke softly.

"Think, Finnabair. What would Rochad want with Medb? She is the enemy of the warriors of Ulster. And as for killing Cuchulainn, my son is his friend, his brother in arms."

"How can I think when I am but a pawn in everyone's game?"

"That is true," she said, simply. "You have a right to feel so, but I am here to offer you my dwelling as your sleeping place. It is safe, and I will use you to no purpose but to keep you warm. Unless you prefer the cold ground."

A dark suspicion crossed my mind. If Rochad did not wish my mother, did not wish to betray Cuchulainn, why then had he bargained for me? Could it be for this alone, that the daughter of Medb would be seduced to Ulster, won over by the kindness and concern of such as these? Did they hope that Finnabair would then turn against her mother, would betray her to the enemy armies? For the

first time since I made my way into the river, cold reality
skimmed through my mind. Here I was feasting, sleeping,
talking with my enemy. With the enemies of Connacht. I
felt my back straighten, a sapling thickening. What had I
done? Had I played into their plans, all ignorance and
wounded pride? In my haste to disentangle myself from
Medb's webs, had I wound myself into theirs? Into the
web of Ulster? Would more of my kinsmen die for my
foolishness? For all my anger, would I place them in the
way of death with my tongue? My mother, my father, my
brothers the Maine? The warriors of Connacht? And I
knew that I could not. Or was all this still a part of Medb's
plan? Had I been moved most skillfully upon her board?
Was I here where I could be most useful to her? There was
no safety. Neither here nor there. Only Medb knew the answers. I felt as a dreamer, awakening from a long sleep.
The time had come to confront my mother. Still, I could
not let these Ulstermen know that I would travel to her.

Oh, truly, I am Finnabair of no country and no people! I
am she who does not belong.

I forced a smile to my face, tore off a piece of the bread.

"Well, you are most kind. And I will think on these
things." I smiled at Cuchulainn and Laeg. "And though the
snoring of the two of you makes for most comfortable
sleeping, I believe that I will accept Niniane's offer of a
place to dwell this night."

"Well and proper," Cuchulainn pronounced. "A
daughter-in-law should grow in love and respect with her
husband's mother."

Niniane's little face wreathed up in a smile, I inclined
my head in thanks, said nothing, but all the while I was already plotting. I needed to know the truth about Rochad.
And to find that, I would need a horse. I would need to
travel to Medb.

4

My father, Ailill, was seated in his scrolled bronze chair by the fire in his war tent. His chin rested on the palm of his hand. The firelight played across his handsome features and still-golden hair. His face was composed, pensive. I knew immediately what it meant.

"Medb is entertaining?"

My father's face brightened at seeing me. "Mouse! Why do you come here in the small hours of the night?"

"I came to talk to you and to my mother about this marriage, this Rochad to whom you have sold me. I slipped away in darkness to do so, a hard day's ride on the borrowed horse of Rochad's mother. But when I did not find you in the bedchamber together, I came here. She entertains?"

The usual shadow passed across his face. He nodded. Pity for him moved in me.

"Why do you allow it, Aither?"

"Allow it? Do you not know your mother? One could no more give permission to the sea to hurl itself against the shore. You know what she says, Mouse."

"I know. She says that she chose you because you were handsome and generous, the son of a king. And a man who would not be jealous. For ever, as she puts it, does Medb have 'one man waiting in another man's shadow.' "

He smiled sadly. "And just so it has always been."

"But if you knew that, why do you let it break your heart?"

"It does not break my heart, Mouse. It batters a little at the walls of my pride. It greens my eyes. But my heart will ever be strong for Medb. I love her. I love her eyes, her fire hair, the way she rides her chariot, her body like milk, her laugh like that of a man. I love every argument we have, even the one that started this foolish war over the bull. Medb is more than any woman, better than a thousand men. Better to be a husband in her shadow than a king with a colorless wife."

This stung me and I bent my head, my hair falling forward.

My father leaped from his chair, gathered me into his huge arms.

"No, my little mouse, not you! Never you. Surely you know that you are beautiful. Your hair is like the winter wheat, your eyes the color of water. You are lissome and silent, unknowable. Do you know how many men vied for your hand? Promised to kill the Hound if only they could wed you and bed you?"

"Should I feel flattered that I was bid upon like a Beltaine cow? And why did you think that so fine an idea, you and my maither, to promise me again and again to all those men? Most of whom, now, are dead at the hand of the Hound!"

"That is surely true." My father shook his head sadly. "We underestimated the Dog-Boy. But still, sweeting. To think that you inspired so many to try the deed, to fight just for your favors! Surely you are your mother's daughter!"

He looked at me in delight.

"I am not my mother's daughter! Do you not know me by now? I wish only one man to love me. One. To Froech

I gave my heart and I gave it loyally and full. No other man will win me!"

"Froech will not return," my father said with certainty.

"How do you know this?"

He shrugged. "He was of the Other; they do not stay with mortals." But his eyes flicked suddenly toward the door that led to Medb's entertaining chamber.

"What did she do?"

He looked back at me. "Do? Why, nothing. I only wish for her to finish at her entertainments. I think of me, daughter, not of you."

"That is ever the way with both of you. But I will speak to her."

"Surely you will not interrupt her."

"I will. And I would speak to both of you. About this Rochad. Will you accompany me?"

I started for the door. He jumped up, blocked my passage.

"Do not do this, Finnabair. She does not like to be disturbed." He looked down for a moment, met my eyes. "And I should not like for you to see her thus. It would shame me."

"You shame yourself."

"Perhaps so, but I will not let you go." He closed his large hands around my shoulders, pushed me backward.

Lightning-fast I swept my right hand down to my side, lifted my small, jewel-encrusted woman's dagger from its sheath. I pressed the blade below the socket of my own eye.

"Do you see this, Aither? Do not think that I will hesitate."

His hand dropped from my shoulders. He raised his hand toward the dagger, his eyes uncertain. I pricked the skin beneath my eye and the blood began to trickle down my face, along the line of my jaw. Ailill stopped, fear plain in his eyes.

"Finnabair, why do you behave so? Do you dislike the

husband we chose for you so much that you would wound yourself? You frighten me! This is not my quiet, compliant child."

"Aither," I said, low and menacing, "do you know where I have been these nights?"

He shook his head. "I thought that when Rochad escaped us . . ."

"Not to the bed of Rochad of Ulster. No, not I. I made a bed of the river, Aither. I faced the wide sky and wished to die. I have been bartered and sold. I have lost my true beloved. I care not if I live or die. Do you believe me?"

He nodded, stood perfectly still, comprehension dawning on his face.

"Good," I said. "Now I will find my mother, and you and Medb will tell me why."

Medb of Connacht, my mother, was at one of her favorite pastimes. Naked, she sat astride a glistening young warrior, while another fondled her from behind. She did not hear me enter the chamber, but she must have seen the change in her young suitors' eyes, for a dagger appeared in her hand from nowhere. Before either of her suitors had even moved to defend her, she turned astride toward me, ready to throw her weapon.

"Finnabair!" she cried, but no anger sparked in her eyes. Instead, her face folded into a delighted smile. "Daughter! Have you come to tell me of your conquest of Rochad?" She unstraddled herself from her gleaming, sweaty warrior, stood to her full height.

Embarrassed and furtive, the two soldiers scrambled for the shadows, dropped tunics and cloaks around themselves.

But not my mother.

No shame was upon her. None. Her face had the smile of a delighted child.

With a single gesture, she waved the two warriors out of her presence. They bowed and bumbled their way from the room, their cheeks stained crimson. My mother never looked at them at all.

She noticed the blood, then, on my cheek. She ran to me, examined the wound. Certain that it was a skin wound only, she licked her fingers, wiped my face, dried at the wound with a long strand of her hair.

Naked in the firelight she faced me, hands on hips. I am bird-boned and small, but my mother stands nearly as tall as my father, large-breasted and wide-hipped. Her hair spilled over her shoulder, past her waist, over her buttocks, almost to her knees. Her skin was stunningly white, freckled everywhere, face, arms, legs, chest. She grinned at me.

"So, Daughter, how is the new husband? Does he give you a good ride?"

My father appeared in the doorway. He must have waited until the others left. He lifted her cloak from its peg, swung it around her. She kissed him gently on the cheek.

"It is Rochad that she comes to talk of, Medb. Rochad and Froech and the others to whom she was promised. Our daughter is displeased with us."

Medb looked at me in surprise.

"Displeased? But you agreed to the marriage with Rochad."

"He wooed me at the feast. He whispered sweetings in my ear. He bedded me and disappeared."

"And he did not take you with him?" asked Medb. Now she was angry. "Then he did not keep his bargain. If he has dishonored us, he will pay."

"And what bargain was that? How, exactly, was I pawned?"

My father spoke then.

"We were here in the war camp, all the warriors of Connacht, when Rochad came thundering upon us in his chariots."

"Do you think I will forget that, Father? You horsed me and sent me out among them."

He shrugged. "We knew they would not fight a maid who rode to them alone. In truth, they surprised us utterly. The Ulstermen are in their pains; the curse is deep upon them. You know that they cannot fight while the curse is upon them, nor have they since this war began. They are laid low in their pains, helpless as women in childbirth. If we could only reach them, we could kill them all and take the bull. But between us and them stands Cuchulainn. Day after day, it is the Dog-Boy alone who fights our warriors, one by one. And, one by one, he kills them all."

"And one by one you offer them my favors before they die. They go to battle with him, thinking they will bed me, if only they can win."

My mother sighed in exasperation.

"Well, it is not as if I offer you alone. I promise them the riches of my own thighs as well."

"This is marvelous consolation."

She shrugged, her gesture saying that she would do what she must and so should I.

"We made a dark bargain with Cuchulainn months ago when this war began. Because the curse is upon the Ulstermen and they cannot fight us, Cuchulainn placed himself at the forge. On a spancel hoop, he carved out words of challenge in the tongue of the Druids."

"Why are they cursed?"

"Who?"

"The Ulstermen."

Medb laughed. "A woman placed the curse upon them. I know little more for they guard it as a shameful secret. And well they should be ashamed. Men and warriors laid low as women in childbed, when I, a woman and a queen, can better wield a sword. I like it well."

"You cannot defeat the Hound."

"No, and not for trying."

"How does he speak the Druids' tongue?"

She waved her hands in exasperation.

"I neither know nor care, Finnabair. Druids, faugh!" She

spat upon the ground. "Suffice it that the Dog-Boy carved the words in *ogham*. None could pass, he said, unless they could defeat him. Warrior after warrior, he defeated."

She shook her head.

"At last I went myself to see him. Imagine my surprise to find that he is just a boy. Only seventeen summers hang on him, Daughter! Still, I did what I could. I offered him the sweetness of my thighs, if he would cease and let the army pass. More, I offered, much more. Lands and holdings here in Connacht, gold, the house of a king. But he would have none of it. Instead he bargained thus:

" '*Send against me one warrior each day. While I am thus engaged in combat, your army may move. But when I have defeated him, you must cease and make camp.*'

"Finnabair, I tell you, there have been days when we could not even muster the army to motion before he defeated our champion. The Hound is not human; everyone knows it."

"So why have you not given up and returned to Connacht? Maither, this is a foolish war. A war over a bull!"

Medb looked at me stunned, as though I had spoken some terrible curse, had called upon her the wrath of the Morrigu. Without a breath of thought, she drew back her hand and struck me hard against my cheek. I felt the heat flame up inside the skin, but I took little notice. In my childhood, even my giant brothers, the Maine, had been the recipients of that swift hand, of the fact that our mother left no gap between thought and action.

"How shall you speak to me? I am Medb of Connacht. My name alone intoxicates. I am Queen of Cruachan Ai, ruler of Connacht. Yet your father is possessed of Finnbennach, the White Bull. All know of its powers to breed upon the cows of Connacht. Yet, I have no bull. What will they say of me? That Medb is weaker than her husband? That Medb cannot increase the cattle of Ulster? Balance demands that I own Donn Cuailgne, the Brown Bull, the best breeder in Eire. More pity that its owner is

an Ulsterman, that fool Daire. More pity still that he re-
fuses to part with his bull. He is the cause of this war,
Daughter. A little Ulster cattleman who dares to say me
nay. When Ulster says no to Medb, war must follow! My
honor, my power, demand such a war."

I shook my head in disgust.

"And when did I become a bargaining piece for cattle?"

Medb sighed. "When dozens of our warriors had died,
there came a day when no more volunteered to fight
Cuchulainn. Your father and I talked. We knew we needed
something we could offer, something to fire the blood and
move the warriors to action." She shrugged. "And I know
best that men can be moved through their loins."

"Why not offer them yourself alone? All the warriors of
Connacht long to bed you, long to speak of one night between the thighs of Medb."

"True enough. But they also know that my favors are
temporary." She smiled at my father. "Ailill is my
beloved; they are only diversions. And a diversion is not
enough to move a man against the Dog-Boy."

"Nor am I."

"Sweeting," said my father. "You underestimate your
beauty."

Medb waved her hand. "She speaks simple truth, Ailill.
She is no Medb. But, Daughter, see clearly. You are the
daughter of Medb of Connacht. One who marries you
reaps riches beyond that reward. Your sweet, young thighs
are the doorway; the family of that warrior will be allied
with mine. Riches and power will follow, dwellings in the
great hall at Cruachan Ai, armies to command, gold and
cattle to own. Even my own favors added to your own.
Such a man would be rich beyond all dreaming. For such
riches, a warrior might fight the Hound."

None of this surprised me. It was as I had thought it to
be. I had come to the light at the center of this candle-tale,
the truth I needed to know.

"And so the first was Nadcranntail?"

Behind her, my father cleared his throat and spoke.

"We are sorry for Nadcranntail, Daughter. He was unworthy of you."

"Unworthy!? In all his life, did he ever bathe? He was fat and hairy and the sweat ran from his greasy hair to his matted beard. Blackheads swarmed across his face like ants and all his teeth were black! Unworthy! So ludicrous was he that Cuchulainn ignored him and plucked birds from the air until Nadcranntail flung his sword. Unworthy!"

Medb placed a cool hand against the still-flaming side of my cheek. I knew this to be her apology.

"But, Mouse," she pleaded. "Be glad. For Cuchulainn neatly sliced Nadcranntail's head from his shoulders and spared you ever coupling. And the others who vied for your hand were so much finer. Think of beautiful Ferbaeth, who fed you dainties."

"He dropped them down my dress in a foolish attempt to fondle my breasts. And he is dead; Cuchulainn pierced him through the neck with holly."

"Think then of the twins, Long and Loch mac Mofemis. They were handsome men, and young."

"And now dead, both! Why will you not see? You have forced too many men to die for me! I cannot bear it. To how many was I promised?"

"Some fifty or so." Medb shrugged and waved her hand. "They did not die for you, Finnabair." She shook her head. "They died for me." She smiled at me, pride in her eyes. "They died for Medb of Connacht. And besides, Rochad is not dead. In him you have a living one, though vanished."

"Yes, let us speak of Rochad."

Behind her, my father sighed. "As I said, his chariots swept toward us on that day. We had no choice but to send you among them."

For a brief moment I remembered the eyes of Rochad, watching from his great, black horse, never moving from me as I called out the messages of Medb and Ailill. Another suspicion crossed my mind.

"Why is Rochad not cursed? How is it that he and his army escaped the ancient evil of Ulster?"

"The Curse falls on the warriors of Emain Macha, the warriors of King Conchobar. Rochad is the son of Faitheman from the far north of Ulster in Rigdonn. The curse does not touch him. Cuchulainn called him to battle against us."

"Why? For all these many months, the Hound has fought our warriors hand to hand. Why call a northern army in?"

Medb smiled, baring her teeth in the light.

"Because we came this close." She squeezed her thumb and forefinger together in the candlelight. "This close to killing the Hound. He was wounded nearly unto death."

"Which warrior came so close?"

"Ferdiad, foster-brother of the Hound himself."

"I fed him dainties from the table. I kissed his mouth of wine!"

"Of course. I promised you to him as prize. And my own thighs as well. We can be proud of Ferdiad, Daughter. He fought four days to win us. And then the Hound killed him as well."

I placed my hands at the side of my head and wailed aloud like a wounded dog.

"Stop this foolish war, Medb. The War of the Bull. Too many kinsmen die! Promise me no more."

She tilted her head in the lamplight and looked at me perplexed.

"But Finnabair, you should be proud. You saved the life of hundreds of your kinsmen."

"How?"

My father spoke. "When Rochad came in his chariots, I asked you to ride among them. That was how we captured him and many of his soldiers. I hid my men in the woods at the edge of the field. You gave your pretty speeches, turned and rode away. Before his men could follow, we ambushed them all, killed their horsemen, drove them to the forests, captured Rochad and brought him to our encampment."

"We made the bargain there," said Medb.

"What bargain do we speak of?"

"We asked the son of Faitheman to send his armies homeward. We asked that they would wait to fight until the curse is lifted from the men of Emain Macha, to return to fight in the final great battle." She waved her hands in anticipation of the day. "In return, we offered him any prize of his choosing. He did not even hesitate. He chose you."

My mother seemed surprised by the choice, even in the telling.

I remembered Rochad sitting beside me at the feasting table, remembered the words he had whispered in my ear. "In my eyes, it is the daughter, not the mother, who is the prize." I did not know then that I had already been bartered and sold. Shame stole up my neck and across my cheeks. I lowered my head, hid behind what was left of my hair. More fool I than I had ever believed. For it was those words that had led me to offer him the marriage cup, to lead him to my chamber, to hang his purple cloak on my wall peg, to feel his deep-throated laugh against my neck, to rise at last into the hands of my Ulster enemy. And in the morning I awoke to find he had left me.

I spoke softly. "So, in one night, you sold me to an enemy who wedded me and bedded me and crept away before the dawnlight came."

"We did not expect him to leave, Daughter." My father seemed apologetic.

Medb shook her head. "No, it was a bargain, Daughter. We bartered you to him fairly for fair return. We thought that he would marry to you truly and keep you by his side."

"Well, he did not. He took just what he wanted and he fled."

"Do not fear, Daughter. Such a slight to our honor will be avenged. The time arrives when the Ulstermen will be free of the ancient cursing. They will come against us then. Rochad will be among them. Then we will avenge you and set his head upon the pike outside your door."

"So be it then," I said.

For a brief moment I remembered the hand of Rochad, descending through the drowning water, lifting me up to his horse's back. Why had he done such a thing so soon on the heels of leaving me? But there would be no answers.

"One last question, then. What of our Munster kinsmen?"

"What fools!" My mother punched at the sky. "When they found you had been married, learned they could not have you or their coveted alliance to my name, they turned on me, twelve chiefs with their shaggy armies. But I defeated them soundly. I used the Galleoin armies and all of our Ulster exiles. Think not of them, Daughter, for they will trouble us no further."

I shook my head, weary unto weeping. Silently, I left the room. What more was there to say?

On the bedstand in my chamber were two candlesticks of red and yellow gold, chased with hounds and hinds and all the patterns of the *sidhe*. These had been the gift of Froech when first he asked for me. They were all I had of him now. I wrapped them in my second cloak and slung them over my shoulder. I mounted the borrowed horse of Niniane and rode away.

Some way from our encampment there rose a fairy mound, doorway to the country of the *sidhe*. At the foot of just that hillock, I spread my cloak and lay upon the ground, a candlestick in either hand. I covered myself with the ermine cloak that had been washed by the hand of Cuchulainn. The grass beneath me rustled and a little wind moved at the tops of the trees. Oh, let it be the Others, I prayed, for no one else is left to me.

Perhaps they would open the door and come for me. Perhaps Froech would be among them. I surrendered then to the deep and sorrowing country of my dreams.

5

I dreamed of Froech. He came on his dapple-grey, riding silently into the glade where I was bathing. I never heard him. I rinsed my long hair of its herbs and climbed from the quiet pond. It was then that I saw him. I was a maiden then, but I did not blush in modesty for I knew him well. I had dreamed him from childhood, standing behind the water door of the Other, even then my Bird-Sight moving in me, though I was all unaware. I had thought him only a dream, but here he stood in flesh, his face alight with joy.

"So," I said, "you have come for me at last."

"I have waited for the day," he said softly.

"Why do you wish such a one as I?" I spread my hands and drops of water cascaded from them like rainbows, floated to the ground in slow motion. Somehow he had encased us in their time, then. The time of the Other, where all things move slowly. I met his eyes, felt the tingling in my skin as he stared at my nakedness.

"You are all loveliness," he said. "Great stillness. You are the silence at the center of my heart. I have watched you from the doorway to my world. I would have waited for you for all time."

He dismounted his horse then. I stepped to him, still

wet from the river, completely unafraid. He gathered me in his arms and loved me gently, as the grasses move before the breeze. He loved my spirit into lightness. Deep in my dream, I laughed again to feel it, the way two souls could twine and rise like smoke ascending to starlight.

When we were garbed again, we walked into the glade, his dapple-grey behind us. There I saw he had come for me as kings come courting. Fifty of his court attended, all on dappled mares. Their bridles were of finespun gold and hung with golden bells so that our retinue made music. Seventy slender greyhounds walked beside them, linked with delicate silver chains, and there were trumpeters and harpers, even gaily clad and laughing fools.

We rode to Cruachan Ai and Froech asked Medb and Ailill for my hand, I standing so proud beside him. But, oh, the sorrow soon began. They set a bride price even the Other could not match. Hundreds of horses and cattle, dwellings filled with jewels and gold. Perhaps they were loathe to lose me; I seem to be a bargaining piece that moves their wars along. Or could it be my mother had eyes for this man of the Other, handsome as marble, bright as the autumn leaves? Now I will never know.

That night he came to me in darkness.

"Steal away with me," he said. "Silent we will go, into the country of the Other."

Oh, if only I had gone! But I spoke from pride and from the newfound sense that I, Finnabair, was at last profoundly loved.

"Who am I to sneak away? Should the daughter of Medb and Ailill go skulking? I wish to ride with all the bells upon the bridles ringing."

Froech shook his head. "I fear your mother's treachery. We do not play so ill among the Other. I fear that she will tear you from me somehow."

But I took my ring from my finger, the gold-incised ring of my own clan.

"This be yours," I said, "in token of my deepest love.

But you must hide it, for it is our clan ring and they must not see it missing."

I put a plain, gold circlet on my finger, so they would not see it gone.

He put my ring in the pocket of his tunic, pressed his lips against my hands.

"I will try all for you, *mo ghra*," he said. "But know this now. If ever we are parted, it will not be by my choosing. Will you believe that always?"

And I said that I would, more fool always I.

In the morning, my mother proposed a hunting trip. At midday, when we were hot and weary, we came to a shimmering pool in the woods. At the far side of the pond, rowanberries grew in deep profusion. Medb professed a hunger for them.

"Good friend Froech," she said, simpering and lowering her eyes. "Will you swim across and bring me berries? For all of us are told of how long and deep the Other ones can swim."

Froech disrobed immediately. How do you refuse the request of the Queen of Connacht in front of both companies?

I saw the ring fall from his pocket, saw my mother swiftly scoop it up and fling it nonchalantly toward the water. I thought that was the ruse, but I was wrong.

When Froech was half the way across, the water began to boil and churn around him. A great head lifted itself from the center of the pool and bared the dripping teeth of a sea serpent. Froech called for his sword. I ran to retrieve it for him, but I had gone two steps when my head was yanked backward, almost pulling my braids from my scalp. My own father. Oh, the betrayal of it! For he had wound his spear into the bottom of my braid and thus he held me back.

The men of the Other dismounted from their dappleds, dismayed by the behavior, all perplexed. This was what they had been warned of humans, this treachery! They started for the sword, but I was swifter. I drew my dagger from my belt, hacked the offending braid six inches from the bottom, heaved the sword toward the water. End over end it tumbled, glinting in the light, the mist of the Other spraying from it, fine, like rainbows. Froech caught it, plunged the serpent down. But he was wounded. Bleeding from a deep gash in his arm, he dragged himself to shore. My mother, all solicitous, sent for nurses, bore him back to Cruachan Ai. But I was forbidden to see him.

That night, under cover of darkness, I crept toward his dwelling. I feared for him under Medb's ministrations. I wanted to warn him about the ring. But on my way to him, I saw a thing that I will long remember. From the edge of the forest beyond the dwelling where Froech had been hidden, I heard a strange low moaning. It rose in tone and tongue, became *na caoine,* the keening, the death wail. The *bain sidhe* were coming for Froech. Riveted with fear, I watched as they emerged from the forest, three times fifty of them, their green cloaks iridescent in the darkness, their legs shimmering white like fog. My clansmen began to cry out in fear, running back and forth between the dwellings, but I stood still. I watched as they entered the hut, watched as they bore him away. I dropped to the ground then, limp as water, for I believed him dead, thought that I would never see him more.

But I was wrong.

The next evening he arrived, hale and handsome, bearing with him a great, fine salmon. The ways of the Other are not our ways! My heart rejoiced.

My parents declared a feast to be held in the great hall of Cruachan Ai, in celebration of his safe return. Froech spoke before the company.

"Medb of Cruachan Ai and Ailill, I salute you. I have returned to the pond of yesterday. I have destroyed the serpent. He will never trouble your people again. From that pond, I have brought this fine salmon. I asked that it be cooked for this evening's feast. Here before all the company I ask again for your daughter's hand. Do me the honor of giving me Finnabair to wife and I will care for her in my country as I am cared for there."

I watched as they conferred on this development, leaning back and forth, whispering to each other. At last my mother spoke.

"Froech, son of Be Find of the Other, we rejoice that your health is renewed. We will cook this salmon in triumphant celebration of your return." Cooks bore the fish away. My father stood.

"Prepare for the feast!"

The workers bore in great plank tables and covered them with the finest linen. Candelabra festooned every table, little oak trees of light. My mother's hall at Cruachan Ai is the most beautiful dwelling in all of Eire. Great columns of red yew and oak rise to the ceiling, covered with carvings of fish and foul, of deer and horses. Behind the high dais where my parents sat was a huge wall of bronze, chased with silver. For their table, Froech produced the great candlesticks that I held close to me now and a beautiful *fidchell* board with squares of silver and gold. When all was ready for the feast, my father stood again.

"Now in celebration of our good fortune, we will have a counting of the fortune. Bring before us all the wealth of the clan!"

Now I saw the ruse truly. Always one for counting the wealth, Medb would use this ceremony to trap us. I signalled Froech, held my ring hand aloft, but he regarded me with utter calm. One by one, my father called each of my brothers the Maine before him. With his steward by his side, he called aloud their rings and torques, their jewel-encrusted swords. I slipped the plain gold band from my finger, awaited my fate. When my turn came, I stepped before them.

"Our daughter, Finnabair the beautiful, we have endowed with riches and she has stewarded them well. Call the list." The steward cleared his throat and began.

"One torque, inlaid with rubies and emeralds."

I touched the piece around my neck.

"One armlet, chased in finest rose gold."

I lifted my arm and it flashed in the light.

"Twenty bracelets in silver and gold, with clasps and finest chasing."

They jingled up and down my arms.

"A dagger with a jeweled hilt."

I dutifully produced it, held the piece aloft.

"The finest silver brooch pin."

I pointed to my shoulder.

"The ring of the clan of Medb, queen at Cruachan Ai."

"The ring is missing."

My mother stood, all feigned amazement. "What say you, Daughter? What has become of it? You know that our clan ring is precious. It binds us each to the other."

"In the troubles at the pond, I lost the ring. Perhaps the serpent swallowed it."

"The ring is the ring of our clan," cried Ailill. "It was your duty to protect it. We will send servants to search for it. If it cannot be found, we will drown you in the bog."

The whole company gasped and screamed, but I knew what they played at. Medb herself had thrown the ring into the water. Nor would they drown their only daughter in the bog. This was a play on a *fidchell* board and Froech was their pawn-piece. He stood. I shook my head at him, willing him to say nothing, but he spoke.

"Let us serve the feast. Let us be convivial and warm. If the ring is not found by the end of the feasting, I will offer all the treasure of the *sidhe,* I will give up my place in the country of the Other, to redeem the honor of Finnabair."

Medb and my father conferred again, nodding and smiling.

"This is a generous offer, friend Froech. We accept. Bring forth the platters."

Cooks swept in with loaves of steaming bread and pots of honey, with fish wrapped in seaweed and a great boar with apples in its mouth. Steaming bowls of pungent leeks were followed by cakes dripping with honey. All the while I sat with a stone in my stomach, unable to tell Froech of the treachery of Medb while he only nodded at me across the table, serene in his ignorance of their plans.

At last the cooks bore in his platter with the great steaming salmon.

Froech jumped to his feet.

"This is my gift to Medb and Ailill. I myself will fillet it for them at the high table."

The cooks set the steaming platter between them and Froech brandished his fine dagger. Light flashed from the jeweled hilt as he held it up. He plunged it into the side of the fish, peeled back the skin and lifted up the first fillet. There, gleaming against the point of Froech's golden dagger, was my ring, the clan ring of Medb of Connacht.

"Behold what the salmon of knowledge brings us!" cried Froech to the assembled company. "Even the fish of the rivers of Eire bless the union of Finnabair and Froech!" He faced me with the ring gleaming on the tip of his dagger.

I stepped forward and placed it on my finger.

"Tonight, *mo ghra,* I will take you with me to the country of the *sidhe.*"

The company burst into applause and song. Already the bards were composing the story for telling, the great miracle of the clan ring of Finnabair. My parents were caught in their own perfidy. What else could they do? They made great show of apology, clapping Froech about the shoulders, hugging me in front of the company. At last my mother stood and raised her cup.

"We rejoice at our daughter's good fortune and wish to give her the wedding that befits the daughter of Medb of Connacht. We owe her great apology, as we do you,

Froech, son of Be Find. Do not take her from us tonight, hugger-mugger in the darkness. We ask only that she be allowed to remain with us, in our loving protection, until three days from this time, when we will celebrate the marriage of Froech and Finnabair with a great and worthy feast. As our apology, we will reduce the bride-price that we have asked of Froech to one small task which we will convey to him in private council. When that task is completed, we will proceed with a wedding feast like none that we have ever seen at Cruachan Ai!"

Great shouts and cheers went up from the company. Froech put his arm around me, touched the side of his head to mine.

"I like it not," I whispered.

"Fear not, love. I have bested them now. Whatever little task they wish, I will achieve it. We will be married in three days' time." Then he kissed me with such tenderness and gentle love that the kiss made its way to the center of my soul, where it will remain forever.

Froech disappeared on the following day and I never saw or heard from him again.

Now I awoke on the damp, dewy ground, the cold and slippery candlesticks clutched in my hands. The hill of the *sidhe* was still closed to me. If indeed the Others were beneath it, they had not opened their door, had not taken me in. I was alone in the great world of the living, joyless as dust.

I sat on the ground on my wet ermine cloak and cried in great, heaving sobs. I did not even hear the chariot until it was almost upon me. I opened my eyes to the pounding of the horses' hooves. In the little distance, I saw the charioteer turn the right side of his chariot toward me, the mark of greeting and honor. I stood. They wheeled in closer and I saw skinny Laeg, swinging and arcing the reins behind a

pair of horses, one black, one grey. There beside him was
Cuchulainn, in a fine cloak chased with running deer, his
spear in hand. They swung near and Laeg reined in the
heaving pair. Cuchulainn jumped from the chariot and ran
to me, sweeping me into the bearlike arms.

"Where have you been, little Stinkweed? We looked for
you all night. Niniane is terrified for your welfare."

"You looked for me?"

"Of course we looked for you. Are you not the wife of
Rochad mac Faitheman, my own warrior companion?"

I stepped back. "Did he send you for me?"

Laeg and Cuchulainn exchanged glances. "He did not.
His little mother sent us, mother bird, worrying for your
safety all the while. Now climb aboard." He was already
wrapping up my candlesticks, gathering my cloak. Laeg
looked around furtively, sniffing the air like a dog. I understood why.

"You are in terrible danger," I said. "You are in my
mother's country, deep behind enemy lines. Her war camp
is a few minutes' chariot ride from here."

"We are not stupid, Stinkweed. We have informants. We
know her war camp well. We knew that you were there and
we knew that you had departed. So we searched. Hurry
now and get aboard."

Where else did I have to go? I climbed into the chariot,
braced hard by Cuchulainn and clung to the wickerwork
in terror as Laeg thundered us back to the territory of the
Ulstermen. All the while I was filled with wonder. They
had come looking for me. Looking for me in enemy country. Looking at peril to their very lives. I was daughter
enough of Medb to wonder why.

6

Cuchulainn and Laeg dumped me unceremoniously from the chariot in the clearing of Flavius the Nubian and rode at thunder speed toward the ford. Niniane was waiting in the clearing. So, to my surprise, was her great son, Rochad. Only Niniane, however, ran toward me with her arms outstretched.

"Finnabair ni Medb. You have returned to us. I was so afraid that they had stolen you from us."

I regarded her in bafflement. She seemed genuinely joyful to see me, so relieved that tears shimmered, unshed, in her eyes. My questions must have shown on my face because Rochad stepped forward. "My mother would have nothing but that Cuchulainn and Laeg should look for you, nothing but that I be sent for from the north, so afraid was she for your welfare." His mouth was set in a thin line of disapproval. His reaction met my expectations. I drew myself up to my full height and nodded down my nose at him, at Niniane.

"I am sorry that you were so inconvenienced. I had business in the war camp of my mother."

Rochad stepped forward.

"What business would that be? For did not that same

mother bargain you to me in marriage? Are you not now of Ulster?"

"Haughty, arrogant bastard. I am of my own country. Neither you nor they can claim me."

"Stop this!" Niniane commanded, taking a swipe at her huge son with her tiny hand. "Do you think to make her feel welcome with a claim at law? She is back with us and safe. I will hear no more!"

Despite being twice her size, her warrior son had the grace to look ashamed, to lower his eyes to the ground.

"Fools, men, all," she said as she took my hands in hers. "Except Flavi. Come, we have prepared a feast for your return."

Inside the hut Flavi turned a haunch of deer on a spit. Niniane had baked bread, and a large pitcher of honey simmered warm at the ash edge of the fire. Flavi beckoned me to a seat that he had placed by the fire. Tender as a nurse, he wrapped me in a soft, plaid blanket and hung my cloak, ermine side out, to dry by the fire. He unfolded my candlesticks and regarded their chased patterns for a long while. His eyes shifted to mine and regarded me for a moment, then spoke to Niniane.

"What does he say? What tongue does he use?"

"He speaks in the Roman tongue. He says that the candlesticks have come from the country of dreams."

"He is correct. They are the only thing that remains to me from my beloved. He was of the Other."

Rochad made a sharp intake of breath, somewhere between a snort and the deep fricative noise that men make before spit. But his mother took my face gently in her hands. She regarded me with such loving kindness.

"He is lost to you, then?"

"He returned to his own country."

Rochad broke in.

"So you learned the skill of vanishing from the Other? Drowning in rivers, fleeing from those you are contracted to."

Niniane caught her hand in the back of his long braid and lifted.

"Ouch! Maither, you know that I hate to have my hair pulled!"

She lifted the braid until he was forced to scramble first to his knees and then to his feet.

"You are a great, dumb ox, my son, and you are not welcome at this feast. Depart now, until you can keep a civil tongue in your head before your new bride."

I wanted to laugh aloud, but contented myself with flashing him a look of triumph. How could so loathsome a creature come from so loving a mother? The sound of his horse's hooves thundering away toward the ford filled me with relief.

Niniane said something to Flavi in the Roman tongue. He bent his great height low to hers to hear her, listened intently. Then they both burst into laughter.

"What is funny?"

"I have told Flavi that now my son will commiserate with his friend Cuchulainn over the strange ways of women."

Flavi gave me the haunch of deer, that part reserved for honored guests, for poets and Druids. I had a whole loaf of bread and warm honey. Niniane used one of the irons from the fire, holding it in the cup of mead until the mead sizzled and was warm. How strange we were—a Nubian, dark as silk with eyes as fathomless as water, a Welisc woman, tiny as a bird, and me, the daughter of the high queen of Connacht wrapped in the plaid of Ulster. I should have felt strange, demeaned, dining thus below my rank among my enemy, but I knew the truth. We were all three of us strangers in strange country. I ate and drank and felt—I do not know how to describe it. I felt something that moved in me like the warm mead, so surprising that twice I pressed my hands against the sides of my temples and closed my eyes to contain it.

At the gesture, Flavi said something to Niniane, all the while regarding me.

Niniane turned to me and smiled.

"Flavi says to tell you this: In this dwelling you are safe. In this dwelling you feel contentment. You need not close your eyes to contain it." She smiled and patted my hand.

"Contentment," I said softly. I felt almost drowsy with it, like a drunkard with his first cup of mead. Flavi gestured to the sleeping platform where they had placed me on the night I had tried to drown in the river. I nodded my head.

"How does he know what I think?" I asked Niniane.

"Flavi is a healer. He watches you. He listens. He reads what your body and your gestures tell him. Now he senses that you are weary and need rest."

"How did you come to be together?"

Niniane patted the sleeping platform.

"Come, lie down and we will tell you our story."

I curled up on the sleeping platform under the plaid cloak. I sighed aloud for the warmth and the food, for Flavi lifting the cloak beneath my chin and Niniane holding my hand in her tiny hand.

They began the story of their journey, Niniane speaking to me in the Gaeilge, Flavi chiming in to her in the Roman tongue, seeming to follow the process of the story, even in our tongue. And, oh, how strange and sad a story it was.

"I have told you that I am Welisc. My mother was born of the tribe of the Cymri, the small people who dwell in the hills and hollows of Wales. She grew up wild as the shaggy ponies that she rode, but at the age of seven she was fostered to our distant cousins in the clan of the Atrebates near the eastern sea of Alba, far distant from our own village." Niniane shook her head and sighed.

"Why do you sigh? Fosterage keeps the clans strong."

"It does, but when my mother was fourteen years old, in the last year of her fosterage, when she should have been returning home, Julius Caesar came to the shores of

Alba." Niniane's voice took on weight and fear. She regarded me wide-eyed. I shook my head.

"I do not know this one. What is his clan?"

"He was the ruler of Rome. A mighty warrior. He was feared by all. He and his warriors landed on the eastern coast in their flat-bottomed boats, the oars manned by dozens of slaves. They sent among us Commius." Here she paused and spat on the ground. "He was of the tribe of the Atrebates, but he was loyal to the Romans. A client-king." She regarded me.

"A traitor to his people," I replied.

"Exactly. To mollify the Romans, Commius told his tribesmen to offer hostages to the Romans. My mother's kinsmen did so."

"Oh, you gods. They gave your mother to the Romans."

She nodded. I felt a wash of kinship with her vanished mother, understood the terror, the betrayal, bone-deep. I sat up on the sleeping platform and drew my arms around her tiny body.

"Oh, your poor maither. The terror of it."

"Just so she said." Niniane drew back. "But, Finnabair, hear me now and respect the length of my life path. For sometimes great good will arise from great sorrow. My mother was shipped to Rome and given into the service of the household of a Roman legate—a great warrior with many soldiers who served beneath him. They were not cruel to her, though she was treated as a servant of the household. Slowly she learned the Roman tongue. Several years passed.

"The legate had a son some five years older than my mother whom she had never met, for he was off fighting the Gauls.

"One day the wife of the legate sent her to the garden to prepare vegetables for the evening meal. My mother had almost twenty summers then. She was seated at a little table beside a bright fountain. She leaned her hand into the stream of water to rinse it and water sprayed into her hair and onto her cloak. She laughed out loud with delight.

"As fate would have it, the son of the legate rode into the courtyard at that moment on his fine, great horse. He saw my mother, her hand in the water, her head tipped in delight. He heard her laughter. He made a single noise and my mother turned to look at him. She told me that it was as though the fountain froze in its descent. The horse stood still in midprance. They regarded each other and they knew. They had always known.

"And so it was that the son of the legate, my father, Gaius Ammianus Julius, met Brynna ap Huw, my mother. In one fluid gesture, he dismounted from his horse and kissed her, as though he were returning to his lost beloved. My father was a Roman; they are not much given to romance, but he told me that in that kiss he knew for the first time that eternity existed.

"They were married with very little protest, really. The Romans intermarried often with their clients and conquered folk, and my grandfather was no fool. He saw the looks that passed between them.

"A year after their marriage, my father's legion was posted to Egypt with the forces of Caesar."

"This is a place that you have mentioned."

She smiled. "How to describe Egypt? If you think of the burren, stony and bare, and you fill it with sand, that is Egypt. It is a vast desert. But my parents were in a garrison near a great river called the Nile and they were happy. Far away in Rome, Julius Caesar was assassinated, but his—chieftain—Marc Antony ruled the armies in Egypt. My parents had been barren for many years, but then they were introduced to an Egyptian healer who gave them herbs and powders."

I pointed toward Flavius but Niniane shook her head and laughed. "No, he was a boy then himself, with less than twelve summers upon him and still dwelling in his own country."

I gestured her to continue with her story.

"Well, two years after Caesar's death my brother, Marcus Dyffed, was born, and then two years past that, I was born—Niniane Julia. We were that most rare of things in the Roman world, a happy family. My parents truly loved each other. My father had risen in the ranks of Marc Antony's service and was himself a legate, as his father had been before him. We had a fine house in Egypt, beautiful garments. We ate choice figs and olives and goats' cheese and drank watered wine. I suppose we were wealthy, although a child does not measure happiness by wealth, taking their surroundings for granted, but feeding off the air between their parents and the love and care that comes to them.

"My mother had suffered from some childbed fever after my birth and had still some uncomfortable aftereffects. When I was five years old, into our life came a Nubian healer, a young man of twenty years with medical skills and gentle hands and eyes, but no voice for either speaking or singing."

Here she smiled at Flavius.

"No voice? But then how . . ."

"Flavi will tell you, for his tale is equally a labyrinth as mine. By the time he came into our household, he was a freedman who had been a Roman slave. My father hired him into our household as physician to my mother and he brought her back to full and happy health."

She grew silent; though she still held my hand, her eyes had grown faraway and lost.

"Something terrible happened, did it not?"

She looked back at me, seemed almost surprised to be there in the hut with its thatched roof and central fire.

"Yes. Something terrible. Nothing is as certain in life as change, Finnabair. Some of it, surely, is terrible.

"Marc Antony had grown large with power. His beloved was Cleopatra, queen of all Egypt, ruler of that part of the world. She was a woman both beautiful and beguiling. But

Antony was married, in the Roman law, to Octavia, sister
of Octavian Augustus, emperor of Rome. Antony had two
sons with Cleopatra. One day Antony staged a great enter-
tainment for the people of Egypt and for the Romans stationed there. He brought forth his son Alexander dressed
in the costume of the Medeans, crowned with a tiara. His
son Ptolemy he had dressed in Macedonian short boots
and cloak. Seated on gold and silver thrones, Cleopatra by
his side, Antony granted to Alexander and Ptolemy, one
after another, all the known countries of the Eastern
world.

"I was there with my parents, a child of some eight
years. There was feasting for all, music and clowns. I
thought it the most beautiful ceremony my childish eyes
had ever beheld. But I could hear my father muttering to
my mother that it was dangerous, that they must think of
our safety, my brother's and mine.

"In the way of politics, Marc Antony had gone too far.
In faraway Rome, Octavian was infuriated at the slight to
his sister, at the threat to his empire. Things grew tense
then in our household; war was pending and my father
was Antony's legate.

"My mother decided to send my brother and me to her
family in the Welisc hills. We pleaded not to leave them,
but she wrote letters of passage in the Roman tongue, gave
to us each brooches by which her clan would know us. My
father found a centurion who was loyal to him and who
had been with Julius Caesar when he invaded Britannia.
You have never known the centurions of Rome, Finnabair,
but they were fierce fighters and men of high loyalty and
honor. The centurion assured my father that he would accompany us all the way to our village. My father wished
my mother to leave him, too, but she would hear none.
'Gaius Ammianus,' she said, in her no-nonsense voice,
'we have been together forever. Do you think I would let
the politics of Rome separate us in your most dangerous
hour? We will join the children later.'

"Oh, Finnabair, all their plans were not enough, not swift enough, not devious enough for Rome. The armies of Octavian descended. Marc Antony committed suicide and the beautiful Cleopatra stung herself with two poisonous asps and died. My father and many of his legion were killed in the fighting; one of his men brought us word in flight, screaming to my mother to flee with her babies, but it was too late. The soldiers of Octavian were swollen with bloodlust and promises of riches in Rome. Or perhaps Octavian told them to destroy all the followers of Antony. They swept from house to house of the legion, killing women and children.

"My mother screamed to Flavi to hide us. He gathered us into his arms, ran with us toward the trapdoor in the kitchen that led to our cellar, the place where we stored our roots and vegetables, our flour. But my brother, Marcus, was twelve and cried aloud that Roman soldiers do not abandon their women. He took a knife, a mere kitchen knife and ran to help my mother. I tried to scramble after him, but Flavi held me in an iron grip, clasped his hand over my mouth. He knew what the Romans would do to me, a girl child."

"I do not understand."

"It was Roman law that they could not kill a virgin, Finnabair. So to make a girl child ready for slaughter, the Roman armies would deflower her, one of them after another."

"But this is monstrous; none in Eriu would ever treat a woman in such a way, virgin or no!"

"But the Romans did." She paused, pressed her hands against her lips. I knew that she was gathering her strength to tell the rest of it and I girded myself to hear it.

"When the house was silent at last, we came from our hiding place. My mother was dead, her head almost severed from her neck. My brother, Marcus, had been killed with a Roman shortsword through the heart, a death of honor for a warrior boy."

Even now, these many years later, the horror of it was on her face. She continued softly.

"For many days Flavi hid me, here and there, sometimes among the furtive and scrabbling men of my father's legions, sometimes in the back streets and tenements of the Egyptian city. He gathered my mother's letters and her Welisc brooches and he looked everywhere for the centurion. He cut a healer's cloak with its many inside pockets to my little height and in the pockets he put all of these, plus herbs and medicaments. By day, when we were in hiding, with gestures and markings, Flavi instructed me in their use for the journey. At last he gave me two amphorae in a pack that I was to wear over my shoulders. He instructed me never to remove them, for they contained the gold of Rome. In the amphorae were pepper and cinnamon. From the neck of each bottle hung a little spoon and Flavi taught me how to measure the amounts, what to ask for the sale."

"Cinnamon I remember from your porridge, but I do not know pepper."

She went to one of Flavi's niches, took down a graceful jar, and lifted off the stopper. She placed it beneath my nose. I inhaled deeply, then sneezed and sneezed again. Flavi and Niniane laughed aloud and I felt glad to have lightened the burden of their story.

"At last the centurion and Flavi found each other after more than a month in hiding. I begged Flavi to accompany us, but by gesture and drawings he convinced me that he would be dangerous to my journey, he being a man not Roman and with no voice. I was a young girl; Flavi, a young man of only twenty-five years, though from the perspective of a child I thought him old and all-wise."

She smiled at Flavi and he bent his head.

"The centurion was one Ammianus, a good old man, though gruff, a soldier with no experience of a girl child. By degrees, disguised as a trader and his daughter, we made our way across the world, sailing first to Rome, where we purchased more spices, then gathering our resources for a trip across Gaul and then across the Gaulish ocean to Alba. On shaggy ponies through rain and wind, we made our way to my mother's village; the journey took us three years. My grandmother, who was still alive, had thought her daughter to be dead all these long years. She welcomed me with love. The old centurion, Ammianus, remained there with my people where he was much beloved for his Roman skills with roads and water and his fierce defense of my small, dark clansmen."

"Then how did you come to be here?"

"In the simplest and oldest of ways. Irish raiders came from the sea looking for slaves. Rather than fight them, the chief of my village offered to negotiate with them. For a small price, he would give them slaves and no resistance. None of the raiders would be wounded or would die. I was a girl of nineteen years by then. My grandmother had died, as had old Ammianus; I had no blood ties left within the clan. I was a logical choice. He sold some eight of us by that reckoning. We were dumped unceremoniously into the Irish longboats and taken to a market near Emain Macha. There, naked and shivering, our necks clapped into *cumhal* torques—slave collars—we were sold for purposes of field and farm and house.

"As it happened on that day, Faitheman mac Eochaid, chieftain of his clan, was there to bargain for horses. He was a man nearly twelve years my senior, a fierce warrior with one dead wife behind him, no child, and no desire to wed again. But he must have taken pity on my tiny, naked frame in the cold wind. He bought me, wed me, and freed me all in one day." She chuckled. "It was a fairly momentous day for me."

"How can you laugh?"

"Do you remember, Finnabair, that on the first day we met I told you that twice in my life I wished to die?"

"I remember it well."

"The first time was on the day I saw my mother and brother slaughtered at Roman hands. The second was on that day in the market as I stood there naked and enslaved, shivering, a lower being than the horses around me."

"Both times I can well imagine that death would have been welcome."

"But I also told you that life surprised me. As it turned out, Faitheman was neither cold, nor all warrior, just a lonely man who did not know how to approach women. For two months I cooked for him and cleaned, complied with him in the marriage bed where he asked little of me, kept silent, listened to the tongue of Eriu. Then one evening I was bent above the fire, stirring at a rabbit stew when he swept through the door. The light must have been in my curls. Like my son, Rochad, Faitheman was a huge man with great hands like haunches of deer. But with immense gentleness, he lifted a curl in his hands and then watched as it sprung back into place. Like a three-year-old boy, he burst into laughter. With all the Gaeilge I had to me I said, 'If my curls delight you I am glad.' Faitheman began to laugh aloud; he could not stop laughing. He laughed so much that I joined in. Eventually I climbed into his lap and we mixed our giggling with sport. From that day forward he was my beloved; when my Gaeilge was good enough I was his advisor in all matters of his clan. Finally, one night, years later, I asked him what had made him laugh so hard on the night he touched my curls. It seems that when I had intended to say 'curls'—catach—I had said cadog instead—'haddock.'"

I laughed with her then, the capriciousness of fate and circumstance gusting up through me. Flavi regarded us quietly, smiling all the while. I realized that the story was not finished.

"Where is he now?"

"He died of the winter consumption just a few months

after Rochad returned from fosterage. Rochad had seventeen years then."

"But that was more than ten years ago."

"Until Flavi returned to me three years ago, I was alone."

She did not seem troubled by this, smiled in Flavi's direction. He regarded her with his great liquid eyes, all tenderness.

"And what of Flavi? How did he come to be with you again? And his voice? For I have heard him speak."

"Indeed you have." She spoke softly to Flavius, perhaps asking him permission to tell his story. He nodded in my direction once, placed his fingers against his lips. Niniane responded with a single word. She turned to me.

"We will tell you Flavi's story."

Behind her, Flavi began to disrobe, lifting his tunic over his shoulders. Though he surely had fifteen summers more than Niniane's fifty or so, his body was large, well-muscled, gleaming and beautiful.

"Why does he do this?" I asked Niniane.

"He will show you his journey, sweeting. For our story has but begun."

Flavi stepped into the firelight. Beautiful tattoos streamed from the sides of his cheeks down his neck and over his upper arms. He pointed to one that resembled an arrow or spear, spoke to Niniane.

"Flavius is not his true first name. He is a Nubian; his people lived along the banks of the Nile River in Egypt. Farther south than the country of Cleopatra, but still desert, dry and sunny."

"I know of nothing beyond Eriu; so much of your story fills me with wonder."

"Flavi's name among his people was Taharqa. It is a royal name, most ancient. Flavi's father was physician to the great queen of Meroe, the capital of that place. I have never been there, Finnabair, but Flavi says there were palaces of rose-colored stone, carved with statues more beautiful than anything in Rome. The women wore fine silks and beautiful jewelry and ate and drank from cups and plates of gold encrusted with jewels. The people were as beautiful as Flavi is, and they sang of their joy in each other and their land and made music of it on great drums and flutes."

Behind her, Flavi nodded. He went to a chest in the corner of the room and drew out a wooden flute and a small, gold ornament that looked like a ring holding a triangle. From the base of the triangle dangled tiny, golden leaves. These he handed to me gently.

"The flute belonged to Flavi's father, the ring to his mother."

"How is it that he has come this far with them?"

Again, he pointed to the arrow tattoo.

"The Romans invaded Egypt. The queen of Meroe was forced to defend her people. The Nubians were known all over the world for their skill at archery, but few can stand against the might of Rome. Flavi accompanied the army into battle as surgeon and physician to the royal house. In the terrible fighting, Taharqa was wounded; a Roman soldier slashed him across the throat deep into the muscles and the box that hold the voice."

Flavi unwound the gold and turqoise scarf that still covered his neck. There, hidden from view beneath the silken layers was a thick scar, jagged, raised and puckered. Flavi nodded toward Niniane and she continued.

"Speechless and bleeding badly, Taharqa was captured. He did what he could to heal his throat, but the voice was gone. Among the people of Meroe, the healers give medicines for the body, but they also sing to the spirit, call it forth to assist in its own healing. Taharqa had lost half of his healing powers. He had lost the very power which might have called forth his own spirit, which might have healed his voice. More ignominy followed. He became the slave of a Roman legate, but one who was vicious in his treatment of both his troops and his slaves. He named Taharqa Flavius and tried to beat out of him his royal Nubian bearing and his knowledge, which far exceeded that of the legate."

Now Flavi turned his back to me and I saw the crisscrossed scars and raised welts.

I gasped aloud. I scrambled from the bed and ran to him, placed my cool palms against the skin. He turned to face me, smiling gently, spoke to Niniane.

"He says that he shows you not to trouble your heart, but so that you will know our journey and come to trust us."

"Why should that matter?"

"We will speak more of that, Daughter. But first let us tell you of our journey."

I settled back onto the sleeping platform, drew the warm cloak around my shoulders, listened warily, for I suspected now that the telling had something to do with me.

Flavi drew his tunic back over the gleaming body. The pictures of his journey were hidden now. He rewrapped the beautiful scarf around the disfiguring scar. He spoke softly to Niniane.

"In time, the legate died in battle. It was a Roman custom to grant manumission to slaves upon his deathbed, but because the legate died in battle, none of his slaves was freed. The legate had no wife or children, so the slaves were sold in the market in Egypt.

"You must understand the slaves of Rome, Finnabair, for here, in Ulster, you have a scattering of slaves who work their way to freedom, or marry freedom, or purchase freedom, and once they do, they share all rights of Eriu before the law."

"That is so."

"But the slaves of Rome were all of the conquered people of the empire and though they could earn or purchase freedom, they could not be citizens of Rome. My father told me once that the slaves of Rome outnumbered the Romans threefold. My grandfather told me that in one day in the Gallic Wars, Caesar sold more than fifty thousand Aduatuci people into slavery. The slaves of Rome spoke every tongue, boasted every color of skin and hair. The custom at the time of their sale was to stand them naked in the market with a sign around their neck. On that sign was the country of their origin and their profession. The slaves of Rome were its doctors and its scribes, its gladiators and its actors. Just so, tall and naked, silent, with a sign that read, FLAVIUS, NUBIAN, HEALER, was Flavi sold. He was purchased by a decurion and taken to the country of Cleopatra. The decurion realized quickly that Flavi was a learned man. He granted him manumission, made him a freedman, hired him as the surgeon and physician for his own household. When the decurion died, my father hired Flavi into our household."

"A most strange and wandering journey."

"Stranger still, Finnabair, for what happened to Flavi when I left him is more amazing than any story I can tell you."

From across the room Flavi said something, short and low. Niniane responded, her tone a question. He nodded his head.

Niniane looked at me her eyes shining.

"Flavi will tell you his story himself."

Flavi came and knelt on one knee before my sleeping platform. He spread his arms out and tipped his palms skyward. In perfect Gaeilge he said, "Be not afraid." Then he placed his great palms on either side of my head. Joy rushed through me, fearless and warm, stunning in its intensity. I gasped aloud and pressed my hands against his to hold the sensation inside me, to keep it forever.

"Finnabair," he said softly, his voice musical, still in Gaeilge. "Hear my tale."

I leaned in toward him, my breath coming in short gasps, for I knew that what I would hear was what I could feel in his hands, the pulse of it so warm, so full of joy.

"I am listening," I said.

And then the hoofbeats thundered into the clearing.

Rochad mac Faitheman burst unceremoniously into the hut, his face a mask of anger.

"Finnabair ni Medb!" he thundered. "Your mother sends yet another against Cuchulainn at the ford."

I stood before him.

"As ever she will, for she is Medb! Has not the Hound bested them all? Why do you come to me with this?"

"Because she sends your brother, Maine Mathramail. Cuchulainn says that if you wish to save his life, you must come and talk sense into him."

Panic rushed through me. Not Mathramail. Any of them but Mathramail, my beloved brother. Immediately I felt ashamed of the thought.

I had pinned the cloak of Ulster to my shoulder before Rochad ever finished speaking, the end of the story of Niniane and Flavi forgotten utterly in my haste to reach my brother. I took Rochad's massive hand, flung myself up behind him on the heaving black horse. The cloak billowed out behind me as we rode like the wind for the ford.

7

I have seven brothers. Or I should say had, for Cuchulainn has already disposed of one of them. Though, in truth, my brother had twenty years upon my age and I did not know him well enough to grieve his passing. I suppose in my mind he was just one of the Maine, warrior sons of Medb. Among my people, my brothers are known as the Maine and each is possessed of a special quality. Morgor was the duty-minded and it was he whom Cuchulainn first dispatched, as Morgor did his duty for Medb. Andoe is the swift, for he can run like a deer or a wolf. Moepirt is known for his honeyed speech and his gift with women. All of them are older than I; none of them know me, their silent little sister. None, that is, but Mathramail.

When I was a child it was Mathramail who would clean and bandage my little scrapes and kiss the tiny bruises. It was he who would place me on his shoulders at the *feis* so that I should see the chariot riders. At night when I was alone and wept in fear of the dark, it was Mathramail who would shoo away the nurses Medb had hired and cuddle me, singing silly songs and telling stories until he had me laughing. His care of me had earned him his nickname—

Mathramail—the Motherlike. And it had earned him the derision of his six warrior brothers and of our mother.

It was Mathramail who was mustered at the far side of the river, his tall slender body shivering in the breeze, his face looking determined and terrified at the same time. My heart wrenched with pity to see him.

Rochad hauled his horse to a stop and I dismounted in a single sweep of my leg. I unpinned the cloak and waded into the river all in one move.

Cuchulainn was standing atop his rock in the center of the ford, ready again to defend the passage into Ulster. He watched my brother as one watches a small growling dog, not taking his eyes off of him, but calling to me over his shoulder.

"Make haste, Stinkweed. He ponders his options and I should not like for him to exercise them."

I started to clamber up the rock, wet and slippery, but could get no purchase. Behind me I heard a snort of derision and then Rochad rode the great horse into the river behind me and, from his saddle, boosted me by placing his hand unceremoniously beneath my buttocks and heaving me toward Cuchulainn, who simply reached his arm behind him for me to grasp. Rochad rode back to the far side of the river.

I stood up beside Cuchulainn, shaking at the wet bottom of my tunic.

"I grow sick of this river, Hound."

"I hear you well there, Stinkweed, for I think that your mother means for me never to leave it."

On the opposite bank, Maine Mathramail regarded me in surprise.

"Finnabair? That is you?"

I called him by our childhood name.

"Mahneemawra, I am here before you. I beg you, do not fight this Hound. I know why you are here, but you will fail. Medb will not respect you; you will not earn her love.

No, you will die at the hands of this Hound and then she will laugh at the fireside when the other Maine tell stories of you."

Mathramail hung his head at the truth of it.

Beside me Cuchulainn shifted and groused. "I put on all of my warrior garb for this."

I looked sideways at him. In truth, he was resplendently garbed. The battle harness that covered his chest was made from layer over layer of waxed skin tunics, more than two dozen of them from what I could see. Over that was a fine silk apron with a border of gold. He wore a fine battlebelt of tanned leather, and from it ranged a mighty collection of weapons from eight daggers to small spears and a great sword with an ivory hilt. In his hand he held the *gae bolga,* the vicious spear with its killing barbs that opened in the body. A deep crimson shield with a slicing edge was strapped to his left arm. A collection of extra javelins and spears ranged around him on the rock.

"Why are you garbed so?" I asked him in amazement.

"I was told that your mother sent one of the Maine against me. I remember Morgor; he was a fierce fighter, a worthy opponent. I did not expect such a one as this."

He gestured at Mathramail. Tall and thin, Mathramail was shivering on the opposite bank. He wore a tunic and cloak, a small battle apron, his ordinary sandals. His long, curly, golden hair lifted and moved in the breeze. He stood with his shoulders hunched forward a little, his hand moving up and down spasmodically on his javelin. I turned to Cuchulainn.

"What mean you to say?"

He turned to face me.

"Only that this is no worthy battle opponent for so much gear."

I balled my fist up into the tightest curl I could make. I put all my weight behind my arm and punched him as hard as I could just below his left eye.

For a moment something happened to him. He seemed

to enlarge somehow. The eye retreated into its socket while the other seemed to bulge. His mouth opened and a terrible sound began to issue from it. On the opposite shore Mathramail witnessed the transformation. He hurled himself into the river, javelin raised high.

"Finnabair, leap from the rock. Jump, my sweeting. Jump!"

Cuchulainn turned toward my approaching brother. A low humming sound issued from his throat and he seemed to force himself back into his body. He beat the hilt of his sword once against his shield. It made a sound like a great drum. He called aloud.

"Halt! I will not harm your sister."

Mathramail stopped midwater, regarded the Hound. He swung his javelin in an arching side-to-side motion, suspicious.

"I do swear it; you have my word."

Mathramail let the javelin descend.

Cuchulainn turned toward me.

"He loves you, this green sapling. He was willing to throw himself at me to save you." He touched the spot below his eye and grinned at me. "And he is obviously the brother that you love. Tell him to cross to the opposite bank. We will sit down and talk this over. He has my surety that neither you nor he will be harmed."

Cuchulainn made his usual leap to the bank, a single airborne bound that carried him to shore. I started to work my way down the rock by footholds but Mathramail thrashed toward me and helped me down. Meanwhile, Rochad sat his horse on the opposite bank and watched the proceedings with a look on his face that hovered between amusement and surprise. Whatever Cuchulainn said when he reached Rochad caused him to ride away into the forest. He did seem to be always leaving. I shrugged. Good riddance. My brother and I reached the far bank, wet and bedraggled, to find that Cuchulainn had already snared a rabbit and was building a fire and spit. I wrapped myself in my Ulster plaid cloak under my brother's disapproving eye and sat by the fire.

"Why did you come here, Mahneemawra?"

"Medb can find no one to fight the Hound since you left us. She cannot promise you as prize and after the debacle of the Munster chiefs no one would believe her."

"So she sent you?"

"She did."

"What of the other Maine?"

My brother was uncomfortably silent.

"I see the way of it. None of them wishes her approval enough to try the Hound. None but you. And why do you need her approval? Because of me. Your care of me."

Beside the fire, Cuchulainn sighed.

"There you go again, Finnabair, taking all the failings of your mother onto yourself."

Mathramail regarded him in surprise. Cuchulainn looked up at him.

"Oh, I know what you have heard of me in your camp. I disappear into the *riastradh*, the warp transformation."

"They say you are terrible to behold."

"I am not so wonderful to behold even now," he said, grinning.

My brother regarded him in amazement.

"Well, you are better than the stories. They say you grow taller than any man, that fire spits from your mouth and your hair, that your eye bulges . . ."

"Oh, I have heard it all. I am vicious with both friends and enemies. My weapons are invincible. And on and on. But I am as trapped here as you two, the offspring of Medb. And I am glad not to kill you, Mathramail, for I would wish to kill no more brothers."

"I do not understand this."

"The Ulstermen are in their cursing. You know this. They cannot come against the armies of Connacht. Yet who will defend them until their curse is lifted? I am left alone here at the ford. I struck the only bargain with your mother that I could think to strike—single combat, one warrior at a time until the Ulstermen arise. But your mother harries me nigh unto death. Do you know that she once sent more than twenty against me at one time? Her reasoning was that they were all of the same clan and therefore counted as only one man."

"And I am told that you killed them all," said Mathra-mail.

Cuchulainn snorted. "No such thing. Half of them went slinking away into the forest and will not show their sorry faces until this War of the Bull is over. And Rochad mac Faitheman is always my good right arm. I tell you your mother is deceptive. She dishonors our bargain. She tries to sneak warriors against me in the night to harry me and weary me when I am sore wounded. And then she sent my foster-brother against me, Ferdiad, my own brother."

His voice broke at the name and I saw tears stand out in his eyes. From across the clearing Rochad rode up on his horse, the saddle baskets bursting with loaves of bread and the drinking vessels that I recognized from the dwelling of Flavius. Beside him Laeg wheeled in his chariot. So, the Hound had sent them for food. I looked at the Hound, that Rochad might not think that I hoped for his return. Cuchulainn regarded their approach, bent his head toward the fire.

"Tell them I have gone for a deer."

He loped away into the forest without another word.

Rochad swung down from his saddle and lifted the baskets. He set them by the fire and turned to me.

"What did you say to him?"

I bristled. "We said nothing. We were speaking of Medb, of the warriors she sends against him. He told my brother"—I gestured toward Mathramail—"that he wished to kill no more brothers. Then he spoke of Ferdiad and ran away into the forest."

"Ah, Ferdiad. There was his heart broken in this endless war. Your mother has a vicious heart."

My brother pointed toward Rochad. Mathramail's anger was palpable.

"Who is this one?"

"Know you not, brother? This is Rochad mac Faitheman. This is he to whom our mother sold me in marriage. All to avoid a battle. All to keep this single combat with Cuchulainn continuing without end until she finds her great bull."

"I am sorry for what she has done to you, Finnabair. Obviously, this Rochad is not worthy of you."

"From what I have seen, he is not worthy of much. But he has a good and gentle mother."

Laeg shifted his position against the side of his chariot, recrossed his legs on the ground.

"Cuchulainn would not like to hear you speak ill of Rochad, for it is only Rochad and his warriors who assist him in these wars."

Rochad grinned lazily.

"You need not defend me, friend Laeg. Finnabair recalls at least one occasion where she well knew my worth."

I felt the hot blood rushing up beneath the roots of my hair, staining my cheeks and chest. My mind went unbidden to the thickness of the great upper arms, to the long hands, surprisingly gentle. I dropped my head and let my hair fall forward.

"Will you shame me before my brother?"

Mathramail came immediately to my defense.

"No shame in you, little sister. For well we know that what Medb wills, we all must do, regardless how distasteful the task."

Rochad made a small explosive sound in his throat somewhere between exasperation and laughter.

Behind my hair, I allowed myself a small smile of triumph.

"Well, he is an Ulsterman, Mahneemawra. We all know that they cannot rise when the occasion demands it."

I glanced out from behind my hair. Rochad was regarding me with a peculiar look, the way one regards a little dog who has just growled for the first time.

Laeg spoke again, ignoring the implications in what I had said.

"Rochad's tribe is not affected by the cursing. Only the warriors of Emain Macha are so cursed."

"It sounds to me like a most convenient way to avoid fighting Medb and her armies."

"Do you know the story, Finnabair?"

"Only that Ulstermen are cursed and cannot fight."

"It is much more than that."

"Tell us then, for lately I have wondered."

His voice became cadenced, rhythmic, and I realized with surprise that the charioteer was a born storyteller.

"Long, long ago, there lived in Ulster a lonely man named Crunniuc. He was widowed and lived alone with his two small children in a hut not far from the ford of this very river. One day he returned from hunting and entered his hut to find there a woman of great beauty. She had laid the fire and cooked a sumptuous meal. She had bathed his children and had sung them to sleep with lullabies. Without a word, she took Crunniuc to bed and loved from him all the sorrows of his losses. And so she remained, loving him and tending to his home and children, singing snatches of beautiful songs and speaking very little. In the evenings, just before last light, the woman would run beside the river, her black hair streaming behind her, and Crunniuc would watch in awe at her speed and beauty. Crunniuc was too happy to question his good fortune. His joy reached its zenith when the woman told him that she was bearing his twin children.

"At last, it came time for the great *feis* at the hill of kings. The woman packed Crunniuc's bags and prepared him for the journey. Just before he departed, she gave him this warning: *Do not speak of me at the* feis. *Do not speak of me at the feasting. Do not speak of me by the fires.*

Crunniuc solemnly promised that he would not speak of
her at all and departed for the great festival. For the first
two days of the festival he was able to keep his promise,
but on the third day, a great race was held at the crest of
the hill. Charioteers from all over Ulster drove their finest
horses pell-mell and headlong around the circle. Of
course, the great black pair of the High King of Ireland
won the race. That night by the fire, everyone discussed
the races, relived each turn of the track, praised and ana-
lyzed the merits of each horse. At last Crunniuc could
bear no more. Before the high king himself, he did the
very thing the woman had instructed him not to do.

" 'I have a woman who is swifter and more beautiful
than all the horses who have raced today. I wager that she
afoot could defeat even the pair of the High King.'

"The laughter and friendly banter of the company
dwindled to silence. At last the king rose. He regarded
Crunniuc with barely disguised disgust. Disbelief in his
voice, he issued the challenge.

" 'Bring her before us and let her race.'

"Now Crunniuc panicked. He stood before the crowd,
palms out.

" 'I boast only. Surely we all know that no woman could
outrun a horse. It is too much mead that is talking.'

"But the damage was done. The king would hear nothing but that she be brought before the company. He dispatched a contingent of warriors and they returned,
dragging her between them, her seven-month belly pro-
claiming her state to all.

"To Crunniuc, she gave one look only, a look so
scathing, so filled with loathing that he shrunk away in terror. To the king she made appeal.

" 'Look at me, O King of Ulster, a woman heavy with
child. Do not use me as you use your horses, lest you bring
down wrath upon yourself. Does the king of Eriu treat our
women so?'

"But the horses of the king had been challenged and he would hear none.

" 'You will run,' he said, 'or the head of your boasting husband will pay the price.'

"The woman did not even glance in Crunniuc's direction.

" 'Bring my team!' the king commanded. Between the great, heaving black horses he placed the woman. At the sound of the drums, the race began. And, oh, how the woman ran, her hair streaming behind her, her heavy belly heaving with the effort. She left the horses far behind, far behind. But at the end of the track, she collapsed to the ground, heavy in labor. Screaming in pain, she cursed the men of Ulster.

" 'Woe to you, men of Ulster. For this ignominy to a woman, I curse you now and for nine generations to come. When Ulster is most in need, when warriors are called to defend her, down they will fall, cursed by the pains of labor.'

"In screaming pain, she gave birth to two tiny twins. She stood and gathered them into her arms.

" 'From this day forward, you will call this hill by my name. Know me now as Macha.'

"Screams of terror arose from the hill, for all knew her now. She was Macha, the shapeshifter, one of the three sisters of the Morrigu, goddess of darkness, goddess of panic, goddess of war.

"And so, to this day, the hill is called Emain Macha and the men of Ulster fall down in pain in their time of need. Only Cuchulainn is exempted of all in Ulster. And the boys were exempted, too."

"What boys?"

"The boy troops of Ulster. The beardless boys."

"And where are they now?"

Laeg looked away across the field towards the woods line. Rochad spoke instead.

"Finnabair," he said quietly. I looked at him directly for the first time since the night of our marriage. His eyes were grey, sorrowful.

"There is much you do not know. When Cuchulainn fought Ferdiad, his foster-brother, he was wounded. Sore wounded, almost unto death. The boy troops of Ulster stood in for him, rode into battle against the warriors of Connacht."

"Oh, you gods," I said. "I fear that I will hear a terrible truth now."

"You will," said Rochad.

Beside me, Mathramail reached for my hand.

"Your mother gave command. Her warriors slew them all, all the beardless boys."

"No. Oh, no."

"He does not tell you all," said Mathramail. "For Cuchulainn was so incensed at their death that he went into the warp spasm. Around our warriors he rode, this sapling driving." He gestured at Laeg. "One after another he slew them until they were toppled head to heel, a human fence of all the slaughtered."

"Mathramail, why did I know none of this?"

"Medb gave command, Sister. You were not to know, not to hear anything that would make you rebel against her plan. She feared that you would stop her from offering you. The stream of warriors who wished to curry favor would dry up."

"I have part in all of this. And you." I pointed at my brother who nodded woodenly. "And you." I gestured at Rochad, who shrugged, but had the grace to look ashamed. "And him."

Cuchulainn emerged from the woods line, a deer slung over his shoulders. I did not know that I was running at him, so swift did my feet move over the ground. I ran as the Macha ran. I ran full of my own cursing. I reached him and without stopping at all I stretched out my arms and toppled him. The great hero of Ulster fell to his back in the field, the bloody doe behind his head like a pillow.

I beat on him with my fists.

"Stop it, Hound! You must stop it! It must cease! All this bloodshed for a bull. Hound, make it cease!"

Rochad and Mathramail pried me from him, held me kicking and flailing. Cuchulainn sat up, nonplussed. He smiled at me, no anger in his eyes, no bafflement upon him.

"Finnabair," he said. "That is why we have purchased you."

And so we would come to it at last. I prepared myself to hear the truth of my betrothal and marriage to this stranger of Ulster.

8

We had before us the makings of a feast, a deer roasting on a spit, bread and honey, rabbit and mead. We were a strange gathering at the fire: my brother and I, enemies of Ulster, children of Medb; Laeg the charioteer; Rochad, my erstwhile husband; the Hound of Ulster.

Like hosts at a great feast, Cuchulainn and Laeg made sure that all of their guests were served whole loaves of bread, brimming tankards of mead. Cuchulainn made great ceremony of giving me the haunch of deer, the hero's portion, pointing to the little blue bruise beneath his eye and winking as he did so. He seemed almost proud of me. When we were all seated in a circle, the Hound heaved a great sigh.

"How to begin?"

"Begin with the truth and simply. I have heard it so seldom in my life that I promise you I will recognize it aright."

He laughed, turned toward Rochad.

"She is witty, this one. I love wit in a woman. For wit, I wed my Emer."

For his part, Rochad was still regarding me fixedly, as he had been since first I punched Cuchulainn in the eye, as if he were seeing a sea creature he had never encountered before.

"Please, Cuchulainn."

He nodded.

"Very well. I do not promise that you will like it, but I will tell it to you unvarnished."

"Do so."

"Your mother sent Ferdiad against me."

"So I have been told."

"Ferdiad was my foster-brother. Together we studied at the warrior school of Scathach. Together, we learned the feats of war." He smiled at me, but the smile was sad. "We competed with each other, laughing at who would best the other. The salmon leap, the breath feat, the lance point, the spear points. Together we fought in the war against Aoife. I loved him, Finnabair. He was my foster-brother, my friend. How did she persuade him to come against me? What could she have offered?"

I hung my head, the shame creeping up my neck.

"Ah," he said. That was all. No blame, full understanding. The simplicity of it released my tears from behind my eyes and they dripped down the front of my tunic. My brother came to my defense.

"Such was Medb's strategy for that while, Hound. One warrior after another and my sister in her diaphanous dress, feeding them tidbits at the feast. Medb as part of the offering, also. And for Ferdiad she offered the riches of a kingdom, land and dwellings at Cruachan Ai, armies and serving folk, great riches."

"And for those Ferdiad went against me?" The Hound's voice was wounded, almost childlike.

"No," said Mathramail. "Medb is wise in the ways of men, Hound. You say that your boyhood games were all competition. What was your best feat?"

Laeg spoke. "At all feats of war he excels. Why?"

"Because on those feats Medb incited Ferdiad to war. When all her other enticements had failed, she said that

Cuchulainn had jeered when Fergus warned him that she would send Ferdiad against you. She said that you had boasted that you would not need even your best feat to defeat Ferdiad."

"So she trapped him with our boyhood pride."

"She did."

Cuchulainn looked down at the ground, his food untouched. When he looked up at me, his face was almost warped with sorrow.

"For three days we fought, Finnabair. Side by side as we had fought as boys. By day we fought with hurling spears, stabbing spears, broadswords. By night we shared our food and our medicine. Our charioteers hobbled our horses side by side. For three days we fought thus. But on the fourth, Ferdiad wounded me grievously."

He lifted his tunic. Crawling down his side was a puckered, red snake of a scar, thick and sinuous, hideous in its healing. He stood, agitated, his arms beginning to windmill at his sides. He was fairly screaming now.

"I told him that he should not have come against me for the thighs of Medb and her winsome daughter. I told him so! I cast the *gae bolga* at him, Finnabair. The *gae bolga*. He died full of my fishhooks. I carried him here to my side of the river. He died in my arms."

He began to spin in place. He was transforming before us and I could do nothing. Cuchulainn began to howl, an unearthly wailing, a howl of pain and grief that I recognized. I actually stood to comfort him, terrible as he was, but Mathramail dragged me backward from the fire, held me tight by the upper arms.

"Medb of Connacht," Cuchulainn cried aloud. "Hear me. All of your war was but as child's play to me until this. Ferdiad! Ferdiad! Curses on you, Medb of Connacht."

He was spitting and whirling. He danced into the center of the fire and the sparks rose around him and seemed to issue from his mouth, to sprout from the top of his head. The howling took on the sound of thunder, rolling and turning around us. Spinning and sparking, he lowered his body, began to whirl his arms in our direction. His face was horrible to behold, one eye bulging and bloodshot, the other deep within its socket. He was sweating and panting like a great dog. He pointed a huge hand at Mathramail and me. I closed my eyes and prepared to die.

Laeg began to scream.

"Fid Duin! Fid Duin! Fid Duin!"

The whirling Hound of Ulster turned toward the forest. He leaped into the air and ran for the darkness of the woods.

9

"What did you say? Where has he gone?"

"I have sent him to the Fid Duin. To the Dark Forest. There the Partraigi will care for him and calm him. They alone can calm him. The Partraigi and Emer."

"I do not know of this place or these . . . Partraigi?"

"Nor would you, being of Connacht." Laeg smiled. "They dwell in the dark forests of the north. They are as much unlike us—the men of Ulster—as the moon is unlike the sun."

"How so?"

"It is a hard thing to explain. We call them the People of the Stag. They live in the forests as the deer do, invisible, light as air, most ancient. I think that they are not of the Celts, nor ever were. The story is that they came from across the water. They are dark and silent, deep as the water they traveled on. Among them, the Hound's *riastradh* is quieted."

"Did Emer come to him when he was wounded?"

Laeg and Rochad exchanged a glance. I read it instantly. "You did not tell her!"

Laeg shook his head. "We did not. Understand, Finnabair, this battle with Ferdiad—it wounded him nearly unto death. His side was pierced just as he has shown you, but there was more. Every inch of his skin was nicked and cut. He had to hold his clothing away from him with twigs and grasses. His breathing was shallow, and in the days after Ferdiad's death, he rose and broke fevers, one after another. When the Hound is at war, Emer lives in the south, at the Gardens of Lugh. Emer loves him well, but she fears his warrior life."

"As well she should. So you nursed him back to health."

Again they exchanged a look, said nothing.

"Laeg?"

He responded with silence.

I turned to Rochad, looked him full in the eyes.

"Too many threads are untied here, Rochad mac Faitheman. The Hound has said that you purchased me to stop this war. It is time for you to tell me all."

Still he said nothing.

I pulled out my best weapon.

"Niniane would wish this of you."

He sighed. "You begin to surprise me, Finnabair."

Mathramail chuckled. "Do not underestimate my sister, Ulsterman. Her fires are banked; they are not put out."

I looked at him, askance that he would say such a thing to our enemy. But he was watching Rochad avidly, awaiting his response.

Rochad looked from one of us to the other. He heaved a long sigh.

"Very well. It cannot hurt to tell them the truth, now that the danger is passed?" He looked to Laeg for confirmation. Laeg nodded, spoke quietly.

"You are the children of Medb, so I will tell you that your mother almost got her fondest wish. Cuchulainn was hours from death, Finnabair. He had bled too much and his heart was beating erratically and slow. More than that, his spirit was broken. Ferdiad dead by his hand. I bathed him over and over with the cold river water, squeezed droplets of water onto his tongue. He raged with fever, murmured Emer's name. Once, in a moment of cold clarity, he said, 'Take my head to her that my spirit may dwell beside her.' 'Nonsense,' I said. 'You will rise again and beat off the warriors of Medb.' I did not believe it, but my saying so rallied him some. That was when he asked me to send for Rochad."

His eyes grew wide with the memory.

"I left him alone, Finnabair, helpless by the water, covered in wounds, fair game for the wolves or for the marauding warriors of Medb. I rode as though the Hound himself was on my heels for the hut of Flavius the Healer. Flavius rode north and brought the warriors of Rochad."

Rochad took up the story.

"When we arrived, the wolf was guarding him." He gestured toward the woods line but the vigilant, dark shape of the Morrigu had vanished. Rochad continued.

"Cuchulainn was like a torch in which there is no more wick, only grey and smoky residue. But he raised himself up on his elbows, whispered to me. 'Your clan is not subject to the cursing. Will you ride among the camps of Medb? Will you buy me time to heal?' Before I could answer, he drew me down to him, whispered low, 'Think well, for you will lose many of your clansmen.' But there was no thinking. He was the Hound. Alone, he had defended Ulster day after day. Our honor demanded that we aid him. With all our chariots and horsemen, we rode among your armies. But riding toward us on the plain we saw not warriors bristling with armor. No, we saw the treachery of Medb, sending toward us a slip of a girl in a dress made of clouds."

His face was full of anger. He turned toward me, pointed his forefinger.

"Do you think I was taken in by that, Finnabair ni Medb? Besotted by your beauty, by what I could see beneath your gown? I am not a pimply boy, all my juices like sap in the spring trees."

Laeg spoke up, sarcastic as always.

"Do you think to woo her with these fine words, Rochad?"

Rochad had the grace to look embarrassed.

"You came to us, Finnabair, your spokesman . . ." He waved his hand in the air.

"Mac Roth."

"That one. The herald of Connacht we call him, with his linen headband and his hazel rod, bargaining, always bargaining for Medb. And this time he offered us you, with sureties of truce, promises of land, requests that we save ourselves for the last battle when the men of Emain Macha arise from the cursing."

He turned and spit on the ground.

"Faugh. That is what I would say to Mac Roth, to Medb."

My brother spoke from his seat by the fire.

"And yet you took the bargain, married my sister."

"I did. You asked for truth and I will tell you why. To my right was Laeg, who whispered, 'Take her. The bargain will buy Cuchulainn time.'"

Laeg nodded. "So I said. And to his left was Flavius the Nubian. Hear me, Finnabair. Something happened when Flavius saw you. I heard him. 'Ahh,' he said, on a long note, as though he recognized you. And then, 'This one?' As if he had received answer, he turned to Rochad. 'Marry this one,' he said. 'For she will bring peace to Ulster.'"

"I? How would one such as I go against Medb?"

Rochad shrugged. "We all know that Flavius . . . sees things. I did as he asked. And then the treachery of it. The treachery. Your kinsmen hiding in the woods, the ambush of my clan."

"You paid them back, Rochad. You bedded me and vanished in the darkness."

Laeg shifted uncomfortably. "That was my doing, Finnabair. I sent a messenger to him in darkness. I told him to return."

"Why?"

"Cuchulainn was healed."

"In three days? And why did you abandon the Hound? To battle my clan? Did it never cross your mind that my mother could send assassins against him in the darkness? Murder him in his weakened state?"

Laeg and Rochad exchanged glances.

"She would not have found him. He was not here."

"He went among the Partraigi?"

Silence. Then at last, "No." Nothing more.

"Where did he go? Speak, man."

Rochad shook his head. "It is a story you may not believe. We are still not sure what we saw."

"Make us see it. Let us judge the telling."

"Very well. The night that I arrived," Rochad shook his head. "I would not have given one *eric* for Cuchulainn's life. I thought that we would return from our battle with Medb, to find him gone, his spirit flown the body."

Laeg continued.

"But as we sat beside the river in the dusk, we saw coming toward us a troop of women. They were shining, beautiful, in cloaks of green shot through with silver. And the silver shimmered like stars as they moved. Among them was a woman, Fand, who was the most beautiful woman I have ever seen, so beautiful that were I asked to give up earth and sea to dwell with her, I would do so."

"They did not walk," said Rochad. "They drifted toward us as water runs toward the sea or as fog insinuates itself into a valley."

I looked at him.

"And their legs were white as the fog and seemed smoky, insubstantial as the air."

"You have seen them!"

"When my beloved was wounded. They came for him, carried him away."

Rochad gave me a dark look that I could not read.

"Were they accompanied by a man of light?" Laeg asked.

"No, they were women only. More than a hundred of them."

"When they came for Cuchulainn, there was among them a tall man. He wore a green cloak and under it a gold tunic, covered with embroidery, birds and fish, leaping and entwined. He carried a shield of deepest black, but it seemed that light tried to seep from its edges and he held it in by force of will and hand.

"When he reached Cuchulainn, he bent over him with such tenderness, such love. And then he sang a song, the *suantraighe,* the sleeping music, just as a mother would sing to her infant. We watched as the Hound fell into a deep sleep, watched as the shallow, labored breathing became deep and regular."

"So it is true. We of Connacht have heard that the Hound is not human, the he is the son of Lugh."

Laeg shrugged. "The man of Light did not say his name. He said only that we should return in three days' time, that Cuchulainn would be restored to us. When I returned from the battle with the armies of Medb it was just as he had told us. For the Hound was seated here by the fire, whistling and cooking, as hale as when I first met him, a boisterous boy. He said that he had been among them for a year, that the woman Fand had ministered to his wounds. But three days only had passed. No matter the time, the Hound was well. And so I sent for Rochad. He had done what we requested, Finnabair. He had bought us time and the Hound was healed." Laeg gestured in my direction. "I knew you not, Finnabair. You were only a piece on the *fidchell* board of this great war, daughter of Medb, pawn. I did not call him back to cause you pain."

"Pain? What pain could arise from such a match as this?" I gestured in Rochad's direction. "He is not my

beloved. I did as Medb requested. I bedded him. I gave my
army time to ambush." I shrugged.

Rochad met my eyes. A small smile played at the cor-
ners of his mouth. I looked away. All men are arrogant;
this much Medb had taught me. I struck out at him.

"Nor would you have stayed of your own will among
my people, Rochad. You did not bargain fairly, any more
than I."

"I bargained for what I believed in. For the Hound. For
Ulster. What do you believe in, Finnabair?"

The question was fair and cut to the bone.

"I believe in the truth. So believe me now when I say
that you are released from your bargain, Rochad mac
Faitheman."

"No!" said Laeg. "Flavius would not wish it."

"I do not know what Flavius saw. Nor care. Nor do I
know what the Hound meant by saying that for the purpose of ending this war, Ulster had purchased me. But I
will know, though it bring me as much pain as the death of
Ferdiad has brought to Cuchulainn. I will know the truth
and all of it. So it is to the Hound that I will go first."

Laeg shook his head.

"You cannot go among the Partraigi."

"I am the daughter of Medb. I can go where I will."

"The Partraigi do not accept just anyone, Finnabair.
Many have been known to vanish in their forests, never to
be seen again."

I smiled at Laeg.

"Do you think I fear either banishment or vanishing,
Laeg? All my life, I have dwelled in both of these states at
once." I stood and kissed my brother. "Except for you,
sweet Mahneemawra. And one Other."

Rochad made his usual expletive sound, but my brother
stood and swung his cloak over his shoulders.

"I will accompany you, Sister."

Rochad protested.

"A man of Connacht, son of Medb, far into Ulster territory? You will not survive the journey. Nor will this headstrong fool." He gestured in my direction but would not meet my eyes.

"Finnabair is my sister."

"Oh, by the gods! I will take her!" This seemed to make Rochad terribly angry. He threw the bones of his meal toward the fire, stood with a single motion. "I am an Ulsterman and she is my wife." I turned the full anger of my gaze against him. He amended. "At least in law. For now. And so we will not be troubled by my kinsmen."

"Why should I need you? I am capable of turning a horse's head alone."

"No horse, Finnabair," said Laeg. "Among the Partraigi, one walks, silently, if she is wise."

"Then I will walk wisely. I am capable of that as well."

Laeg rummaged about in the Hound's traveling pack, unearthing a soft deerhide cloak worked to almost white, beaded and embroidered with stars and swirls. This he handed to me.

"I have my own cloak, friend Laeg," I protested.

"It is the Hound's. It is made from cloth from Tir Tairngire, the Promised Land. Or so he says."

"I should take it to him?"

"If you are in danger you should wear it."

"But why?"

"You will know why when you don the cloak."

Impulsively I kissed him on the cheek. He blushed and smiled at me almost shyly. I drew my arms around my brother.

"*Slan abhaile,* Brother. Safe home."

Mathramail hugged me hard.

I started toward the tree line where the Hound had vanished. Behind me, Rochad spoke sarcastically.

"How do you propose to find the Fid Duin, Finnabair, when you have never been there?"

Laeg hissed at him, "She has the Bird-Sight, man. Do you know nothing of her?"

"She does?" A pause and then I heard Rochad's footsteps moving in my selfsame path. I did not look back.

10

At the edge of the Fid Duin sat Cuchulainn's wolf. She turned her wary yellow eyes upon us, looked back toward the forest.

"Why will she not enter?" I whispered, careful to keep my voice low.

Rochad shrugged. "It is a wolf; I do not ken their behaviors."

I looked at him directly. "You know as well as I know what she is; why does she not enter the Fid Duin?"

"Cuchulainn has told you who she is?"

"He has."

"None know this but Laeg and me. None. He must see something in you." He seemed baffled by this thought.

I sighed. "How did such a mother raise such a one as you?"

"What do you mean?"

"Never mind; answer my original question. Why does the Morrigu not enter the Fid Duin?"

"It is said that the Partraigi do not make war."

"Never?"

"Once they were a warlike people, so the story goes. But these among them chose a way of peace. They did not wish to live among their warlike brothers. When our voyagers went to their shores long ago, they returned upon our ships and disappeared into the Fid Duin. It is not a place for the Sower of War, so she does not enter."

"If that is so, it is a place that I could stay forever."

"Really? Why?" Again that note of bafflement.

"I am the child of Medb. She plays at war the way she plays at love, the way that boys play stick war."

He grinned at me. "Then how could such a one as she have raised such a one as you?"

I chose not to answer his barb and entered the Fid Duin in silence.

The eerie dwells around us always. We are spared its presence only because, so preoccupied with the dailiness of our lives, we do not acknowledge it. But it is always there.

In the Fid Duin, one was required to acknowledge it.

It was the deepest forest I had ever journeyed, so old that the trees towered out of sight in the clouds and all the bracken and brush that carpeted the floor of a new forest had disappeared, leaving great trees, deep, breathing, sacred green. I could feel the eyes of the Partraigi watching us, their ears listening for our steps. Once or twice, I heard the sound of a bone flute, distant, round, and haunting.

Rochad mac Faitheman did not seem troubled by such perceptions, moving noisily across the forest floor, grumbling and cursing under his breath over such an "unnecessary" journey. When I could bear no more of his ire, I turned and faced him. He stopped before me, his face a full head above mine. I flexed my right hand, then curved the arm up in a long, swift arc. I caught the side of his face full with my hand, the palm cracking against his cheek. His lip curled back from his teeth and he growled low in his throat. His hands closed hard around my upper arms. For a moment I thought that he would heave me to the forest floor like so much debris. I whispered to him, "As this was an affront to you, so is your crashing and cursing an affront to this ancient place."

For the first time he looked around, drew in breath. Then he looked back at me. His head tilted to the side and he regarded me again the way one looks at a strange animal. I whispered to him:

"Why do you regard me so, Rochad mac Faitheman? Three times now I have seen you stare at me the way one looks at a creature that might prove dangerous."

He answered me just as softly.

"You surprise me, Finnabair."

"How so?"

"I expected either the creature of Medb, all fire and ice, lust and anger, or the castoff of Medb, something broken and dull. It seems that you are neither."

A tiny flame moved, right at my center. I lifted my chin, met him eye to eye, said nothing. He held my glance for a long moment.

When I turned again to walk, he moved beside me the way one should move in a forest, rolling his steps from the outside of his foot in, silent on the forest floor.

Now and again, I turned my sight toward Cuchulainn, trusting it consciously for the first time in my life, altering my direction to move toward him as one moves toward true north. Rochad seemed content to follow my lead, following in the direction I took. We walked in silence. Toward dusk, we came upon a small herd of deer gathered beside a gurgling stream. They watched us with their large, dark eyes. A doe moved between us and her two fawns, stamped a slender hoof three times on the ground.

"She warns us not to come near them," he whispered. I nodded. Rochad looked for a long moment at the doe, then made a sound deep in his throat, something that was a cross between a snort and a cough. What happened then I have never seen. The doe tilted her head sideways on its axis, looked at him in much the way he sometimes regarded me. For a moment, she was still and then she answered, snorting in response, pawing the ground. Back and forth they went, man and deer, until at last he said, "We can go among them and drink."

"You spoke and heard in her tongue."

He nodded, looked away.

I placed my hand against the cheek that I had struck, the same apology that Medb had given me all my life. I let my hand remain until he turned back toward me.

I said nothing. I let my eyes speak my awe at what he had done. His cheek grew warm beneath my hand and then he folded my hand into his own great hand and led me to the stream. We drank in the midst of deer, all around us their musky smell and large eyes. When one of the little fawns nuzzled against the back of my neck, it seemed the most natural thing to stroke it gently, to gather it into my lap. I knew that in that moment we rested in the lap of magic and I was unafraid. Completely unafraid.

We built no fire in the Fid Duin, for it seemed to me that the forest would not bear a fire. We lay down on the cold ground to sleep, silent as we had been for hours, but the damp seeped into my bones. When the last light had nearly fled from the treetops, I drew Cuchulainn's cloak from my own traveling pack and swept it over my own, drawing the hood up over my head. It was a huge cloak, far too long and wide for Cuchulainn, and in its massive folds I felt safe and much warmer. From the ground beside me Rochad whispered,

"Finnabair?"

"I am here."

"I cannot see you."

"I am not surprised, for it is darker here than anywhere I have ever slept."

"Not so. As you are gifted with the Bird-Sight, I am gifted with night-sight. From the time I was a little child, I have seen in the darkness as the owl sees. Were it not for your voice, I would not know that you are beside me. I cannot see you."

I sat up, shrugged the hood back from my hair.

"And now I can."

"What say you?"

"The cloak, Finnabair. When you are beneath the cloak I cannot see you. That must be why Laeg wished you to have it. You will sleep most safe beneath it."

I drew the hood back over my hair, curled back down on the forest floor. When my eyes adjusted to the darkness, I could see his form against the ground, some few feet from me.

"Finnabair," he whispered.

"I am here."

"I am sorry if I hurt you. Truly. Had I known you, I would not have left you."

For a moment, I lay still against the ground, blinking in surprise and something else, something that I could not name. Then I stood and moved toward him, feeling with my foot. When I brushed against his side, I lay down, curled my head into the hollow of his shoulder, drew the white deerhide cloak over both of us.

"We will both sleep safe beneath this," I said. His great arm drew around my shoulders and I fell asleep to the deep and even rhythm of his breathing.

Morning in the Fid Duin came like one of the prayers of the Druids, starting so softly, light trailing down through the leaves like green-and-gold snowfall, spiraling dust motes and whispers of wind. I sat up beside Rochad mac Faitheman. He smiled, the smile moving lazily around his lips.

"You slept well, Finnabair."

"How so?"

"You snore."

"Never say so." I swatted at him and he caught the hand in midair.

"You pack too hard a punch," he said, but he held the hand and did not release it.

"Your hair is beautiful like this," he whispered. "All tangled and gone astray."

My face went hot. I snatched my hand from him and worked my fingers through my hair, drawing it up and twisting it in my hands. He watched me silently, but something moved and sparked in his eyes. For the first time since Froech's departure, I felt an answering spark. I dropped the hair, felt my eyes lock onto his. My tongue felt thick and dry, and my heart began to beat in little drum rhythms that I could hear in the still forest air.

He sat up, the long length of his body uncurling toward me.

And then from far away across the little stream came the sound of a bone flute, round and haunting.

Rochad's head turned toward the sound and the little tune grew on the air. It was a song that I had sung often after Froech disappeared, and it came unbidden to my lips:

> Long ago and far away
> I wandered, wandered, wandered
> Long ago and far away, mo ghra,
> I wondered at your eyes, your lips,
> Your hands, your heart, mo ghra.
> I wondered where your wandering heart had gone.

The little flute answered me, clear as birdsong in the forest, and when I looked at Rochad, his eyes were brimming with astonishment and something else.

"Finnabair," he said, so softly. That was all, but the saying of it was like the sound of the little flute, so round and pure.

He did not touch me, but stood in measured silence and bundled the cloak of Cuchulainn into his traveling pack. He reached for my hand and drew me to my feet.

"It seems that the Partraigi invite us to join them."

* * *

Around a cone-shaped, smokeless fire sat the people of the Partraigi. They wore soft deerskin tunics and pants of soft-worked hide and, on their feet, not sandals but shoes of hide. Their hair was black, long and straight, shining like rivers of light and their skin was beautiful copper, gleaming in the light.

One of their women stood as we entered the clearing. She carried a stick painted in bright colors of green and red, long feathers trailing from it. Some were the feathers of eagles and I recognized them, but others were feathers of such color and iridescence that I knew they must be magical indeed. One was bluer than the seas of Eriu, bluer than the woad we used to tattoo our bodies, brilliant even in the muted forest light.

The woman was neither old nor young, seemed ageless to me, so tall with her streaming black hair. Tiny blue dots began at her right temple and cascaded down toward her cheekbone. Just below the cheekbone, a thick blue river bisected the dots. Across the tatooed barrier of water was a spiral of the same dots.

The woman smiled. "I am Jigahnsa, clan mother of the Partraigi. Welcome, Bird-Sight Woman. The Hound has prepared us for your arrival." She did not seem to notice Rochad at all.

She held up the stick with its dangling feathers. She stepped toward me, held the stick forward. I closed my hand around the bone handle. The wind lifted the feathers and they began to move, to spin. I lifted the handle high, closed my eyes, followed the feathers skyward. Warm light poured down over me, like honey into mead. It lifted all the hairs along my arms and scalp, streamed warm across my skin. I saw below me the Fid Duin, the hill of Emain Macha, the green fields and lakes of Ulster, the hills and stones of Connacht, all so small and green. I opened my eyes, surprised to be standing among the Partraigi, Rochad by my side.

I looked into the eyes of the woman of the Partraigi.

"It is all one," I said.

"It is a story in the telling."

She smiled. She stepped toward me. The little blue dots drew my hand and I pressed my fingertips against them unbidden. I closed my eyes. Beneath my hand they were warm, a path in a sun-filled country. The little river was cool and moist to the touch.

I felt the woman's hand at the back of my head and opened my eyes in surprise. With a single gesture, she drew my forehead against hers. The bridges of our noses touched. She inhaled deeply three times, wafting her hand toward her head with each inhalation. She stopped, kept her forehead pressed to mine. I understood somehow that I should do the same. Three times I inhaled deeply, pulling her essence into me with my hand.

When I had finished we remained quiet, our foreheads touching. Softly, she spoke.

"I carry your journey, Finnabair, Daughter of Light. Your spirit dwells within me; I bear your stories."

Though I had never met her before this day, I knew what to say.

"I carry your journey, Jigahnsa, clan mother of the Partraigi. Your spirit dwells within me; I bear your stories."

We stepped apart. I felt as though a hundred years had passed, as though I had returned from a long journey in a strange country.

At the far side of the fire sat Cuchulainn, grinning at me like the wild boy he is. He looked from Rochad, who still stood behind me, to me, saw something. His grin widened.

"Come, you two," he said. "I knew that you would follow, Finnabair. And so much wandering will surely make you hungry."

11

We stayed for a fortnight among the Partraigi and I gleaned from them many skills I had not known before—how to build a fire that gave no smoke, how to move in the forest like the beasts move. They played for me longing melodies on the bone flute. Jigahnsa and I had exchanged the breath song; more than that, she became for me the sister I had never known among the seven Maine.

"We are a storytelling people," she said. "We tell our stories; we carry those of others. We carry them to the Maker; we tell the ones he sends to us. You have been sent among us to learn to be a bearer of tales."

"What tales could I carry?"

"That I do not know. Only that when the proper tales find you, you will know and you will carry them into the world."

So, as we walked side by side in the forest, Jigahnsa told me stories—why the trees are so tall, how the stag got its name, why the Maker gave the bees the right to sting. She taught me to read the stories in the tattoos of her people. And she taught me the wisdom of faces. "Every face tells a story, Finnabair. It tells one story in repose and another in discourse. In repose, regard the creases beside the eyes and the mouth. They will tell you if the person has lived their life in joy or sorrow, in open-heartedness or disapproval. But in discourse, watch the eyes. Pay no attention to the mouth, to the words. Truth is in the eyes; if they shift away, you have just been told a lie." On my right temple, just above my cheekbone, Jigahnsa tattooed two small blue dots, but no river.

"These two represent the Finnabair of Connacht and the Finnabair of Ulster," she said to me, "but you have not crossed your river yet. When you do, you will return and here we will complete your journey." And she stroked the side of my face, tracing her fingers along my cheekbones. She rested her fingers beside my lips, gentle as feathers. She tilted her head. "Here, Finnabair. Just here. This is where your journey will cross the river."

"What does this mean?"

"I do not know. Only that it will happen. And that you will know it when it does."

Though the Partraigi built long houses with roofs of thatch, they were a people of the forest. Always they were outside in the dappling light. In that play of sun and shadow I began to change. The light that seeped through the trees began to lick my hair; streaks of gold appeared in it. My skin grew freckled and bronzed for being always outdoors.

I could have stayed among the Partraigi forever, for in their deep forest, it seemed that no war raged between Ulster and Connacht. Indeed, those two warring countries seemed to me as long ago dreams.

For his part, Cuchulainn insisted that I learn some warrior skills, and though at first I resisted, I felt pride in how my skills grew. I learned balance, standing first on a stump and then on a sapling and at last, single-footed, on the point of the Hound's spear. He was ecstatic with me for this, calling it the spear-feat, waxing that it had been taught him by Scathach and that few could learn it. To me, it did not seem difficult at all. I simply made myself thin, transparent. Even the wind could pass through me. In that state, nothing could disbalance me, for I was insubstantial as the air. This was a skill I had learned well as the daughter of Medb.

Together, he and Rochad taught me the skill of defending myself. Day after day for hours we worked outside in the open air. In boy clothes of borrowed deerhide braichs and a huge, belted tunic, I stood in the clearing as Rochad approached me from forward and behind. Over and over, the Hound coached me to use my little frame to tip the weight of Rochad, to unbalance him, to work with my elbows and knees. And though I said nothing, I came to like the feel of his arms around my body, the warmth of him against my back. When I was working with the Hound, I would catch Rochad watching me from the edge of the clearing, eyes wide, face flushed. At last there came a day when I caught Rochad midsection and tipped his full weight to the ground. Both of them cheered me then, though Rochad did it with less wind.

"Practice it now," the Hound said. "I will return shortly," and he disappeared into the forest. I practiced again and again, running at Rochad or allowing him to catch me from behind, tipping and turning, my body a fulcrum. But when I tumbled him for the twentieth time, his arms shot up from the ground. He caught me by an arm and a leg and lifted me like a deer on a spit, yanking me unceremoniously against his chest, down the long length of him, all my breath expelled from me in a great gust.

I lifted my head from his chest and glared at him.

"What was that?"

"That was to keep you from becoming too confident," he said, grinning, but his hand had begun to stroke down the length of my back and over my flanks. I shivered with the feel of it, lifted my face above his. My hair fell around us and our faces were curtained inside it.

"Finnabair," he whispered, all the while his hands gently stroking, calming, the way one would tame a skittish horse. "You speak of your beloved. I am told he was a man of the Other. Do you think you could love a man of this world as well?"

I rolled away from him then and sat up, thumping in the dust.

"What did I say or do to anger you?" he asked, curling up cross-legged opposite me on the forest floor.

I shook my head.

"Perhaps I am angered at myself, Rochad, at my weakness. My beloved abandoned me. Perhaps it is time to stop longing for him, to stop believing in promises. From anyone. I am no longer the fool I once was."

Rochad watched me silently. At last, he sighed.

"Finnabair, I am sorry that you have been hurt by the promises of men. I am sorrier still that I played you false. I did not know you. I played for time—for the Hound, for Laeg, for Flavius."

He looked away into the forest, pursed his lips and expelled a puff of air, looked back at me. His face was suffused with color. When he spoke, he looked down at the ground.

"Finnabair, that night in the dwelling—the night of our marriage bargain. I did not play then." He looked up, forced himself to meet my eyes. "Hear me now. I do not know how well he knew you, your beloved. But I know this. A man who knew you would not leave you. Not of his own will."

"What are you saying?"

"I do not know. Perhaps I am a fool to say so. They say he was of the Other; their ways are not our ways. But I think that you should search your heart. Was his love of the kind that would hold you so lightly?"

I regarded him for a long time.

"Now you look at me as at a new beast. What have I said?"

"You have spoken as a man of generosity and wisdom. I am taken by surprise."

He shrugged and smiled.

"As you say, I am the son of Niniane."

"So you may be."

"Would it help if you told me of him?"

"I have thought it through again and again, Rochad. Over and over. He came for me; he spoke for me at the marriage table. He made offer of dowry. He passed all the tests of my parents, even those most devious. They said they would ask of him one small test only and then we would hold the marriage feast. And then he disappeared. I never saw or heard from him again. What do you hear in that, Rochad mac Faitheman, but the blushings of a foolish girl?"

"I hear, 'They said.' I hear a story in which the only treachery could come from 'one small test.' And I see a girl who does not wish to think that her parents would deprive her of her truest love."

I scrambled to my feet.

"By the gods, Rochad! Do not say it! Oh, do not say it. I fear to hear it."

"But you have thought it more than once."

I actually pressed my hands against my ears, so great was the fear, the certainty. So roaring a sound would that betrayal make that I would be like Flavi with his vanished voice, unable ever to hear again.

Rochad came to his feet. He folded himself down around me, holding me in the great arms.

"Hush now," he whispered. "Hush. We will speak no more if you do not wish it. We will never speak of it again."

"All these years I have held my finger in the dam; nothing can stop the water now. Oh, you gods! Have I not feared it all along? Has not my heart feared it to be true? Oh, Froech, *mo ghra.*"

Rochad dropped his arms, stepped back from me, his mouth a round *O* of surprise.

"What have you said? What name have you uttered?"

"Froech. He was my beloved. Froech, son of Be Find of the Other. Why do you start and look so pale?"

For answer, he stepped back from me, made a soft, plaintive call into the forest, *huu, huh, huu,* like an owl calling for its mate. This was behavior most strange. Dusk had begun to coalesce in the Fid Duin, dense and blue-green. I felt a shiver of fear; I stepped back from him. He looked around wildly, watching the trees, even looked up into them momentarily. Cuchulainn arrived behind him, silently, coming up behind his shoulder. I had learned well. I did not betray the Hound's presence with my eyes, with any turn of my head. He was upon Rochad before any sound or sense reached him, and Rochad leaped up and shouted like a child at seek and find.

The Hound looked at him in surprise.

"You called me. Did you not expect me to come?"

"Froech. Son of Be Find."

"I remember him well. What of him now?"

"Finnabair. He was her beloved. Froech was her beloved."

Cuchulainn seemed to collapse in on himself. He spun on his legs, his body collapsing into a seated position on the forest floor.

"No," he said. "Oh, no. Such cobwebs as ensnare us here."

"Speak to me!" I commanded them. "Both of you. You whistle and you collapse. You speak in riddles both. It is most terrifying. Tell me clear. I will bear it. What do I not know?"

"I must bear it, too, Finnabair," said the Hound. He reached his arm up to me and I put my little palm into his great shovel of a hand. I sat beside him. "I must bear it, too, little sister. Until now I had never heard you speak his name. I killed him, your beloved, Froech of the Other."

* * *

We had built one of the little conical fires of the Partraigi. We sat beside the smokeless red cone, staring from one to the other. Cuchulainn heaved a great sigh.

"I knew he was of the Other when first I saw him. I tried to frighten him away. 'Man of the Other,' I called from my river rock. 'You have no powers over me. I am half your stock, or so they say. Depart, for I do not wish to harm one of the people of light.'

"But he smiled a small, sad smile and shook his head. 'I cannot go,' he said. 'I fight for a prize that is greater than my life. It is, they told me, one small task. And I accepted it.'

" 'Then pity upon you,' I said, and I launched the first of my barbs. He did not fight well; they are not a people of war. More's the pity.

"When he was sorely wounded, I gathered him from the far side of the river and brought him to mine. He pointed to a small distant hill. 'Take me there before I expire in this world,' he said. 'They will open the hill. They will restore me in that world.' His eyes were full of sorrow. 'And when they do, I will never be able to return to this world.'

"I put him in my chariot. Laeg drove like thunder and I sat on the floor and cradled him against me so that the ride would not jar him to his death. Rochad thundered before us on the Black, crying 'Open the hill for your kinsman.' Just so they did, a door seeming to open out of the very green. The woman who stepped out was more beautiful than anything I have ever seen with these eyes, 'I am Fand,' she said, 'wife of the Sea, Mother of Waters. Bring him to me that his wounds may be healed.' I carried him to her, his clothes crusted with blood. He was drifting in and out of consciousness then. Beside her, bearers appeared, with a litter that seemed to be made of clouds and light. We laid him on it. His eyes flickered open, panic playing in them, 'Hound,' he said, 'tell her that she was worth more than my life. Tell her that. Tell her I wait for her in the next world. She must know.' But until this moment, I did not know who she was to tell her. Forgive me, Finnabair, for I have cost you your beloved."

"I will never see him again."

"Not in this world, no. In this world he is dead; he can dwell now only in the country of the Other."

Rochad spoke gently, "Perhaps you shall see him again there."

I could make no response.

With my last fragile thread of control, I said, "Hound, I forgive you. This death is not on you." It came out as a small voice, strangled and hoarse, a voice that was almost gone. I could say nothing more.

The weeping began as an intake of breath. I sucked in the forest, the stars, the wind. I exhaled them as great, gusting sobs that shook my body and would not stop. Rochad reached out toward me, but I held up my hand, palm out. This is what I am and what I shall be, Finnabair, the pawn, the one betrayed, the one alone. I shall never be anything more. Something that had begun to bloom in me shriveled itself to a cold, hard seed.

I turned my back toward the Hound and my husband and lay down on the forest floor. I wept like a broken child. The fire burned down to embers behind me and went out. Just so I let die the lie that I had told myself, the last lie, that Medb and Ailill would not betray me so. Just so I let the hope of Froech's return in this life burn out in me, an ember, gone to smoke, gone cold.

I waited until the two of them had fallen into sleep. I drew Cuchulainn's cloak from the bag and lifted it over my head. I moved through the forest, silent as gossamer, invisible as wind. But I think that I would not have needed the Hound's magical cloak, for I was hollow. I was the bone flute of the Partraigi, stripped of all its song. I was a wraith moving toward the source of its sorrow.

Moving toward Ailill and Medb.

12

I was seated on her chair in the great hall of Cruachan Ai when she came in from her morning walk. It had taken me almost a week to reach her on foot and on borrowed horse. By day, I drank from streams and lakes. By night I slept beneath the cloak of Cuchulainn. I ate nothing; I was all sinew stretched on a frame of bone. My hair was matted and dirty, twigs and leaves caught in the errant curls. My skin was crusted with dirt; I stank. I did not care. I looked out at the world through eyes made dry from weeping. Neither the Hound nor Rochad followed me; it was as well.

At the last I reached the river and Laeg, who regarded my tattered appearance with wide eyes and said nothing. He told me that in the absence of the Hound, my parents had abandoned their war camp and returned to the stronghold of Cruachan Ai. Without my asking, he had hitched his team to the chariot, dropped me unceremoniously in Connacht, and fled.

But something strange had happened to me on the silent journey. Froech had returned to me, his gentle smile, the light in his eyes, his tender hands. He had not abandoned me; he had loved me, enough to take on my parents' tests, enough to set himself before the Hound. Enough. They had taken him from me, the Hound had given him back. He had begun to fill me, like a dry well refilling with water. I had been loved, truly and well, not as a pawn of war, but for myself. On the final night of the journey, swathed in the cloak, walking under full moonlight, I had an astonishing thought. One who has been loved can love. One who has been loved is a well that will never run dry.

Medb came in on a rush of laughter. One of her pet squirrels was perched on her shoulder; she was surrounded by her women, who held their little shields around her head as she walked. She saw me as the shields lowered.

"Finnabair! Look what your Hound has driven me to do. I must take my walk surrounded by my women with their shields. Already, the Dog-Boy has killed one of my squirrels and my pet bird with his slingshot. He taunts me that his slingshot could just as easily take my head. Ah well, the fortunes of war!"

She whipped her shawl gaily around her head, waved her women away from her.

She tilted her head, regarded me more closely. She moved in, sniffed the air.

"By the gods; what have they done to you?"

"We need to speak."

With a single gesture, she cleared the room. She sat beside me on the chair my father usually occupied.

"Speak then."

The thought flitted through my head that she thought she was about to receive intelligence of war, that by marrying me to Rochad she thought that she had planted a spy in the camp of Ulster.

"Froech, son of Be Find."

"He who abandoned you. What of him?"

I was still for a moment. I remembered what Jigahnsa had told me, focused on her eyes.

"Did he abandon me?"

Her eyes shifted away.

My father came into the chamber, all delight. "Finnabair! Medb's women told me you had come to us."

"Father," I said, "look at me." I could feel my mother circling, trying to warn him away, but he looked only at me. I asked directly.

"Did Froech abandon me or did you send him to his death?"

And his eyes shifted away.

"So it was both of you then. You knew the 'one small task' you chose for him would kill him. And you sent him to it. Why? And do not lie to me further. I will know if you lie. Perhaps I have always known."

Medb sighed.

"Oh, very well. You begin to weary me, Finnabair, with all your independent thinking. You might as well know. He was unworthy of you at any rate, a worthless Otherling who could not kill the Hound."

"I did not wish for him to kill the Hound."

Medb looked at me in surprise.

"But I did. We reasoned it out, your father and I. Froech was of the Other; perhaps he had some powers that would work against the Dog-Boy, being of his stock. If so, the Hound would be dead and we of Connacht could finish the war against the cursed weaklings of Ulster and win the bull. You would not be necessary then, and we could let you go into his country. But if he could not kill the Hound, then you were necessary to us still as a goad for combat, a prize for our warriors. And then it would work out well. Because Froech would be dead and you would still be here. And so it worked out!"

She smiled in delight at the perfection of the plan. My father shifted uncomfortably.

"Your mother tells it harshly."

"It is a harsh truth, Aither."

Medb stretched out her hand.

"But, Finnabair, we did provide for you another husband."

A moment of silence spun out among us.

"In all of this discussion of strategy, did either of you ever say to the other, 'But he loves her. But she loves him'?"

And their eyes shifted away.

By the time I reached the hut of Flavius, three days later, I looked like one who had dug herself up from the grave. Flavi took a single look at me and simply lifted me into his arms. By the time Niniane arrived, he was heating a cauldron of water to bathe me and had already spoon-fed me a thin soup.

Niniane took one look at me and pressed her hand against her mouth.

"I have renounced my parents. I come to you an orphan and a supplicant."

She raced to me, seemingly oblivious to the stink. She pressed her hands against my face, closed them around my arms and wrists, patted my stomach.

"I look much worse than I feel, Little Mother."

I had called her the beloved name for a mother-in-law. She recognized it immediately and her eyes filled. She began to flutter around the hut.

"No orphan here. Never you mind. We will set all to rights. Flavi and I. You will be fine, Daughter."

She lifted a bunch of fragrant herbs from a hook on the ceiling and crushed them into the pot. The water smelled like spring blossoms.

"Come," she said, "we will bathe you and wash your hair. A bath makes everything better." She set a curved stool beside the fire. Flavi lifted me gently, set me on the stool. Niniane waved him toward the door; before he left he put his great hand against my cheek.

There was more strength in the little body of my

mother-in-law than I could have suspected. She managed to undress me, hold my thin frame against her body, stream my hair into the fragrant pot and sponge my body again and again until I was warm and smelled like flowers. She dropped a fresh, soft, lamb's-wool tunic over my head. She threw my shredded filthy tunic into the fire, but I waved her away from the deerskin braichs and the cloak of Cuchulainn.

"I will wear the pants again when I have washed them," I said. "And I will bring for you a pair. They are much more practical for women."

Niniane nodded.

"Rochad came. He told me. What was done to you." She did not speak my parent's names, accorded them no disrespect, but her eyes burned. "I am sorry for the weight of your loss."

"I am glad for the depth of our love."

Her head snapped up.

"What say you, Finnabair?"

"Knowing that he loved me was like this bath of herbs, Niniane. I can live on the smell of the blossoms."

"Then you grow wise. My son worries for you. He said he knew that you would go to them. And that he and the Hound should not follow. But still he worries."

"He need not worry, for now I am as strong as the oak, which bends in the wind but does not break. But if he wishes to visit me, you may tell him he is welcome." A blush stained up my cheeks; Niniane pretended not to notice.

"I shall tell him so," she said, turning to the bath things and beginning to tidy.

"Here, let me help you."

"No such thing until we fatten you up. You are too meager, Finnabair. Your strength is in your mind, not in those slender bones."

"Niniane, when last I was here . . ."

She stopped her fluttering and looked at me.

"Flavi began to tell me his story. He placed his hands here." I pressed the sides of my face, remembering the feeling that had flooded me. "I should like to hear that story."

She called out a single word in the Roman tongue and Flavi ducked beneath the lintel. In his hand, he carried his little wooden flute. He must have been waiting just outside the door. A look passed between them and he nodded. Gingerly, he lowered his great frame onto my sleeping platform, sitting sideways beside me, like a father who will tell a bedtime story.

In broken fits of Gaeilge, discursions into the Roman tongue, quick discussions between Niniane and Flavi, the story emerged.

"After Flavi sent me away with the centurion, he hid for a while. After a time, the politics of Rome returned, as it always does, to business as usual. Flavi hired himself out to a decurion, a Roman functionary who employs some ten men beneath him. Flavi began to serve as healer for all of these families. Among them was a family who were converts to the Jews."

"The Jews?"

"They are one of the peoples of Rome. Though they do not see themselves as so. They practice a very different religion. They believe in only one god."

"And who is this god?"

"He is the creator of all. They call him so—The One Who Is."

"I was of the household of Medb. We had little enough traffic with gods in my childhood. But our druids say that there is a God above the gods, the one who is maker of all."

"Just so."

"But who controls their sea and their wind, the Jews? Who grows the crops and incites the wars?"

"For them, there is but one god."

I digested this for a time; Niniane and Flavius waited in silence.

"And why would Romans convert to this religion?

From what you have told me, Romans are the rulers of all the world beyond Eriu."

"That is so. But you must understand the Romans. Romans are bureaucrats, Finnabair. They organize their world in ways that are amazing. They build roads and temples. Their houses are heated in the winter with hypocausts—ditches of stone that carry the heat to every room. Even the floors are warm in winter and you can walk on them with bare feet."

"This cannot be!"

"It is, but their strength is also their weakness. They can build and organize, govern and even rule the world, but in their efficiency and organization, they have forgotten wonder."

"They have no gods, no magic?"

"Oh, they have many gods, much magic. They throw coins in wells to their gods, build temples to Saturn, Jupiter, Apollo. The wealthiest families vie for the priesthoods of lesser gods so that they can conduct ceremonies. But it is all for show. In the Roman heart of hearts, no wind moves."

"And is this the way the Jews differ from them?"

"It is. Many Romans admire the Jews. Some convert; others become proselytes or supporters of their temples. They see in the Jews something they do not have."

She grew quiet, watched me as I thought about the complicated story. Flavi played gently on his little wooden flute.

"I think I understand. The Romans contain the world but are contained by nothing. They envy the Jews that containment and so some become their followers."

She repeated this to Flavi, who smiled broadly and replied in his deep voice.

"Flavi says that for one who has never traveled, you have understood the Roman world precisely. He says that he knew you to be wise from the first vision."

Something pricked in me; the hairs raised up on the back of my neck.

"What vision?"

Niniane stumbled. "The first vision of you. When he rode beside Rochad. And then that night. When you came to us wet from the river . . ."

Behind her Flavius said something, soft and low. Niniane silenced.

"What does he say?"

"He says that he will tell you of the Little Brother."

In his low deep voice, Flavi began, occasional words in my Gaeilge interwoven with the words of Rome, Niniane translating.

"Among my patients were those who had converted to the Jews. There was, in their circle, a Jewish family of Egypt. Into their house they had taken a little family who had fled to them across the desert. The little mother of the family was ill. She had had a difficult childbirth and she had grown dehydrated in the flight. They asked if I would see her.

"At first I feared that her heart had lost its rhythm; it beat erratically and out of pulse. Her skin was dry and lifted from her bones like parchment. But I strengthened her with medicines, good fruits, and clear water. Her courses were irregular but those we fixed with women's herbs. Each day, I took her walking in the early morning cool, a little longer each morning as her strength returned. While we walked, I held her child, a boy of some two years. Though she was but a girl, she seemed to me the bearer of some great sorrow. And she was loving gentle to everyone—to her husband, to the family who kept them, to the child—and to me. Her name was Miriam, but in my heart, I called her Little Mother and I came to love her deeply, as a father loves his beloved daughter."

"Why had they made so dangerous a journey?"

He waved his hand.

"Some bureaucrat of Rome who feared his throne had taken it upon himself to kill all the infants who could grow up to take it." He snorted his derision. "As if my little family could have threatened anyone. They were threadbare poor, uneducated. They did not even speak the tongue of Rome. But to Roman lunatics, logic matters not.

"I ministered to her on and off for three years and she grew well and strong. One day, when the boy child was five years old, I was seated with her by the fountain in the garden. She was well and healthy now and it would be my last visit with them. I was glad to see the plumpness of her skin, the health in her eyes and her nails. I patted her little hand and stood to go when the boy child came dashing from the house. He was such a delightful child, always laughing, dark curly hair and eyes. He said something to her in the tongue of their country and she turned and looked at me. She shook her head. But he said something yet again. She must have relented because she spread her hands, palms up. She shook her head at me and left the garden. The boy sat down beside me on the fountain wall and we enjoyed the silence."

Flavi paused. He and Niniane exchanged a few words. He looked at me.

"Finnabair, hear me now."

"I am listening."

"Listen here," and he pressed his hand against my side where my heart was beating.

I nodded. My heart had begun to hammer and my breath came short. Flavi's eyes widened and he leaned toward me, spoke softly.

"Suddenly the boy stood up beside me on the fountain wall. He stretched his hands into the spinning waters. Rainbows broke over his hands and he laughed. I smiled up at his delight. He took his tiny wet hands and pressed them against my cheeks."

I remembered Flavi's hands against my cheeks, the wash of joy. I nodded.

"In my own tongue, Finnabair, in the tongue of Meroe, he said to me, 'Taharqa of Meroe, be not afraid.' But I was terrified. I began to shake like a leaf. I do not know why;

he was a five-year-old child. Still smiling at me, he said, 'Elder brother, is your heart bitter toward the Romans that they have taken your voice?' How he knew, I do not know. Perhaps his host family had told him my story. It seemed so old a question from so young a child. I searched my heart; once when I was young, there had been bitterness there, but it was gone. I had made a life as a healer; I had married once to a woman of Egypt and though she had died, I had loved her well. I shook my head no. The boy spoke again. 'You have a good and forgiving heart; you have been most kind to my mother.' I nodded my thanks at him and smiled."

Flavi looked away; when he turned back toward me his eyes were filled with water. "Then the boy said, 'You should sing.' He arched his hand into the fountain water, pressed his ice-cold, wet palm against the scar on my throat. I felt the scar go warm, felt the warmth travel inward and inward. I slid from the fountain wall to the dust. I began to cough. A voice came out of me, raspy and old, scratchy with disuse.

" 'Child,' I coughed out. 'Healer, what shall I call you? For my grateful heart will speak your name.'

" 'I am Yeshua ben Joseph,' he said, still dancing his hands in the fountain. 'I have called you Elder Brother. So you may call me Little Brother.' He smiled. 'And when the time is right, you may speak of me on your journey.'

"And then he danced away to his mother's voice calling from the house.

"I came to see them one more time when three days had passed. I had kept the secret of my voice to myself, not using it before the decurion, practicing it alone in the dark. But on the third day, I wanted him to hear the gift that he had given me; I wanted to return him thanks. He came to me in the garden and I opened my voice and began to sing. He regarded me with delight, clapped his hands. But from the house, his mother came running. She pressed her tiny hands against my mouth. She whispered, 'Protect him, healer. Protect him with your silence.' And I knew then that the danger that had driven him to Egypt would follow him there, would follow him always. His mother took him by the hand and led him toward the house. When they were almost gone, he turned back toward me. 'Elder Brother,' he said, 'your song has brought me joy.' They were gone the next day, departed from Egypt for their home country. And I knew that if I were to protect him, I would need to depart as well, go to a country where they had never known me as a voiceless healer. I thought of Niniane, of the look of hopeless terror on her face the day I sent her sailing for Alba. Somehow, she had stayed frozen in my mind that way, a child of ten, terrified. I thought that if I could find her, if I could tell her of the Little Brother, all the terror would go. So I wrapped this scarf around my neck and set sail. It took me three years to find her."

Niniane came and stood behind him, her hands on his shoulders.

"Imagine my surprise—imagine the surprise of all—on that day in the great hall of Emain Macha when a Nubian healer came among us and called my name. And, oh, my joy to see him, to hear a voice that I had never heard."

"And imagine my surprise to find not a terrified child, but this beautiful bird, so strong of wing." Flavi put his great hand over hers; her face softened. I saw then with my new eyes, saw what they had not yet seen between them. I wondered when they would know it.

"Flavi, the little Brother. Who is he?"

"I do not know, Finnabair. Only that in his smile, in his hands, moves all the hope and all the healing of the world."

"How then did he bring me to you?"

"I had a dream, Finnabair. I was riding beside Rochad and his war party, a thing I never do, nor ever have done. In my dream there was a young woman on a white horse. She raised her palm to us, and behind her hand I saw a rainbow in the sky. On the day that I rode with them, you did not see it, but it was there, a rainbow arching behind your shoulder. I took it as a sign."

"It is a most slender sign."

"Do you think so? I think the signs are around us always, Finnabair. It is we who do not see them, occupied as we are with the business of the day, lost in our sorrows, reveling in our joys. But the Great Mysterious speaks to us always. It is for us to learn to listen."

"But what gift could I bring to your Little Brother?"

"I do not know that, either. Perhaps it is a gift he wishes you to have, like the gift of this voice. When the time comes, you will know. It is the song that brings him joy, Finnabair. Whatever your song, it will bring him joy."

13

Rochad came to me the way a green sapling boy comes to court. He wore his finest red silk tunic and his belt of leather, worked with an intricate silver buckle. His black hair was washed and combed into place and his cloak of clan plaid was fastened with his warrior brooch. He actually carried a cluster of flowers, drooping over his fist.

For my part, Niniane and Flavius had trussed me up and preened me until I exploded.

"You fuss over me like two grandparents."

Niniane relayed this to Flavius and in a hurt, little voice he said something in the Roman tongue.

"What says he?"

"Flavi says that is how we love you."

This response reduced me to shamefaced silence and I submitted to their ministrations. Even I was surprised at the results.

My tunic was of deep blue silk, woven with silver threads and intertwining braids and knots. Among them, rich birds in blue and green twined their heads against each other. I asked Niniane where she had come by the dress, but she would not say, averring only that it was borrowed for "the occasion." The occasion seemed to exist somewhere in their minds.

Over the beautiful tunic, I wore my cloak lined with ermine fur. It had been cleaned and brushed and rubbed with herbs, and the clasp was an elaborate brooch of three twined swans, their eyes inlaid with glimmering stones in ruby and emerald.

They wound ribbons and flowers in my hair, which smelled like fresh-washed herbs, and Niniane used a fire iron to make my curls more whirling than usual. My cheeks and lips she stained with juice of berries.

When they were finished and she handed me her hand glass, I gasped aloud. All my life, I had lived in the shadow of Medb of Connacht, a beauty of such fire that all flames were swallowed up by hers. But now I saw that I was beautiful, too.

Niniane and Flavi led me out between them and, though I felt like a prize horse, I could not help but feel delight in Rochad's reaction.

"Oh, Finnabair." He looked at me in awe. "How like the Fid Duin you are."

"The dark forest?" I bristled.

"Oh, yes. All this beauty and all this mystery so concealed."

And then I blushed to the roots of my hair.

"Go now," said Niniane. "Walk beside the river." She shooed at us like troublesome children and we did as we were told. For a long time, we walked in silence, me holding the drooping flowers, Rochad, head and shoulders taller than I, pretended to watch the river flow. At last he gave an uncomfortable laugh.

"It is awkward this."

"Awkward?"

"The two of us, of enemy clans, but already wedded and bedded, and walking like strangers with nothing to say."

I smiled up at him.

"We are strangers really, Rochad, for all our wanderings."

We walked into a patch of forest where the light spun down among the trees. Rochad reached for my hand and I let him hold it, let him bring it to his lips.

"Finnabair," he said, "I wish to love you."

I nodded at the obviousness of this. I am not the daughter of Medb for no reason.

"But before I love you, there is something I must know."

He turned me to face him on the path.

"I do not know if you love me yet. I do not know if you will ever love me. If Froech . . . if you can ever love me."

"I have learned a strange thing, Rochad. It is because Froech loved me, loved me well and truly, that I can give myself to you now, here in the world of the living."

He exhaled on a long breath. "Finnabair, I have loved you since that day in the Fid Duin."

"What day was that?" I asked, teasing him lightly. "The day that I knocked you to the dirt?"

He laughed, but shook his head to seriousness.

"The day that you sheltered me beneath the cloak. Your enemy. Your betrayer. And you protected me. You have an extraordinary heart, Finnabair. I was right on the night of our marriage feast when I said that you are the prize. And I will protect you now. Forever, if you will have me. I will never abandon you. Not in this world. Not in the next. Can you love me?"

I allowed the tears to spill from my eyes and run down my cheeks. I allowed him to brush them away, to kiss them away. I allowed him to kiss everything away. And in that allowance, the well of my heart was filled to overflowing.

When we were exhausted, when our clothes were scattered over the forest floor and the little flowers were crushed beneath us like a carpet, I lifted myself onto the length of him and let my hair spill over our faces. Inside the fragrant curtain, I whispered to him, "I can."

"Can what, sweeting?" he asked, sleepy with pleasure.

"I can love you, Rochad. I already do."

And so we began again, the sweet binding of our bodies, the sweet becoming of our interwoven spirit.

We returned to the hut near dusk, disheveled and reassembled.

"We will take a terrible teasing for this," said Rochad.

"And we will deserve it well," I answered.

He laughed aloud.

"Bold Finnabair! Will you have no modesty upon you?"

"None with you," I answered. "They all can know and I will only agree and wish for more."

"Then I am the luckiest of men."

He swung his great arm around me and we curved the bend toward the hut.

What we saw next neither of us had expected. The hut was surrounded by burning torches. In their midst were tables, set with fine covers and plates of silver and inlaid wood surrounded by goblets. A boar turned on a spit. Someone started a bodhran and the assembled company burst into the clearing: Niniane and Flavius, Laeg Mac Riangabra, my brother Mathramail, several of the warriors of Rochad and their women, the Hound, and with him a man who looked much like him, short of stature, with a bulbous nose and a wild, untamed ring of hair around a bald pate.

"What is this?" demanded Rochad.

"It is a wedding feast," said Niniane. "Now come and sit here, at the place of honor."

"And how did you know that we would return in agreement each with the other?"

Niniane shrugged. She and Flavi exchanged a glance. "We have lived long; we have eyes."

We sat. Musicians appeared with pipes and bodhrans

and the hammering drums made my blood race. I looked at Rochad through lowered eyelids.

"Oh, stop!" cried the Hound. "You will embarrass my father. Sualdem," he said to the balding man. "Do you see why I bring you among so few of my friends? They are too randy a bunch for me."

Rochad exploded from his chair, rushing over to rub the bald head of Sualdem.

"Papa Hound," he said. "I have told you before. He keeps you from us because he does not want us to see his future. Here." He patted Sualdem's bald head. "But what say you to my new wife, whom you have not met before?"

Sualdem stood and lifted his goblet.

"I say that you are that most rare of beauties. If you would have such a one as me, I would grow back all the hair on my head." Here, he swiped a wool napkin from the table and clapped it over his head. "What say you?"

I laughed aloud at so much silliness.

I ate until I could hold no more, boar and leeks and bread with honey, little cakes with nuts and fish steamed in grasses and seasoned with Niniane's pepper. We drank mead and wine until I was drunk with more than happiness.

At last the music silenced and Niniane placed an intricate silver cup before me. The company silenced. I stood.

"Rochad of Ulster, I choose you before this company. Will you accept the cup of marriage, the cup of joy and sorrow?"

He stood beside me. He took the cup from my hand and drank deeply. For a moment he seemed at a loss for what to say. Then, he looked deep into my eyes and spoke softly.

"Finnabair, you are the prize beyond all price, the wife of my heart, my soul, my body. I accept this cup and give you for it all my love."

The entire table broke into cheering and applause and I saw Niniane and Flavius clasp their hands together and exchange a look of purest joy. Rochad gathered me into his arms for a kiss that grew embarrassing for its length and intensity.

"Stop!" called the Hound. "We do not wish to end the feast early for your revels."

I ducked my head in a hot blush, but Rochad shouted back at him.

"Envy only, Dog-Boy. We will have you riding hard toward Emer."

"Speaking of riding hard . . ." he called, and the laughter and screaming grew to fever pitch.

When we were too full for feasting the dancing began, couples in sets of four and eight, up and down the clearing with intricate footwork and handholds. I danced until I could not breathe. When at last the company stopped for rest and drink and the conversation at the tables grew quieter, I knew what I would do. I stood with the cup and walked to the table where Niniane and Flavius sat side by side, smiling. I placed the cup between them.

"What is this?" asked Niniane, thinking perhaps that there was some custom of Connacht that she had not learned in Ulster.

"This is a marriage cup," I cried aloud and the company leaned forward and grew quiet. "It is the custom among us that the women of Eire choose their mate and speak for him with the cup."

"Of course it is," she said, perplexed.

"Generally, they know that their intended mate wishes them to speak. But sometimes they are slow to see. I have not lived long, but I have eyes."

"Oh. Oh my."

Niniane was blushing furiously, even her neck spackling with red. Flavius, who had been sitting beside her with an arm on the back of her chair, and his legs crossed, relaxed, sat forward now, his hands folded almost primly on the tabletop. In his eyes was a look of such hope and love that it tore at my heart to see it.

Niniane stood before the company, shaking so hard that she had to support herself with one hand on the table edge. I stepped to her and held out my hand.

"I am here, Maither," I said quietly. She clutched my hand hard and nodded. She raised the cup.

"Taharqa of Meroe," she said. "I do love you. With this cup I choose you as my mate. Will you accept this cup of marriage, this cup of joy and sorrow?"

Beside her Flavius stood, so much taller than her tiny frame. He looked down at her, smiled gently. In our own Gaeilge, he answered.

"I do love you, Niniane. Before this company I accept this cup. I give you all that I am, all that I have been, all that I will be, forever. I gift you the gift that was given to me by the Little Brother."

He began to sing. In all my life, I will never hear a voice like his again, so deep and round. In his voice was the feast and the river, the stars and the wind. He sang us a song of love, a song of hope.

On that most perfect night, he sang for us a song of joy.

14

"It is time for the Red Branch to rouse from their cursing!"

The Hound and his father, with Rochad and Laeg, were seated in the morning light, surrounded by the debris of the wedding tables. Niniane and I moved among them, tidying and gathering, shaking linens. The warriors of Rigdonn and their women had headed back toward the north, and my brother had slipped away toward Connacht. The morning was fine, and I felt full and glorious after a long night with my new husband. But, for the past hour, Sualdem had grown more and more agitated on the subject of the Ulster warriors. The Hound addressed him calmly.

"You have not been successful in getting them to do so yet, Aither. What makes you think you can rouse them now?"

"I do not know. They need a shock. They must be shamed into action."

"Why shamed, Sualdem?" I asked innocently. "Is not Conchobar Mac Nessa an honorable king?"

"He has his moments, some for good and others for bad. He thinks to conserve his warriors by letting my boy here do all the fighting one-on-one. It is good thinking. But look at the Hound. Regard him, Finnabair. What do you see?"

I walked over to their seated group, looked closely at the Hound.

"I see Cuchulainn of Muirthemne. He who has become my friend."

Sualdem yanked up the Hound's tunic.

"Look more closely, daughter of Medb."

I saw now what was troubling him. There was not an inch of the boy's torso that was not covered in scars. They crisscrossed his chest and angled down his arms. The great zigzagging scar of Ferdiad had healed badly, puckered and white, with small legs at the sides, like the hundred-legged insects who come into the huts in winter. I looked away.

"There," said Sualdem, satisfied. "Now you see. They think my boy can do it all. They believe all the tales and predictions that surround him; they think him supernatural and invincible. They sit in the great hall at Emain Macha and tell stories about him, as if that somehow supports him. He can die like any other man. He has been harried near to death, like the dog of his namesake. I have had enough of it."

For his part, Cuchulainn seemed philosophical about it, shrugging his shoulders.

"Aither, I was born to be a warrior, trained to be a warrior. If I die in that pursuit, I am content that it is a death of honor."

"A death of honor because the whore of Connacht wants the bull with the biggest balls in Ulster."

"Aither!"

The Hound stood, his face red with anger, his hand gesturing in my direction.

Sualdem's face reddened.

"Oh, Finnabair, forgive me. I forgot that you are not of Ulster, forgot that she is your mother. It is my boy, my Setanta; I fight to save him now. She has harried him near to death; how much more can he bear alone?"

I looked at the Hound.

"Your father has a point, Cuchulainn. But what means this 'shedanda'?"

"Setanta. It is his name, his rightful name. Do you know nothing of his story?"

"I know him only as the Hound, the warrior my mother cannot defeat with any or all of her best warriors."

"And that is how I wish her to know me, Aither." His voice had a warning edge. "Please do not fill her with all that foolishness about me. Finnabair and Rochad, Laeg and Emer—they alone treat me as just what I am. They call me on my foolishness; they can laugh at me. Do not sully that with bedtime stories."

Sualdem grew silent.

I looked at the Hound.

"How well do you know me now?"

"Well enough to call you my sister."

"Well enough to know that I journeyed a week to Medb for the answer to only one question."

"Oh, horse turds."

"Do you think that anything your father could tell me could stop me from loving you? You have been my true friend, you have saved my brother's life; my husband is your brother in arms."

Cuchulainn sighed.

"I am a warrior, Finnabair. To that profession I was born and to it I trained, hard, at the warrior school of Scathach. The feats I am known for—the salmon leap above the chariot, the spear- and blade-feats, the hero's howl, and the *boi* of swiftness—these and more I perfected with hours and hours of grueling practice." He laughed ruefully. "And they were accompanied by shoulders that separated and toes that broke and plenty of cuffs around the head by Scathach when I did not do them well.

"I am proud of being a warrior. A warrior defends the

weak; he stands in the place of trouble; he serves as a rod for the lightning of war. When I am on my rock in the river and your mother sends yet another warrior against me, I think of the children safe in their beds in Ulster, I think of wives twined in the arms of their husbands. Sleep safe, I think, for I will guard the gates of Ulster. That is what a warrior does. Is your mother's war foolish? Yes. Are so many wars foolish? They are. But there will always be those like your mother who start their wars for gain or for ego or for power. And so there will always be need of warriors like me, who are willing to stand on the rock in the darkness and keep the evil away. I am proud of that work, proud that you know me so. I would not have your knowledge of me sullied by the silly fireside stories they tell about me. If I die in the work of a warrior, I am satisfied."

I stood still in the sunlight and thought about what he had said for a long time. At last, I answered.

"But if you die as a warrior, now, in the War of the Bull, then who will stand on the rock in the river of Ulster?"

Sualdem rushed around the table and embraced me, though he was so short that the hug caught me not far above the waist. When he released me, he waved his hand at the Hound.

"She thinks like a strategist, this girl. You should listen to her. We have to move that sloth Conchobar to action."

"Is not Conchobar the High King of Ulster? Why do you think so little of him, Sualdem? In Connacht, we have not heard him brought so low."

"Have you not? And does your mother not have among her armies one leader Fergus, and with him thousands of Ulster exile warriors?"

"Three thousand."

"And why do you suppose they fight with her?"

"I do not know. I always supposed that she won them to her with her wiles and her promises of wealth."

"She won them to her because Conchobar wreaked treachery upon them."

"How do you know all of this so well?"

"Conchobar is my brother-in-law."

"Your brother-in-law? But wait. This means that the Hound is . . ." I turned to him. "Hound, you are nephew to the High King of Ulster?"

"Do you see now why I do not want you to hear all of this? Until this moment, I was just the Hound, your friend. Now that tone in your voice, that shift in your eyes."

"Well, of course, I understand that perfectly well, Dog-Boy. Oh, now I understand well why Niniane gasped and seemed to pale when first I called you that. Of course, of course. And as for that tone of voice, that shift of eye, I saw those selfsame things in you, toward me, when first I came to you, daughter of the queen of Connacht."

"True enough," said Laeg, speaking for the first time.

"We both are what we are, Hound." I concluded my argument.

Rochad grinned at Cuchulainn. "My wife is too well-matched for you wit to wit. She will hear it. She will still love you. She heard my story and loves me still. Now let your father tell it. Do you see any of us leaving you for it?"

Cuchulainn held his hands up, palms out. "I give up with all of you. I give up. Go ahead, Aither. Spin your tale. But do not expect Finnabair to hear it without a thousand questions because that is what she does. For me, I prefer not to listen."

He dropped his head onto his arms on the table. But of course, I knew that he was listening.

"Conchobar's mother, Nessa, was not always called so. When she was a young girl, she was called Assa—gentle and kind, destined to be queen at Emain Macha. She was much beloved and coddled; twelve foster-fathers watched her welfare. But when she was twelve years old, Cathbad

the Druid murdered all of her foster-fathers, systematically, one by one."

"By the gods! Why did he do this?"

"Cathbad believes that he moves the winds of fate, that
his actions determine the course of great events. He
wished to marry Assa, but the foster-fathers protected her.
He thought that if he could eliminate them, she would
have to choose him. She did not."

"Whom did she choose?"

"Not whom, but what. She chose the life of an outlaw.
She became bainfennid—a wild woman of the forests.
Some say that she lived among the Partraigi, but I think
not. She did not bear the marks that you do, nor the ten-
dency toward healing and tenderness that marks them. No,
Assa became Ni Assa—not gentle—Nessa. They say that
Cathbad eventually bewitched her into marriage, but I
knew the old woman well. I say that she became enough
like him that it was a match of kind. From him she gave
birth to Conchobar and to Dechtine, his sister.

"Nessa was ambitious for her boy child. When he was
but seven years old Fergus mac Roich, High King of Ulster, began to make eyes at her, for Nessa was a dark-eyed,
dark-haired beauty. Fergus managed to get her away from
Cathbad and managed—by Nessa's wiles—to disrobe her.
When he was hot to bed her, she made her bargain. 'I will
bed you every night and every day for as long as you wish,
for one favor only.' Fergus was too hot for her. 'Name the
favor,' he cried. 'Make my little son king for just one year,'
she demanded. To stupid, besotted Fergus, that seemed a
bargain for the sport he would receive, and he agreed. He
named Conchobar king and romped with Nessa day and
night. While he was thus engaged, she went to work. From
the household of Fergus she stole gold and silver,
weapons and dishware. And then she gave it all away. To
everyone in Ulster, she presented gifts, saying, 'This is
from Conchobar, who loves you well.' By the end of her

year with Fergus, he could not have won back the kingship of Ulster by any means, for he was poor and his people were rich. And so Conchobar became High King of Ulster."

"But in Connacht we hear of him that he is a great and mighty warrior."

"Conchobar is a huge man and handsome. He is savvy and political. He curries favor with his smiles and his handshakes and, following his mother's example, buys it everywhere he goes. He surrounds himself with the trappings of power and the people regard it all with awe. He presides in Craobh Rioga, the Royal Branch. It is a beautiful place, Finnabair, more than 150 inner rooms, paneled in red yew. And Conchobar's apartments are something to behold, huge rooms, walled with great screens of copper and silver and bronze, all incised with gold and silver birds and inlaid with jewels from the wide world over. And the Craebderg, with its rows of heads and its heaps of the spoils of war. And of course the Tete Brec, the twinkling hoard of weapons and gold. Over the head of Conchobar, wherever he goes, there is a beautiful rod of silver, bearing three apples of pure gold. When he lifts this above his head, the assembled company all goes silent. And in the middle of it all Conchobar Mac Nessa, the treacherous, High King of Emain Macha.

"Because the people wished for him to have a son, he was never permitted to go into the forefront of battle. Surrounded and protected by layers of warriors, he made a show of war. Just so, he makes use of my boy. And there is more. Do you know the marriage custom in Ulster, Finnabair?"

I shook my head.

"All men give their brides to Conchobar on their wedding night. He beds them first. All fathers give him their daughters."

"Even Medb of Connacht does not go this low. Those who bed her are hot to bed her."

Rochad spoke from the table.

"He dare not be hot to bed you, Finnabair, for I am not a man of Ulster. My people are of Rigdonn; we live by older, simpler laws. Conchobar will never approach you."

"On that I will rely," I said, nodding toward my husband. "But still, Sualdem, the threads of your story are not weaving a rug. Why is it all so personal to you?"

"Dechtine, the sister of Conchobar, is a woman most beautiful and fine. She served as his chariot driver and saw to his every whim. But Conchobar's lust is bottomless."

"Oh, no; such a love is forbidden everywhere in Eriu." Sualdem shrugged.

"To forbid a thing does not always stop it. Dechtine was with child, but no one knew. It was a rumor only, but it was a persistent rumor. Conchobar held a great feast and gave her in marriage to the one man he could find who would not trouble him—a man squat and ugly, bald and unprepossessing. He gave her to me. That night, before we were to . . ." he looked at his son, with his head still dropped on his arms, "consummate Conchobar's bargain, Dechtine began to bleed. I held her in my arms and she wept like a lost child. I promised her that no one would ever use her again while I had breath in this body of mine. We were allowed three weeks together and then Conchobar must have seen that Dechtine and I had become the one thing he never expected—beloved, each of the other. He arranged for her to be sent away. The night before she left she came to me. In my arms, I loved her as a woman should be loved, gently and with all respect. The next morning with one hundred women, chariots and horses, Conchobar sent her away."

"And you never saw her again?"

"No such thing, Finnabair. What Conchobar did not know was that on our wedding night, she had lost his child. He circulated a story that at the feast she had drunk from a cup that contained a mayfly. He averred that the fly was Lugh, Man of the Light of the Other. In drinking him, he said that Dechtine had become pregnant and was carrying the child of Lugh. Only I knew that no such thing had happened and that she had lost Conchobar's child. I wondered how he would explain it when nine months later she returned with no child."

Now Sualdem began to laugh and Cuchulainn lifted his head and grinned at his father.

"This is the part that delights him, Finnabair."

Sualdem rubbed his hands together.

"Oh, it does. For no one was more surprised than I when nine months later Dechtine returned to Emain Macha, bearing in her arms a boy child she called Setanta. Conchobar made so much fuss over the boy—Amargin to teach him poetry, Finnchaem to nurse him, Sencha to teach him oratory, and so on. Setanta was fostered out to Amargin and Finnchaem and reared at Imrith Fort on the Muirthemne Plain. I was glad for his fosterage. For one thing, it kept him from the cursing of Ulster. But for another, the moment I looked into his blanket and saw that nose, that ring of wild hair, I knew whose child Dechtine bore. Setanta was my own boy, safe in the story they had invented for him."

"But as he got older . . ." I gestured to both of them. "Surely all could see the resemblance."

Sualdem shrugged.

"By then they did not dare touch him. By then he was the Hound."

From his place on the table Cuchulainn groaned aloud.

"It was just a dog; why does everyone have to make such a fuss over it all?"

"What dog? Is this how you got your name?"

"It is. When I was a boy, I played at hurley. I loved that game! The day came when we were invited to a feast at the *rath* of the smith of Culann. I was very excited because I knew that my mother and father—Sualdem and Dechtine—would be there and I would be able to spend time with them away from the prying eyes of Emain Macha. But I had a hurley game to play. So I promised my foster-parents that I would follow them down the road, and so I did, hitting my hurley ball before me with my stick.

"Unfortunately, Culann the smith had forgotten that I was coming. He had closed the gate to his rath and put before it his great mastiff. My parents had no idea of the danger I was in. The dog came at me with his great teeth bared and I did the only thing I knew to do. I hit my hurley ball. Down his throat it went and the mastiff choked and died. All would have been well, but Culann was as stupid over the dog as that dog was stupid."

Here both Sualdem and Cuchulainn fell to laughing aloud and I marveled at how much they looked alike in laughter.

"So true," said Sualdem. "Culann waxed on and on about that dog, how he had raised him from a puppy, how none other could guard his rath so well. At last he worked himself into such a froth that he said he would kill Setanta, Dechtine, and me if we did not compensate him."

"So I did," said Cuchulainn. "I told him that I would be his dog, that I would live in the dog's house beyond the gates, that I would guard his rath from all comers while he trained another mastiff. Only an idiot would take up a boy of seven years on such an offer. Culann did. He had the doghouse cleaned and I bedded down there that very night."

"And you let him live like a dog for a year?" I turned on Sualdem. Father and son exchanged a look.

"We will tell you what we did, for Rochad and Laeg know already. But you must never breathe a word of it in Ulster."

"I will not."

"I rode far north to Rigdonn where I had friends among the tribes of Faitheman. There we set up a plan; in the forest outside the rath of Culann we built bothies. The warriors of Faitheman and I surrounded that woods. We watched for animals; we gave Setanta warning of human arrivals. He guarded his gate and we were his eyes and ears."

I nodded my approval of his plan.

"And at the end of that year he earned his name, Cuchulainn, the Hound of Ulster. With that name came all the protection, all the immunity that I wanted for my endangered child. So he became the warrior of Ulster and was sent to training school with Scathach. All the rest has passed into history."

"With a few embellishments," said Cuchulainn drily. "But I will tell you this, Finnabair. In that year at the gates of the Culann there came from Rigdonn two boys who were apprenticing as warriors." He pointed to Laeg and to Rochad. "So you see what gifts we are given, even in the worst of times."

It was not until we were preparing for bed that something occurred to me.

"Rochad," I said, "when the Hound was wounded, in the battle with Ferdiad . . ."

Rochad, busy with unpinning my cloaks and ribbons, simply snorted a response.

"Did you not tell me then that the men of the Other came and took the Hound away?"

He stopped and regarded me, his eyes widening.

"If Cuchulainn is Sualdem's son, why would they come for him? Why would the people of the Other carry him away?"

15

I arose to find Sualdem binding on his leather armor, Cuchulainn helping to tie him into the bracings. At the table sat Rochad, running a sharpening stone against the wicked-bladed edge of a round, black shield.

"What is is that you do?"

Sualdem answered.

"I go among the Ulstermen. I will do what I must to rouse them from their torpor. No inch of my son's body remains that has not been nicked by a dagger or pierced by a spear. Twice he has been near death. One thing I must say for your maither, Finnabair. She has been true to her bargain, for the most part. With one or two exceptions, she has stayed to single combat. But it has gone on for three months. Winter has passed, spring has come, and my son will spend the rest of his life on a rock in the middle of a river.

"Medb will not wait forever. My son cannot live forever. The Ulstermen think they are safe behind their mountains and their bogs, hidden in their forests. But the time has come. Let the armies of Ulster and Connacht face each other now."

"How will you make them hear you?"

"Perhaps I can shame them into action."

"And what of the curse?"

"Oh, Conchobar uses the curse to his advantage. The woman, Macha, laid upon Ulster a curse that it would never know peace, and thanks to your mother that would seem to be true. But the pangs that lay its warriors low? By the terms of the curse, they are to last for one week of each month only, four nights and five days. Conchobar has made the 'curse' last for nigh onto three turnings of the moon."

"Why would he do such a thing?"

"Conchobar husbands his resources. If he can have but one warrior fighting, he preserves his army."

"Is that not considered cowardly? Though, from what you have told me of Conchobar, he bears but little shame."

"Cowardly enough after all this time that soon the 'curse' must be lifted. I go to hasten that process now. Before my son pays the price for this king's delays. And you must ask Fergus Mac Roich about the cowardice and treachery of Conchobar Mac Nessa."

"You never told me the story of how Fergus and his exiles came to be among my mother's army."

"Niniane will tell you while we are gone."

"We?" I could feel a rising panic.

Rochad spoke softly from his seat. "I follow him, Finnabair, in case he should need my help."

"And the Hound and Laeg?"

"We will return to the river. Events will move swiftly now, and Medb has spies. She will send more warriors against us."

I whirled in a circle, met Niniane's eyes where she watched me in the doorway. She held out her hand and I ran to take it like a child.

I wept for a while when they had departed, at last rubbing the heels of my hands against my eyes and shuddering to a stop. Flavi brought all of us something warm, spiced with cinnamon and we sat at the table and drank it in silence. At last, Flavi spoke to Niniane in his deep voice.

"What says he?"

"He says that you do not have the heart for war, but you have the heart for healing. He says that we will teach you the healing arts, if you will learn them. Then, when we pass, you will continue our work."

I nodded at the wisdom of their words.

"It is well. I would feel glad to undo some of the damage these foolish wars bring. And this work will keep me occupied. But I have a request of you as well. You must teach me the language of Rome."

"Why would you wish to know it?" asked Niniane. "For surely you will never travel there."

I smiled. "I would wish to understand you both without translation. I would wish to learn from Flavi without our language in between."

Flavi spoke to her.

"He says that we will start today," said Niniane.

We did so, gathering baskets, walking into the forests. As we collected plants and roots, Flavi named them for me in the tongue of Rome and I gave him the word in my tongue. I knew that they did all of this to keep my mind engaged, to stop me from thinking of Rochad, the Hound, Laeg, and Sualdem and I tried to concentrate my attention on the tasks at hand.

When my attention wandered toward a distant sound in the forest, Niniane tried another distraction.

"I must tell you the story of Fergus and the Ulster exiles."

"Yes," I answered, turning my head back toward her. "How they came to my mother's camp."

"It was all over a woman, Finnabair. A woman and treachery, though not her treachery. Deirdre was her name. Poor, poor child."

She settled on a fallen log among the greening spring shoots and I sat on the ground before her. Flavi continued in a circle in the forest around us, widening and widening, collecting things in his basket. Niniane told the story.

"When Conchobar was young, he and his warriors would often go to drink and eat at the home of his storyteller Fedlimid mac Daill, for it was said that he could spin a tale like no other. Fedlimid's wife was heavy with child and on this evening, she was serving the roisterers meat and mead when Cathbad the Druid came to join them. Her belly brushed against his side while she was serving and Cathbad turned to look upon it wide-eyed.

" 'Cathbad,' cried the woman, 'what is it that you see? What is it that you hear?' for on his face was a look that frightened her.

" 'A golden girl with copper hair I see, and lips of ruby red. Deirdre is her name and she will be more beautiful than any woman Ulster has ever seen. But, woe on Ulster for the sorrow she will bring.'

"The words were so upsetting to the little mother that they drove her into labor then and there, and she gave birth to a tiny, beautiful girl child. Cathbad whispered into Conchobar's ear that he should kill the child and the warriors of Conchobar were calling it aloud, for they had heard what Cathbad prophesied. But Conchobar declined.

" 'Find a wet nurse for her, and a tutor. We will wall her up in a rath in the forest and I will keep her for myself. For if she is such a beauty as prophesied, she should be mine alone.'

"And so Deirdre grew up in the forest with her nurse, her nurse's husband, and Levarcham, her tutor, a woman with a tongue for truth and satire. From time to time Conchobar would come to visit her, watching in anticipation as she grew beautiful and ripe, but Deirdre did not know that she was promised to the bed of the visitor she saw only as an old man.

"Then, one day, Deirdre was walking near the walls of her little prison when, from the forest nearby, she heard the voice of a man, chanting. Frantic to see what face attached to the beautiful voice, Deirdre clambered up the vines of the wall and looked over into the woods. There she saw a young man of such beauty and sweetness that she fell in love immediately. Deirdre ran to Levarcham, who had her pet raven sitting on a glove upon her hand.

" 'Levarcham,' she cried, 'I have fallen in love with a man of just these colors. He had hair of raven black, cheeks of red, and pale, white skin. He sings a chant of great beauty.'

" 'I know this one, Deirdre. He is Naoise, one of the three fine sons of Uisliu. But he cannot be yours.'

" 'He is already promised?'

" 'No,' said Levarcham. 'You are the one who is promised.'

" 'I? I know no man but my foster-father.'

" 'Do you remember the one who visits us?'

" 'The old man of Ulster?'

" 'The old man of Ulster is Conchobar, High King of Ulster. He has raised you here for his own pleasure.'

" 'Hear me, Levarcham,' said Deirdre and her voice was low and serious. 'Before that man lays hand on me, I will choose to die by this little hand.'

"And Levarcham, who loved only her raven and her little charge, Deirdre, helped the girl to a cloak and bag and led her into the forest to find the son of Uisliu. For Naoise's part, he had seen her on the wall, had asked his brothers of the beauty in the woods, and they had told him well.

" 'She is Deirdre, promised to the High King Conchobar. Think no more on her, brother, for she would bring death upon us all.'

"When Deirdre and Levarcham found him, he turned from them and ran into the forest, calling over his shoulder.

" 'Do not approach me, beautiful Deirdre, for to love you would bring death to me and mine.'

"But Deirdre was a headstrong girl. She caught Naoise by his braid and pulled him back to her. She placed a kiss upon his lips and he was lost. And so their tragic journey began. Conchobar hounded them from end to end of Eriu, riding them down in forest and field, sending trackers and warriors. Even the brothers of Naoise were not safe from the wrath of the king, and they joined Naoise and Deirdre in their restless flight. At last, Deirdre begged them for a home, for a place of permanence and rest, and the brothers talked amongst themselves and decided that the only solution was in exile. So they crossed the water to Alba and there they hid from the king and gathered to themselves a few years of peace. But Conchobar never gave up. When he could not find them, at last he sent spies to Alba where he discovered that the brothers had hired themselves as mercenary soldiers to the king of Alba.

"This angered the warriors of Ulster.

" 'Conchobar,' they cried, 'where is your sense of justice? It is not right that our Ulster brothers should die in Alba, in a war that is not our own. You are acting with your lust and not your wisdom.'

"And Conchobar pretended to hear them. He pretended that he would put Deirdre aside. He sent Fergus mac Roich, all unaware, to Alba, with promises of surety and safe passage, with promises of a feast of forgiveness. And Fergus and his warriors brought Deirdre and the sons of Uisliu back across the water to Eire.

"No sooner had Fergus brought them across the water, but he and his warriors were waylaid by messengers from the king. They were needed on urgent business of Ulster. The king's party would return Deirdre and Naoise and his brothers to Emain Macha in all safety. And that they did do. But with Fergus and his warriors absent, Conchobar had suborned Eogan mac Durthacht and his warriors to the killing ground. The three sons of Uisliu were swarmed by dozens of the soldiers of Eogan and Conchobar, and they were killed. Alone at Emain Macha, only one warrior was brave enough to try to protect them, to cry foul. That boy was the son of Fergus mac Roich and he died for his trouble."

"Ah no, no, all for Conchobar's lust."

"Just so. Fergus learned what had happened and he and his warriors rode hard for Emain Macha. There was a great battle, a horrible battle. Finnabair, it made me glad that we were of Rigdonn, that Conchobar's actions were not my husband's war. Hundreds died. And when it was over, Fergus and three thousand Ulster warriors who could no longer bear the ways of Conchobar took themselves to Connacht and allied themselves to Medb and Ailill."

"For lust and for foolish decisions, their new clan was not much improvement."

"The politics of men and war are never good, Finnabair."

"But what of Deirdre? Was she killed with her beloved?"

Niniane shook her head and little curls bobbed with emphasis.

"He kept her for a year, the lustful king, tied up in his chambers. She would not eat, nor sleep. She did not comb her hair or wash or ever smile. He did not force her; perhaps his lust for her died in his guilt, though I may be too generous there. Perhaps he truly loved her, though such a selfish love is hard to fathom. They say he sent musicians to her, but she would drop her head to her knees. When a year had passed, he knelt before her.

" 'Do you hate me more than any other, Deirdre?' he asked.

" 'No,' she replied. 'Not more than any other. For in my heart the hatred I bear you is matched by my hatred for Eogan mac Durthacht, who murdered my beloved and his brothers.'

"Conchobar rose up in a rage.

" 'Then I will give you to him for a year, and when he is finished with you, he will send you back to me. You will be like a sheep between two rams and so will it be forever.'

"And he called to him his charioteer and bound her into

the wickerwork and told the driver to hasten her to Eogan. And when they were thundering toward Eogan, poor Deirdre saw a boulder in the road. Crying, 'Naoise, I will come to you again,' she leaned out the side of the chariot and dashed her brains against the rock. And so she died. They are buried now side by side, surrounded by his brothers."

"It is a most sad and selfish story."

Niniane nodded. "But now you know how Fergus and his warriors came to be with Medb."

"Conchobar does not seem a worthy king for Ulster."

"Or any other place."

"And now my mother, with her desire for the bull, will fight with Conchobar, who is himself a rutting bull. I fear that few will survive."

"I fear it, too, daughter-in-law, and if I could give you further wisdom it would be to also stay far from Conchobar's Druid. Though he fathered Conchobar on Nessa, neither of them speaks of it. But Conchobar relies completely on Cathbad's visions and predictions."

"Is Cathbad a true Druid or does he play on Conchobar's fears and superstitions?"

"Cathbad does have some powers, truly; do not ever let him touch you if you do not wish for him to see your destiny. Flavi knows the Druid well."

"How can that be?"

"Because for a man who can predict the future of others, he sees only one path for himself and that is a path of illness. Every itch in his eye, every twinge in his elbow, every cough, and he is convinced that he is dying and rushes to Flavi for a potion."

"How odd a pair to rule a kingdom."

"How odd it is that so often the unfit rule."

"That is so," I sighed.

Perhaps Flavi sensed our sorrow, for as he circled back toward us through the forest he began to sing. Niniane and

I smiled at each other and entwined our hands as we awaited his arrival.

Rochad returned at dusk. Not a mark was upon him, but his face looked tired and broken.

"Sualdem is dead," he said without preamble.

"Conchobar killed him?" I asked immediately, so low was my opinion of the king of Ulster.

"No. Conchobar's inaction killed him. That and frustration. He rode among them chanting:

> *Have the heavens torn asunder?*
> *Has the sea o'erwhelmed the land?*
> *Is the end of all upon us?*
> *No, it is Cuchulainn crying out,*
> *The Hound, himself, alone.*
> *Men murdered, women captured, cattle stolen.*
> *The Hound defends alone*
> *Though he is sorely wounded,*
> *Though his cloak is stuffed with mosses*
> *Though his joints will come asunder*
> *Before the men of Ulster rise.*

"You would have thought that it would have whipped them into frenzy, but no. They sat and discussed it like old men in their mead cups. Cathbad the Druid said, 'Is this man annoying you, Conchobar? If so, we should put him to death.' And Conchobar said, 'Well, what he says is true; for three months now they have harrassed us for the bull. But why is Sualdem so upset? Do we not still have the sky above us in Ulster? Does the sea not still surround us?' And he shrugged. He sounded as though he were discussing rain for the crops of Ulster.

"Sualdem was crazed with frustration. He berated them and chanted and they regarded him as though he were the camp fool. He ran toward his horse, crying out, 'Men murdered, women captured, cattle stolen. The Hound defends alone.' But he tripped in his haste and his anger. And that shield, that wicked, black shield that I sharpened . . ."

Rochad shook his head.

"What has befallen, husband?"

"Oh, Finnabair, it severed his head quite nearly from his shoulders."

"Oh, you gods. Poor Cuchulainn."

"I have taken the body to him where he weeps and cannot be comforted. But, Finnabair, the armies rouse."

"How so? It seems that they ignored him."

"So they did. But something so strange occurred. When Sualdem fell and died, a voice continued, a voice deep and loud like a roaring wind.

" 'Men murdered, women captured, cattle stolen,' it cried. 'The Hound defends alone.'

"On and on it went until the men of Ulster grew afraid. They are saying that it was the voice of Lugh of the Other. Conchobar has called his chieftains to him. He has forsaken hiding behind the curse. He musters the armies for war."

A great trembling began in my legs then, and they wobbled beneath me. The feeling traveled to my stomach and up my arms. At last my body would not hold me and I simply folded to the earth. He knelt beside me and I leaned over into the shelter of his arms.

"There can be no victor here, Rochad. On the one side of this war are my mother, my father, my brothers the Maine. On the other side the Hound and Laeg. I cannot choose among them." I looked up at him. "We will go among the Partraigi," I said, hopeful that he would hear me. "Among them, there will be no war."

He was silent a long time. When he spoke his voice was sorrowful.

"The Hound is my friend, Finnabair. In his hour of

need, I have roused my warriors to his side. I cannot do less now."

I did not weep, the inevitable being unworthy of my tears. I stood and let my legs firm up beneath me. I reached for his hands.

"Come, husband," I said, "I shall try that my little love will protect you. But first there is a story I must tell you, of one that Flavi calls the Little Brother. I wish for you to have it before you go into this war."

16

On the night before the battle, Flavi and Niniane took me to the river. How different it was from the early days when there beside the water it had been the Hound and Laeg, Rochad and me. In my current state of terror, that time seemed to have to it almost an innocence, a youthfulness of purpose.

Now there were thousands of soldiers amassed around the river. Bothies had been erected and everywhere were fires and the stamping of horses. Rings of chariots surrounded the camp and there were camp women cooking and giving succor or sport to the warriors. Cuchulainn, Rochad, and Laeg were closest to the river, at the place the Hound now called Ferdiad's Ford. They would cross first on the morrow and head southwest toward the plain of Slemain Midi. There the final battle would take place. In the western distance, their fires visible to the eye, were the armies of my mother.

Rochad gestured toward the armies of Medb.

"Ailill and Conchobar have done the talk toward truce. It failed."

"Of course it failed, when all of them are lusting after war."

Rochad was garbed as a warrior in his cloak of purple with its intricate gold clasp. He carried a wicked javelin with a black blade and his war belt bristled with daggers and shortswords. His longsword lay on the ground beside his curved silver shield, with its elaborate engravings of birds and hounds and wolves. I swallowed hard when I saw him, for the fine handsome presence that he made, for the many days we had been apart, for the terrible fear that I might never see him again.

He and the Hound worked at strategy, planning their own movements in the midst of Conchobar's armies.

"I fear only that Fergus and his warriors will come against us," said Rochad. "For they are warriors of Ulster and will know the strategies we of Rigdonn use."

"For that reason, I will remain with your army," the Hound replied. "Fergus is my foster-father. He will not come against me."

"Why will he not?" I asked. "He is loyal to my mother now."

"He cannot," said the Hound. "He has made an honor price."

"What honor price would stop him?"

The two men shifted and looked at each other uncomfortably.

"We should tell her," said the Hound. "It will ease her fear a little."

"If it will ease my fear, then you must tell me."

"Do you know the sword of Fergus, Finnabair?"

"*In Cadabolg.* Who does not know it? It is the Great Slayer; they say it calls the lightning down."

"It is the skill of Fergus that calls the lightning down," the Hound said wryly. "Ever since Conchobar killed his son, he fights like the very Morrigu, as if his rage could purge the pain. But, nonetheless, he cannot fight without that sword."

"What of this?"

"Well, there came a day when Fergus was among your

mother's armies that he was making sport with a woman. He had set *In Cadabolg* on the ground behind him and one of your mother's warriors crept up on him and stole the sword."

"My mother would not hear of this for sport. Surely she ordered its return."

They were both silent. I regarded them.

"Unless the woman he was sporting was my mother."

Silence.

"Unless the thief who stole the sword was my father."

More silence.

"Ah. But then how would this stop his charge against you?"

"Of course, your father knew that he was swordless. To punish him a little, he sent him out against me, to the river, one on one."

"Without *In Cadabolg*?"

"Your father had hidden it in Cruachan Ai. But Fergus did not know the thief, and did not want Ailill to know that he had been sporting Medb."

"I cannot see why not; it would not surprise him."

"Fergus and Ailill are warrior brothers; it would not do to shame him."

"And so he came to you without *In Cadabolg*."

"He did. And I said that I did not wish to fight him, and would not fight him anyway without *In Cadabolg*. So we had a nice haunch of boar and a cup of mead and he returned to the Connachtsmen having made me a single promise—that on the day I would request his withdrawal from battle, he would do so, and take his Ulstermen with him."

"And that day will be in this battle?"

"If the need arises, it will. It is always wise for a warrior to have a fallback plan."

Flavi stood among us and began to gather our things. Panic assailed me and I wanted to reach out and clutch at Rochad, to hold him to me and inhale his scent, to plead with him to return to Flavi's healing hut. But that was the old Finnabair, fearful of being alone, desperate for someone to love her. The new Finnabair was well-loved; she could afford to offer her beloved his dignity.

All of this I told myself as I stood between Flavi and Niniane.

Rochad's eyes met mine.

"Carry this with you," I said softly, "that you are my beloved, the light of my heart. Carry also the story I have told you."

And I walked away into the darkness, clinging to Flavi's strong, still arm, feeling Niniane's hand closed so tightly around my own, her fears for her son poured into the hand of her daughter-in-law.

From the trees above me as I walked I heard the cawing of a crow and I knew that the Morrigu watched her Hound, waited for the day of battle, lusted for the feast of carrion that would ensue.

The work of a healer in war is less than the impact of a raindrop on the sea. We set up a field camp of the healers of Ulster not far from the battlefield. Wounded men were brought to us one by one and we bound and stitched, applied poultices and splints. And while we worked, up to our elbows in blood, our stomachs churning, we would hear that eight hundred had died at Slemain Midi, that a thousand of Medb's soldiers were dead, that Conchobar, Medb, and Ailill were well protected at the rear.

All the while the Morrigu, goddess of war, was feasting, sending her ravens to the battlefield. By day we could see them circling, wide about the river, gluttons for the food of men.

For many days we heard nothing of Cuchulainn or Rochad. Then word came that the Hound was sorely wounded at Fedan Chollna and we three packed our bags to go to him.

He was gashed and bleeding everywhere, his shield arm twisted at the elbow in an angle most grotesque, the wound that he had received from Ferdiad reopened and already festering. Though the armies had been bringing him food and water, no healer had been brought to him by Conchobar. He raged fever and did not recognize us. He kept murmuring, "Be wise, friend Laeg, and bring me news." Flavi and Niniane pulled the elbow back into place while he was still incoherent. Then all three of us stitched and bathed and bound the wounds with herbs and gave him strengtheners to drink and to break the fever.

When all the work was finished, Flavi held his hands above the body of the Hound and began to sing. Soft and low he sang, all through the night, binding up the spirit of Cuchulainn.

By morning, the Hound knew us and he began to rage that he could not return to battle. And then I could ask him of Rochad.

"Laeg drives for him, now that I am wounded. Rochad leads the warriors of Rigdonn. When last I saw them, both were well. But that was days ago."

My heart grew hopeful with the news. We fed the Hound a rich broth made by Flavi, designed to strengthen him; he gained in color. Toward dusk, I heard the thundering of horses' hooves and I ran to the door of the hut, my heart alive with hope that it was Rochad. When Laeg swept into view, skinny and sliding on Rochad's great black horse, I had to duck my head so that he would not see my disappointment and my fear. He swept past me into the hut, knelt beside the pallet of the Hound.

"Tell me all," the Hound commanded.

Laeg looked at the three of us, circled around the Hound, with a look so piercing that my heart froze. But he did not hesitate to tell it.

"Rochad mac Faitheman is sorely wounded. The armies of Fergus have nearly severed his shield arm. I brought my chariot from the rear, as I have done for you in battle, and I plucked him from the fray. We have bound up the arm, but it bleeds profusely. He insists that still he will ride in my chariot at the head of his armies. Fergus and his armies will meet us again tomorrow."

From his place on the pallet, the Hound regarded my face, looked clear and strong into my eyes.

"Not without me there," he said, and he struggled to a seated position.

When the battle was over they said that the Hound had called forth the promise of Fergus when Fergus struck at the shield of Conchobar. Let them tell their tales. The truth is that the Hound rode one-armed, bleeding, and broken into battle on Rochad's black horse. Among the Ulster exiles he rode until he found Fergus and Rochad. In a voice like thunder, he called forth Fergus's vow; Fergus lowered *In Cadabolg* and took the Ulster exiles with him from the battlefield. Medb created a barrier wall, but the men of Ulster broke through it and killed eight hundred of Connacht, among them two of my brothers the Maine. Medb's armies were depleted and at last she sued for peace.

The War of the Bull was over but for the mourning. And, oh, the mourning. For days and weeks, it was naught but keening, the wailing of the women of Ulster and Connacht for their husbands and their brothers and their sons, the wheeling in the sky of the dark ravens of war, sating all their hunger.

To the right of Rochad was Conchobar of Ulster. To my left at the high table were my father and Medb. Between Rochad and me sat the Hound of Ulster. He had insisted that we be on the dais, that he be between us, as though he wished to proclaim himself still at Ferdiad's Ford, still on his rock in the river. I wondered momentarily what a warrior born and trained would do in time of peace, but I shrugged that thought away. The times of peace do not last long enough for such a worry.

Though the Hound had regained his strength quickly, Rochad was pale, with great dark circles beneath his eyes. He had lost much blood and his body had not restored itself to health. His grey and sweating skin were testament to his weakness. His shield arm hung by his side like a useless straw appendage, though Flavi swore that he would teach him Roman ways to bring it back to use.

This was the Feast of Truce. So far, it did not go well at all. The men of Ulster argued that Medb should pay the greatest war price, having begun the war so many months ago. I thought they had a good point, but those among the Connachtsmen cried foul, saying that the war could have ended so much sooner had the Ulstermen just fought in battle like men, instead of hiding behind their curse, forcing the Hound into single combat with the warriors of Medb.

Back and forth they argued, and each point had to be cheered and jeered, hooted at and applauded, as though it were some wondrous hurley match between the teams of Ulster and Connacht. I sighed, deeply weary.

I looked down the many tables that stretched away at right angles. Seated at one of them were Flavi and Niniane. Flavi was regarding me intensely, with a strange, unbroken gaze. I met his eyes; they flicked toward Medb and back to me. I turned to look at her. She had risen before the company and was saluting her warriors with her mead cup. As usual, she was flirting and lowering her eyes, swinging her copper hair around her. In a moment, Conchobar would follow suit, saluting his warriors, lest a mere woman get the best of the great king of Ulster. Like two children. I shook my head.

I looked back at Flavi. Still he regarded me, unblinking and unbroken. I had a sudden, strange thought. I wondered what Flavi's Little Brother would make of two such silly, selfish creatures as Medb and Conchobar.

I looked at Medb again, her mead cup raised. Suddenly, for the first time, I saw her clearly. Medb was a well of wanting, a great empty cauldron. And nothing would ever fill her up. No bull, no amount of men, no great wars, not all the land and jewels and riches in Cruachan Ai could ever fill the well of her wanting.

And in that moment, I forgave her. Pity welled up in me. All that she had done to me, all that she had done to my father. I could not forget them. But I could forgive. I felt forgiveness move through me, clear like water. It was not a state, but an act, chosen and deliberate. And when it had filled me up, I stood. I had no idea what I would do. I raised my cup. The crowd began to grow quiet, to watch me. Medb ceased her toasting; her cup still raised, she turned in my direction. A fearful look came into her eyes. I knew she reckoned the damage I could do to her arguments, the secrets and betrayals that I carried in my memory. Rochad leaned toward the Hound and whispered; they both looked up at me. Silence tumbled back and back through the hall. Complete hush. I fixed my eyes on Flavi.

"Hear me now! I am Finnabair, daughter of Medb of Connacht."

Around me the Connachtsmen exploded in cheering, in thumping of the mead cups on the tables, sure that I had chosen for their side. When silence fell again, I spoke.

"I am Finnabair, wife of Rochad of Ulster, friend to the Hound."

Again an explosion and cheering and thumping from the Ulster side.

"Here am I of neither and of both. Here I stand on the rock between the waters. This I ask: Connacht, are you ready for peace?"

Screams and applause, men and women rising, raising their cups.

"Ulster, are you ready for peace?"

Again the wild roaring approbation. I let it settle, like dust motes into quiet.

"Then hear me now. Here stands the High King of Ulster, who will surely choose wisdom for his people."

A look of pure amusement flickered over Conchobar's face and he stood and raised his cup to me.

"And here stands my mother, greatest warrior woman in all of Eire. Surely she will choose wisely for Connacht."

I turned toward her; she had heard me. For a moment, for just a moment, my praise had filled the well of her longing. She raised her cup to me and her face was filled with pure delight.

"Now hear me all. For Ulster and Connacht these two wise rulers will negotiate a truce. For Eriu will they speak together. Will you trust their wisdom to prevail?"

The hall exploded in shouting and cheering. What else could Medb and Conchobar do? I sat down abruptly. Conchobar raised his cup toward my mother and she answered the gesture, swinging her copper hair, lowering her lashes. His eyes widened; her cheeks stained a little with red. I knew that they would talk very well together indeed. Peace—and quite a bit more—would prevail.

From beside me, the Hound leaned in to whisper.

"Oh, you wise and dangerous woman."

Rochad reached across his lap to squeeze my hand.

As for me, I looked for Flavi's eyes. And when I met them, I held them in profound thanks. For I knew the truth; in choosing to forgive her it was I who had won peace. And it filled me up like water.

BOOK TWO

The Rosc of Finnabair

THE ROSC OF FINNABAIR

Daughter of sorrows
    Finnabair the wise
Small one, silent one
    Deep water is our Finnabair
Friend of the Hound is she
    Sister of Ulster
Praise for our healer
    Who drinks the cup of friendship
Peace-maker, Bird-Sighted woman
    Sweet the wisdom
She speaks between the counties
    Deep forest is our Finnabair
Daughter of forgiveness, child of light
    She who binds the counties
Hungry for war
    Was Medb the Red Queen
Fierce for vengeance
    Was Conchobar of Ulster
Between them our sister
    River who crosses all borders
Journeyer, Mysterious one
    Finnabair the Wise.

17

What I have learned is that a time of war is a dark binding for the spirit. It is the Morrigu who rules in such a time; darkness and panic, death and terror. She feasts on human weakness and on the carrion sorrow of the mourning. For human beings, the harvest of war is bitter and small; it leaves the spirit hungry.

In the end, my mother got what she wanted, the great Brown Bull, Donn Cuailnge. But in their childlike stupidity, my parents penned the two together, my father's White Bull, Finnbennach, and the Donn. They were bulls; I do not know what my parents thought would happen, but they behaved as bulls behave, kicking and butting, biting and charging. No one dared to go between them and so it went until each of them was sorely wounded. The Donn killed Finnbennach first and my father gave command to his men to kill the Donn. But Fergus mac Roich intervened, saying that too many men had died for the great bull for anyone to kill it. He released it from its pen and it shambled, wounded, around the countryside with warriors trailing it, until at last it died.

It seemed to me that there were great teaching stories in this ending, but my mother and father did not see them.

Only Fergus mac Roich dared to voice the public opinion that the whole war had been about following the rump of a misguided woman over the rump of a now-dead bull, but his was a small voice. The rest of Connacht, glad to have the war over, praised Medb as both warrior and beauty and she preened herself on the praise.

And in the end, with both bulls dead, my mother and father were left, after all, with equal hoards.

Cuchulainn decided to leave us to ride south for Emer, who would come to live in Ulster now that her beloved was no longer in daily danger of death.

As for me and mine, we decided to go deep into the Fid Duin, among the Partraigi, Flavi wishing to learn their healing arts and Rochad needing time for his arm to heal. And so we closed up the hut of Flavi and Niniane, loaded ourselves with herbs and medicines like packhorses, and went among the Partraigi silent and on foot.

We came to them in the evening, rolling our feet against the forest floor, not speaking at all. It was early summer and the long light seeped through the trees like honey. They knew, of course, that we were coming. Before we even reached their longhouses, I heard tiny bells ringing and the soft sounds of clicking beads. We stepped into a clearing which had been prepared for welcome. Long strands of beads and bells hung from the trees and the wind moved them in perfect music. Jigahnsa was dressed in white deerhide, embroidered with every twining flower of the forest. She held the feathered stick.

When she saw me, she studied my face, her head tilting sideways. I waited before the scrutiny, silent and still. At last she nodded, stepped toward me, pressed her forehead against mine.

"Welcome, Little Sister. For I see that you have crossed the river."

What began for me there was the time of peace. For me it was the long years of learning; among the Partraigi, it was, for the first time, the years of belonging.

On the very next day, they gave me my tattoo, the two dots on my temple descending to two sinuous ropes of river. Below the water, next to my lips, was a triangle of three dots. A ribbon tied those three dots together and as their cap, a braid of the winding, endless knotwork of my own people. When I asked Jigahnsa for the meaning, she said, "You crossed the river with your forgiveness. With your wisdom you bound together Ulster and Connacht. This is your story, Finnabair, the story of speech that is wise."

"But why are there two rivers?"

She looked away for a moment and then regarded me directly.

"You will cross another water, Finnabair. When and how I cannot say, for that is in the mind of Maker."

My life began in that forest, my true life, in which my spirit turned from war and fear toward light, toward learning. All of us were happy there.

Flavi learned the medicines of the Partraigi; to him, they inclined their heads, calling him Elder Brother. Niniane went among them as she went everywhere, with hugs and laughter and much tousling of her curls, which none of them possessed in their shining rivers of black hair. For me, I felt as the field when rain comes at last. I learned the language of the Romans and the tongue of the Partraigi. I learned the medicines of both. I feasted on the stories of the people. My Rochad gained his strength, but slowly. The men of the Partraigi worked his arm with a hunting bow and had him push against the trunks of trees, holding his body weight with the weak arm until it shook, until his brow beaded with sweat. Flavi had him thrust and slash with a Roman shortsword. In the evenings, I would rub the arm with an unguent that would warm the muscles. Gradually, the limp arm gathered form and muscle. Gradually, the color returned to Rochad's face.

One evening, late in the summer toward Lughnasa, I had stripped him of his shirt to rub the arm when suddenly he slipped it around me. While he didn't exactly crush me to him as he had of old, I could feel the returning strength of the arm. I smiled up at him. His lips were upon mine so suddenly that I was taken by surprise, there in the clearing among the longhouses, surrounded by all the evening movements of the people.

I stood and held out my hand. We walked into the deep, green forest. There, among the fairy ferns and fragrant violets, we made between us Tahar, our little warrior boy. I birthed him, supported between the arms of Jigahnsa and Niniane, my face bathed by his grandfather, Taharqa, so little pain, such joy upon me that I did not think the world could contain it.

And so, a little more than a year later, none of us expected any problems with the second birth. But from the first moment of my laboring, it was clear that both the child and I were in grave danger. Great waves of pain rolled over me; I screamed and the water poured down my face and soaked my hair. But no child would come. The water gushed as it should; the birth door opened; no child would come.

Flavi examined the birth canal; I screamed with the pain. He withdrew his hand and shook his head at Niniane, made a little circling motion with his finger.

"What is it?" I cried. "You must tell me; it is my child."

His eyes regarded me with sorrow.

"The cord is wrapped around the child's neck; I cannot loosen it and the child cannot come forward."

I cried aloud for Rochad. He came behind me, gathered me in his arms. Jigahnsa leaned her forehead into mine; three times she breathed her spirit into me. She placed her fingers against the second river on my cheek and whispered words in her own tongue. Tears streamed down her face. I laced my arms backwards around Rochad's neck. I squatted into the pain. With all the strength that I possessed, I pushed my child toward the world. I felt something tear loose, felt the great rush of blood. My little girl came sliding into the world, blue and cold. Too much of my blood came behind her. I slid up out of my eyes and swam behind her into the west.

We were crossing the water; in the distance there was a beautiful light. My infant child swam before me, but as I followed her she seemed to grow older and older. I swam into the light. I was standing now on a long green field that swept down to the sea. I could feel the mist from the water drifting against my face, clinging in tiny droplets to my hair. How it cooled me! Around me spilled the light, falling over me in rainbows, luminous and warm.

A young woman stood before me, facing out to sea. Her hair was thick and chestnut brown, the curling strands held back by a ribbon of black. I stepped behind her, tapped against her shoulder. She turned to me smiling. Her face was my face.

"Daughter?" I asked.

She nodded, smiling.

"I am the one your heart calls Julia."

And I knew that she was my own child, for indeed it was the name that I had chosen, Niniane's second name.

"What is this place?"

She placed her fingers against the second river on my cheek and smiled.

"We have crossed the water."

"And this is Tir Nàn Og?"

She inclined her head.

"That is one of its names."

"And I will stay here now with you."

She shook her head, but the smile never left her face.

"It is not your time. In the land of Tir Inna m'Beo, he who would be my father weeps. They who love you like their child are lost. And I have a tiny brother."

"But you are also my child. I cannot leave you alone."

"Listen."

I stilled to listen; the whole of that country was suffused with song; it moved the wind; it arched across the sky. In the distance there was laughter.

"I hear, but I do not see."

"Nor should you, for it is not your time. Hear me, Maither. I will return to you."

"When will this be?"

"In a time of sorrow, I will return."

But my heart reached toward her, a *chailin bhig*, my little girl, and I did not wish to leave her.

"I cannot go," I cried.

She smiled gently. "Hear me now, Maither. Nothing is wasted. That Which Is does not waste even a mote of dust. Nothing is ever lost. One way or the other, we are always crossing the water."

Before I could beg to remain with her, I was skimming back across the water, floating above the sea like a gull.

I was a long time healing in the forest. For many weeks I could not stand or walk. Flavi packed me with poultices, Niniane rubbed at my belly with warm oils. I drank herbal teas and swigged at tisanes of alkymelich. Jigahnsa and Rochad took turns bracing my back against their chests while I placed Tahar against my swollen breasts. I wept too much, whispering my child's name. They fed me soups made with venison and boar to try to strengthen my blood. Little by little my strength returned. I slept but little and I could not staunch my weeping.

At last there came a day when I could walk a little way. Jigahnsa led me into a clearing of the forest where the light streamed down between the trees in a perfect circle of long beams. She sat down with her back against a tree and braced me before her, wrapping her arms around my chest. I leaned my head against her shoulder and she rocked me gently, gently.

"I will tell you a story, Finnabair."

I nodded drowsy with the rocking, mesmerized by the streamers of light.

"There came a day when First Mother fell to earth through a hole in the roots of the tree of life. Down and down she came. When she landed here in the darkness, she could see, far above her, the doorway into the First World above. But she could not reach it to return. Frightened, she began to weep. She wept so much and for so long that a sea grew up around her. Now she could not rise to First World and she could not walk away in this world. Years passed and at last she ran out of tears. Far below in the water, she could see a window of light. 'It is only a reflection of the opening to sky world,' she said. But it did not move or change when she swirled her hand in the water. First Mother dived into the water and swam for the light. When she reached it, she passed through the tunnel and came up standing in the First World. The Maker was waiting for her by the door. 'Why did you force me all these years to look up toward the Light? Why did you not open this doorway for me years ago when I fell?' she demanded.

" 'We did,' said the Maker. 'There are many doorways into First World. We opened this one at the moment you fell. But you were weeping so much that you could not see it.' "

"I hear you, clan mother," I sighed.

She said nothing more and simply rocked me. I closed my eyes and drifted into sleep.

Across a little stream my daughter stood. She smiled at me.

"Mama," she said, "dreams are the doorway. I will come to you in dreams."

"When?" I asked her.

"Whenever you need me to come."

We had been among the Partraigi for almost four years when change came to us. I was in the forest with Tahar, three years old and sturdy as a pony. We were gathering roots and wildflowers for Flavi when I heard someone, stumbling and cursing, moving in the forest like a drunken old man.

"Mama," Tahar whispered, "is it a wild boar?"

But I had recognized the voice of old.

"It is not," I whispered. "I think it is a water reed, a chariot driver without his wheels, a man who never accustomed himself to walking."

And then he stumbled into view, skinny as ever, his cloak torn and tattered, leaves and sticks caught in his hair. He did not see us until he was almost upon us, and then he looked up, exclaiming in surprise.

"Damnable forest. Wretched place. They should clear it all down, make way for the chariot wheels. Who is this little fellow?"

"This is Tahar, Rochad's son and mine."

He saluted my little boy.

"It is time for you to meet your uncle then. Surely they have told you of the famous Hound of Ulster."

18

To be human is to leave and be left. All of our lives, departure shadows over us like the wide wings of hawks. Why then does it become no easier as we grow older?

I wept when we left the Partraigi, though I had always known that one day we would return to the world of Ulster, that our life in the forest was an interlude, a little dream.

My forehead bounced against that of Jigahnsa for the strength of my weeping and when I inhaled her essence, I brought her scent into me again and again, the mingled essence of smoke and pine that spoke her name, so that for the rest of my life, I could call her back to me with scent.

I knew that we would never meet again; she echoed my knowledge with her own tears.

At the last, before our departure, I went to the little cairn where the bones of my infant girl were buried. I planted violets in the ground around her rocky grave, in the dirt between the stones. There they would take root and grow; someday a passerby would notice nothing but a hillock of blue spring violets.

We left as we had come, silent and on foot, passing through the Fid Duin as shadows, and then we were gone.

Near Emain Macha, close to the hut of Flavi, Cuchulainn had set up camp with Emer. It was a village by the time we came to them, with a *grianan* for the women, pasturage for cattle, a smithy, bakeshops, and weaving halls. He had even built a dwelling for Rochad and me, close enough to Flavi and Niniane that I could be with them in moments, far enough away that we were private. It was our first dwelling alone of our married life, though we had been wed for five years.

Emer had come to dwell with the Hound, bringing with her all her women and their mates. The village was full with sound, with children. Emer herself was beautiful, with copper hair and milk-white skin and her famous wit and tart tongue.

"So this is Finnabair. Oh, the stories they tell of you," she said, arching her eyebrows at me and laughing. "I should be jealous were it not for Rochad the Beautiful."

Though I thought that she was teasing, I could make no response. My return to Ulster was my return to being Finnabair.

In my years with the Partraigi I had become as they were, soft-spoken, quiet in laughter. With them, I was not Finnabair the Mouse, daughter of the bright sword of Connacht. Nor was I Finnabair of Ulster, wife of Rochad, friend to the Hound. I was only myself; among the Partraigi that was all that was required. I had become the very river on my cheek, a woman still and deep. I did not like my return to the world of civilization, to the place where I was defined by the ways that everyone else knew me. Desperately, I wanted to run back to the forest.

But Rochad was delighted with the company of warriors. He reveled in being able to ride his huge black horse again, delighted in thundering along with our four-year-old son before him in the saddle. I spent little time with him, preferring to work in the hut with Flavi and Niniane, pounding at my herbals and medicaments. I had become, I suppose, somewhat of a recluse.

At night when we slept in our dwelling, I woke often, mindful of the village noises, fearful as I had never been in the Fid Duin.

Niniane, observant as always, spoke to me.

"After Faitheman died," she began, "I was no longer of Rigdonn. Or so I felt. Though I had a child of Rigdonn, I was the Welisc woman who had married him, the stranger from a different country, who spoke a different tongue. Quieter and quieter I grew. Until Flavi came among us, I suppose I was a shadow, Finnabair. Then Flavi came and he became my family. And then my beloved daughter-in-law."

I knew that she held up the story as a mirror, knew that she reminded me of our relationship because she could see the distance that grew between Rochad and me. But I could not unlock my silence.

"You are my family now. You and Flavi. Here we will have our healing practice." I pounded at my cluster of dried herbs.

"Look at me, Finnabair!" She spoke angrily, something I had never seen her do. I looked up at her, startled. "Look at me!"

She stood before me. Grey was threading through her auburn curls. Her face had grown pouchy and her cheeks drooped a little by her mouth. Dark spots of age speckled her face.

"Now look at Flavi."

Flavi was on his sleeping platform, napping in the afternoon having become his custom now, in his eighth decade of life.

"I see you both. You are the parents of my heart. Why are you so angry with me?"

"Because we will not be with you forever. I must speak to you directly, daughter-in-law. Flavi is old. I am following. I love you, Finnabair, as if you were my own child. I know that you did not wish to return to Ulster. I know that you mourn the death of your child, the loss of the people of the Partraigi. Here, you are daughter of Medb of Connacht, wife of Rochad of Ulster, caught in the politics of power. But my son is a warrior of Ulster and the Hound called both of you back. You have grown strong and wise, Finnabair. Do not stay behind your wall of silence; I do not wish for you to be lonely when we are gone."

She clamped her lips shut and pounded so furiously at her dried herbs that Flavi awoke from his nap.

To welcome us back to Ulster, Cuchulainn and Emer held a great feast. Rather than the embroidered silks and plaids of Rochad's clan, I wore instead the white buckskin dress embroidered with flowers that had been my parting gift from Jigahnsa. The deep scent of the Fid Duin was worked into the softened hide, into the winding flowers. Though I knew that Niniane was right, I could not shake off my longing; I sat silent at the table in the midst of all the feasting.

Niniane tried to cheer me; she chattered brightly at the table about the many women of Emer and their men, about the warriors of Rochad who had come from Rigdonn to welcome their wounded brother home. I knew that this was her way of apology, that she was sorry she had been so angry with me. I smiled at her and nodded politely at all she said, toyed with the salmon steamed in seaweed and the honey cakes with nuts.

Only when I saw the tall, thin blond figure duck through the lintel of the door did my spirits lift.

"Maine Mathramail!" I cried, running from my seat at feast to greet him.

He threw his skinny arms around me, then held me off at arms length.

"So it is true what they say of you."

"Who says? Says what?"

"It came to us as rumor, hard on your return. They say that Finnabair is a beauty to rival Medb, that she is water-deep and wondrous wise, a woman not of Ulster, not of

Connacht, but of her own country. Some say that you have gone into the west and have returned across the water. They say there is now no border that you cannot cross."

I blushed and ducked my head.

"I am none of those but only a woman who has known a portion of sorrow, a portion of joy."

"Well, do not wear that dress or curl your hair so when you come to Medb, for she was jealous even in the hearing."

This made me laugh aloud; I felt surprised to hear my own laughter. Had it been so long?

"And why would I go to her, Mahneemawra?"

"We hear she has a grandson; she commands you to bring him to her."

I pointed in the direction of Tahar, who wound his way among the tables with a cluster of girls and boys.

"He looks much like her," said my brother.

"He does," I said. "But he is kind of heart, like his uncle Mahneemawra." I called him to us and he came running, allowing himself to be scooped up for a momentary hug before wriggling free to run again.

Mathramail looked around.

"And where is Rochad?"

I pointed among the warriors. "And at the dais, Flavi and Niniane, who have taught me their arts of healing."

If he noticed how quickly I moved his attention to them, he did not say, and I gathered his hand and took him to the table with me.

Niniane and Flavius hastened to make him a place where he sat beside me, enjoying all the gossip that I had been inclined to ignore.

Late into the evening, when the torches grew smoky and so many of the revelers were deep into their mead cups, we were visited by the High King of Ulster. He came among us accompanied by a band of his warriors in their Royal Branch plaids. Beside him in white was an old druid, thin-faced and sharp-eyed, his hair long ago vanished from his bald pate. I suspected that this was Cathbad the Druid and I shivered at the thought that he might touch my hand, see some future that I would not wish to know.

Conchobar moved among the warriors, clasping arms and clapping shoulders. He welcomed Rochad back among them, but over and over, his head swiveled in my direction.

"What is it?" Mathramail whispered when he looked our way yet again. "What does he wish with you?"

"I know not and I like it not. He is too much like our mother, or so the stories say."

"They got on well in the peace discussions," he said noncommittally.

"I'm sure they did," I answered wryly. I met his eyes and we both burst into laughter. It was while we were thus, our heads together, our laughter ringing from the table, that he approached us.

We stood, of course. He ignored Mathramail, perhaps did not even know him as the son of Medb. Over my hand he bent low and his eyes came up toward mine. He was grinning.

Conchobar mac Nessa was a man of more than fifty years, but he was handsome, tall as were the men of Ulster, well-muscled, dangerous. His nose had been broken and above it his hazel eyes could shift from joy to sorrow, from welcome to anger in a single second. His hair was threaded through with silver, his beard still thick and dark. He eyes were quick, his mouth a sensuous curve.

He drew my hand up toward his lips, pulling me toward him all the while, until we were leaning into each other across the table. My heart began to trip like a hammer; I could think only of poor Deirdre.

The hall grew very still; all of Ulster watching.

"Finnabair ni Medb," he said. "Why did you leave us so soon after the truce feast? I wanted to thank the wise little woman whose words brought an end to the War of the Bull."

I inclined my head, said nothing.

"And now I find that she has become a beauty."

There was nothing to say. I reddened from the roots of my hair all the way down the neck of my dress.

"Your mother was . . . most accommodating in the peace talks between Ulster and Connacht."

"Then it is well that you negotiated with her, Ard Ri. For I am not my mother."

A little gasp went up from the hall. Conchobar bared his teeth at me, his whole face delighted and amused. By the gods! The man thought that I was issuing a challenge. He had thought that the daughter had the same easy thighs as her mother. Here was a sense of self as great as my mother's or greater. Rochad stood and began threading his way toward me, his face a mask of glowering rage. Cathbad the Druid began to move toward Conchobar, sensing, I suppose, some fulcrum, some fork in the road of destiny and wishing to be in the midst of it all.

It was Emer who saved me.

"Ard Ri," she called. He turned his head toward her, like a bear being distracted, but he did not release my hand.

"What is the one thing that can take you across the water faster than a spear point?"

He grinned at her, shook his head.

"One of your famous riddles, Emer?"

"Indeed."

"Then I know not. Do tell me."

"But you should know, great king. Or have you not heard? You hold it in your hand."

He looked down at my hand in his.

"I think not, Emer. Unless we speak of another death entirely."

"Finnabair," called Emer. "What say you?"

I turned my head toward her; I did not know what game she played, but I was willing to play along. As I faced her, my tattoo came full into the view of the High King. His free hand came up to the side of my face; his fingers brushed along the river, stopped on the circles of Ulster and Connacht. He drew breath, pulled his fingers back from my face suddenly. He looked down at their tips as though he had inserted them in fire. His eyes met mine. He bowed low but I knew that we were not finished. I willed myself to absolute stillness, met his eyes. I saw a little flicker of fear and something else, something I did not like at all.

He whirled, almost tripping over his Druid who stood just behind me. I met the Druid's rheumy blue eyes; his pupils went very wide.

19

"And now you want me? Why? Because you will match
your desire to the High King of Ulster?" I hissed at my
husband in the darkness.

Rochad was pressed against me, his body stiff with
wanting. His arms held me hard against the side wall of
the hut, my arms extended above my head. I could feel all
of the strength that had returned to his shield arm.

To silence me, he pressed his mouth against mine.

I bit his lip.

He reared back from me, regarded me with a mixture of
fury and desire. He bared his teeth.

"What, husband? Do you think to mark your territory
like a wolf? If you mark me, the High King will smell it
and let me be?"

I struck the right cord for he deflated and stood back.
He hung his head.

"Yes. I like him not, the way he looks at you."

"At least you are honest, then."

"How so?"

"Not once have you come to me since we returned to
Ulster but a little month ago. All of our twinings in the
green wood of the Fid Duin are nothing here in Ulster. It

was you who insisted we should come, that the Hound would need your good right arm, the people of Ulster would need our healing skills. I left behind my beloved friend, my forest people. I did not know that our love remained behind also in the Fid Duin."

"I do not come to you because you are not the Finnabair of the Fid Duin. She was a woman warm and laughing. She moved in the forest more silent than the leaves. With her, I did not need to plead for favors; one look and she would shrug her shoulders and drop her gown to the forest floor. My Finnabair was hungry for the mating. Now I feel as though you are the Finnabair I hauled from the river so many years ago, hungry only for death."

Now it was my turn to hang my head in shame. I shrugged my shoulders.

"I cannot think what to tell you. I feel like that Finnabair of old, trapped between Connacht and Ulster, never of either place, longing for the forest people."

"But you are of me, Finnabair. When we were in the forest, I did not long for Ulster because you were in the Fid Duin with me. You are my country, not Ulster, not Rigdonn. It is here that I wish for you to belong, here against my heart. Let me be your country." He pressed his hand against his heart. On his face was a look of much longing. My heart softened toward him. I leaned in against his chest, let him wrap his arm around me.

"I do not know what to say to you, husband. I am empty and sad. I cannot make desire bloom in the burren. Why did you insist we return?"

He heaved a great sigh.

"I will tell you, because I do not like this space between us. And I do not like the look in the eyes of the High King. But what I tell you will not ease your burden."

"I did not ask to have my burdens eased, husband. You do not protect me with silence, you make me more alone. A woman binds herself to her man with words."

He shrugged.

"You will not like these words. When Laeg came to us in the forest, he did so because there are rumors. In Connacht, many say that Medb's desire robbed them too soon of husbands and sons, that her war has sundered two generations of Connacht."

"This is true and I have said as much. Why should those words trouble me?"

"Because it is also whispered that Medb blames these misfortunes on the Hound, that she schemes some dark revenge."

"No! We have had peace! Almost five years of peace!"

He spread his hands.

"This is the message he brought me in the forest."

"We shall see about this; on the morrow I will seek to know. Medb of Connacht shall not move against us in secret. She will not ambush me and mine."

He was grinning at me in the darkness.

"Why do you smile?"

"This is my Finnabair, wife of fire."

"Here is fire for you," I said softly, swinging myself across him. "Come, now, husband, let us choose each other anew."

In the morning, I went to the river, to Ferdiad's Ford. It was strange to see the great rock empty, the Hound not seated upon it. I held my tunic up over my knees, waded out to the rock, climbed and slipped and scrambled, bracing myself on the thin spire that was its companion until I was seated cross-legged in the sunshine on the rock's flat surface. I stretched my bare legs in the sunshine, tilted my face to the light.

For the first time in many years, I deliberately used the Bird-Sight, looking long and long toward Connacht, again long and long toward the east. I saw one thing only, a small boy being rowed across the water from the coast of Alba. He snapped his slingshot at seabirds, while at his side a huge man, deaf, mute, and slow, turned the oars. It was too strange a vision for clarity; I could make of it no knowing, no connection to my mother.

I decided that I would go to Connacht, ostensibly to let Medb meet her grandson. I stood, gathering the folds of my still damp tunic, wishing that I had worn the buckskin braichs of the Partraigi. I prepared to climb down the rock and wade, pulled the tunic up between my legs, winding it into my belt, making a short, blousy pair of braichs. From the bank behind me a voice called out.

"So fine and pale a pair of flanks should never be hidden beneath a tunic."

I whirled.

The High King of Ulster sat astride a fine dappled grey, his light summer cloak shifting in the breeze. He was completely alone.

I yanked the tunic from between my legs and let it flutter damp around my ankles.

"Ard Ri," I said, bowing and collected my light cloak from the rock beside me in one motion. I wrapped it around me, my fingers fumbling with the brooch. "I had thought myself alone."

"Of course, you did. That was the pleasure of watching."

He eased his horse into the water; he pranced lightly toward my rock.

"There is no point in your wading back and wetting your tunic further. I shall be glad to offer my assistance."

There was nothing for it but to accept.

He rode up beside the rock, held out his arm. I swung myself behind him on the saddle. He took off for the shore by urging his horse into a leaping motion that almost threw me backwards. It forced me to grab his waist for purchase. He chuckled.

"I am sorry, Finnabair. He is a feisty one, my mount."

There was no answer I could make that would not feed his innuendo. I was silent.

At the shore, he turned west, away from our little rath.

"My King," I protested feebly. "My healing duties call me."

"Can they wait but a little while? I so much wish to know you better."

Gallant and dangerous, courtly and deadly. There was no declining the Ard Ri of Ulster.

"You are the king of Ulster," I said. "What time you request I will give you."

He laughed and patted my hand.

"Good girl," he said. "Wise daughter of Medb."

I closed my eyes. Maybe it was better to get it over with. Perhaps he would tire of me with one bedding, move to another. He had obviously bedded my mother during the peace talks, enjoyed the romp, moved on to others. But she was Medb; that was her expectation. And she equaled him in power. I knew what she would recommend. 'Romp with him a few times,' she would say. 'He is a man; new thighs will call him. And when they do, he will think of you with gratitude. You will have purchased the goodwill of Ulster's king.' For the first time I understood my mother's politics of sex, the control it gave her to be the one who chose.

And then I thought of Deirdre.

What if he did not tire of me? Deirdre had been a great beauty, but I was young and new and the daughter of Medb. What if Conchobar brought Rochad to his death? What if he turned against the Hound? Niniane and Flavius? No or yes, how would each affect my child? All of those I loved? What if his lust had no bottom?

I looked around in desperation. A little way before us on the empty plain, I saw the chariot of Laeg. My heart leaped up with hope.

I leaned in against the king's back; he laughed and welcomed the pressure.

"My king," I whispered against his shoulder. "I have always wished to ride once like the wind on a great horse like this one."

"Done!" he said laughing. "We will take on the wind on the plain before us here."

We rode out onto the great plain and he opened up his horse's gait. Swiftly we moved from canter to gallop, thundering across the space. The wind picked up my hair and my cloak and spun them both behind me where they wound together and apart as we twisted and turned. I clung to the king, who laughed aloud and shouted out his delight. "By the gods, Finnabair, you are a woman of fire." He did not know the icy terror I was feeling there, clinging on behind him, my mind moving faster than his horse.

He did not slow when the chariot hove into sight, riding up at full gallop toward Laeg and the Hound, wheeling his horse to a stop in prancing circles. From his back I watched as the Hound and Laeg realized who rode astride behind him, as their pupils widened. I gave my friends a look both desperate and terrified. After that soul-jolting ride, it was easy enough to do so. And then I prayed that they would understand.

The king was laughing.

"This is a wild girl," he said, whirling and prancing, shouting over their heads. "All the years you called her Mouse. You great fools! This is a woman for the wind!"

"Healer," cried Cuchulainn. "Well met! It is you we search for."

"Why?" asked the king. "She is mine for the afternoon."

"But Ard Ri," said the Hound. "It is your druid, Cathbad. He is sick unto death with the catarrh."

Cuchulainn held my waist as he rode for the healer's hut. He spoke into my ear, constant and unrelenting.

The king had dropped me down to them immediately upon hearing the news, Cuchulainn shouting up that they would take me to my hut, gather all the tools of healing.

"Hear me now, Finnabair. Conchobar lives by Cathbad; Cathbad is both his Druid and his father. Conchobar believes that the Druid controls his fate, warns him of obstacles. He will not believe that he can conduct the business of Ulster without him."

"Then how fortunate that you were looking for me."

Cuchulainn snorted.

"We were not. We were out hunting birds with my slingshot."

"Cathbad is not sick?"

"He has a cough. Now you must make him think that he is dying."

"How?"

"I will send Emer to you. She tricked him well when first we wed and he has never troubled her since."

"Perhaps it is his fear of you that keeps him from her," I said. "For who will defend Ulster if the Hound will not? And who will defend Conchobar if the Hound is angry?"

"Conchobar thinks little when his lust is large. Emer will tell you."

I was stuffing my herbals into my bag, telling Niniane and Flavi my story.

"How shall I do to protect us all? Counsel me."

"Worry him," said Flavi. "Cold cloths to his forehead, a few well-placed sighs. Knit your brow. For a man who suggests so well for others, he is powerfully suggestible." He continued working on something at his medicine table, measuring, pouring, and tying.

"So Niniane has told me."

"But for the lust, I cannot think," said Niniane, and then Emer thundered into the clearing. She burst into the hut, all fiery hair and scent of flowers. Though we had spoken but once and she had riddled me from Conchobar at the feasting, she threw her arms around me in a warm embrace.

"Finnabair," she said, "that rutting stag of a king again. I will tell you my story quickly and we will plan."

I nodded.

"When Cuchulainn and I were to wed, he brought me here to the Craobh Rioga before all the warriors of the Royal Branch. I knew the moment I laid eyes on the king that trouble was before us. He would not take his eyes from me and he was rigid with desire. In the way of men, the Hound saw nothing. While the Hound was busy presenting me to one and all, parading me before the Ulster warriors, I saw Conchobar whisper to an old man in the company.

"Later when we were raising the cups, the old man, Bricriu mac Carbad, stood up.

" 'Emer ni Forgall,' he called aloud." Aside, she said to me, "Forgall was my father, Finnabair, and the way Cuchulainn wooed me from him is a story for a much less urgent day."

I waved her story on.

"So he called my name and raised his glass and then he cried, 'To first mating, to Emer and Conchobar! And may our king make her ready for the Hound.'

" 'What is this?' I asked the Hound, for I did not know that loathsome Ulster custom. But already you know my husband, Finnabair. Anger does not sit upon him as it does on other men. He began to spin and whirl. The feathers came away from his cloak and began to spit in the air. He spun in the central fire and the sparks rose up around him. It was terrible to behold."

"This I have seen, Emer. I know it well."

"And yet we were trapped. For Bricriu had announced it before all of Ulster. Conchobar would be dishonored if I did not comply. Worse, it was Conchobar himself who had begun the quest to find the Hound a wife. Though the Hound himself found me, wooed me, and won me, Conchobar felt entitled to bed me. Should I decline, he would not pay my bride price. The Hound and I would have been forbidden to marry. What was to be done?"

"Tell me quickly," I said, as I finished stuffing my bag

and threw it across my shoulder. "For poor old Cathbad is dying of catarrh."

She grinned at me.

"And there you have it. For that night, they sent the women of Conchobar to me. They put me in the finest gown and wove my hair with flowers.

"I knew that Cathbad would be waiting outside Conchobar's chamber and I bowed before him. 'Druid,' I said, 'I bid you farewell before we die.'

"'Die?' he answered. 'None will die. Conchobar will bed you well and you will wed the Hound.'

"'Conchobar will bed me,' I said, 'but I will not wed the Hound.' He bristled then and said it was the custom.

"'Of course it is,' I answered, 'but you saw Cuchulainn; he has entered the *riastradh*. I am the only one who can abate it; once I bed your son, I lose that power. His rage will grow and spread. Soon we will all be infected.'

"'Infected? It is but his war rage.'

"'Why do you think your son sends him to herd cattle when the rage war comes upon him? Do you not see how many cattle die before it abates? Why do you think Laeg sends him to the Partraigi? Have you seen any of them—ever—emerge from the Fid Duin? It was the chasteness of my love that could abate the riastradh. After this night, none will calm his fever, Cathbad. It will spread and grow; the anger of the Hound will not be quieted; soon he will not be able to stand vigil at his stone, to defend Ulster in its cursing. At last it will turn against Ulster itself.'

"Finnabair, once I had said it, I knew it to be true. I started to Conchobar's chamber, full of sorrow.

"Cathbad was beside me before I had taken another step.

"So swollen with rutting need was Conchobar that it seemed to me a kind of riastradh. But somehow Cathbad managed to convince him that honor would be served, and all of Ulster preserved, if I would sleep between them with no mating night at all. As a witness they brought in Fergus

Mac Roich—this was before he became your mother's exile—and he sat beside the bed all night and watched, then witnessed to Cuchulainn. The worst of my bedding night was that the old Druid snores and smells like an ancient goat. But I was never bedded, then was truly wedded to my Hound. And Conchobar has never troubled me again."

"But how shall I do, for Rochad is only a man?"

"It was the loss of my female powers that frightened Cathbad." She thought for a moment. "What if we tell them that Medb placed you with Rochad that you would be of a healer's family?"

"How will that stop Conchobar?"

She blew out a long breath.

"Then what of this? We shall say that your Bird-Sight is required to see a healing for Cathbad. We shall say you must be chaste for it to work."

"And what will the king make then of all the years that I have bedded Rochad? What of my son?"

She pressed her hands against her lips. Her eyes were wide with worry.

"If only we had some time to think it through."

From his workbench, Flavi stepped forward, completely calm. In his hand, he held a small skin bag filled with calf's blood.

"Here is what we shall do," he said. "When you have ministered to Cathbad in all the proper ways, you will say that he requires a sing. You will send for me. Meanwhile, you will wind your tunic up into your belt, as braichs, as you did on the rock. You will place this bag in the fold. When I come for the sing, we will insist that Conchobar join us, that he bind hands with us. We will tell him that we cannot break the circle. Finnabair when we are bound in circle, you must use your legs to break the bag. Can you do that?"

I saw what he intended. Emer saw it at the same moment.

"Flavi," I said, "I cannot let my danger fall onto you."

"You are my girl, Finnabair. What healer would I be if I did not protect you?"

It was Emer who spoke.

"I would give all the years of my childhood for a father like you," she said.

And in that moment, I knew that I had found a friend.

I was surprised to discover that indeed Cathbad had a deep and racking cough; it produced no poison he could expel. It was easy enough to worry him with it, for I knew it had to break and I did not like the sound. I ministered to the Druid with pine bark tea and smoke inhalations. I put a poultice of hot leeks against his chest. The cough did not loosen and by the time I called for the sing I was wet with sweat, my face steaming and my tunic soggy. While we waited for Flavi, I wound my tunic up between my legs and hooked it in my belt, tucking the bag inside. I tied my hair in a wild knot on my head. Already I looked wet and weary and I hoped that Conchobar would see just that.

Flavi came and called for Conchobar. I shook my head at him and his face creased with worry. I would have felt guilty for worrying the king were both the cough and his lust not quite so deep.

We joined hands and Flavi began a song in the tongue of Meroe; the verses had no sense for me, but I repeated them just as he sang them. While we sang I worked the muscles of my legs against the bag; it burst in the third verse, gushing all over the wound-up white tunic.

Conchobar saw it first; he tried to break hands with me.

"Do not break the circle of song," Flavi intoned in Gaeilge, singing the admonition as a verse.

"But her moon-blood comes," said the king, his voice a little strangled.

"Do not break the circle of song," Flavi intoned again.

All night long Conchobar held my hand as the blood stiffened and dried, as its tangy, coppery smell pervaded the sickroom. The look of revulsion on the king's face was all the healing I would ever need.

Toward morning Cathbad's cough broke and we gathered our medicaments and left Emain Macha. Emer met us by the way; she had been waiting in darkness with my husband and the Hound.

"Flavi," I said, as we stumbled toward our own hut, "what was the chant we were singing?"

Flavi grinned at each of us and threw his huge arm around me.

> A fool sits under the baobob tree
> And will not move for asp or flea,
> And when the branch falls on his head,
> He complains because the tree is dead.

"It must possess powerful healing," I said. "Cathbad was ever so much better."

"Well surely that is because we sang it at least a thousand times," said Flavi, laughing.

20

"May I travel with you to meet her?"

I looked up from packing my things and Tahar's. Emer stood in my doorway, her red hair glinting in the light.

"My mother?"

"Who would not wish to encounter Medb of Connacht?"

"I seldom wish it, Emer."

She laughed aloud. "You delight me, Finnabair. Your wit hides beneath a layer of silence." She paused. "Unlike mine, which speaks its mind before I know what it will say."

It was my turn to laugh.

"I do not wish to cause you trouble," she said, hesitating. "It is my curiosity only. Perhaps Medb will not like me much."

"Why would she not like you?"

"Because she tried to bed my husband and failed."

"You knew that?" The hot blush of shame rose up in my face for my mother.

"Cuchulainn tells me all."

"Well, do not trouble yourself on that account. She will regard you in amazement; she will think what fool the Hound for choosing you instead of her."

"So she does not lack for confidence."

I burst into laughter.

"Go pack your things," I said. "I should like to hear your take on my famous mother."

We rode in the warm sunshine, flanked by the warriors of Rochad. Tahar had not wished to ride before me, a little warrior man of five years, so he rode perched before one of the warriors of Rigdonn. From time to time, he flashed me a proud smile.

In one of those moments, I caught a look of pain on Emer's face. So swiftly had she become my beloved friend that the look wounded my soul.

"What is it, friend?"

She shook her head.

"Did you know that the Hound has a son?"

"I did not, but by your saying, I think that the boy is not your child."

"He is not. He is the son of the warrior woman Aoife. His name is Conlaech."

"And I hear in your voice that you wish for a child between you."

"More than anything I wish it. The Hound is a warrior. That is how he will die."

I put my hand up in protest, but she silenced me with a gesture.

"Hear me, Finnabair. It was predicted for him thus when he was twelve years old."

"By Cathbad, of course?"

"Of course. But what need have we of predictions? How else should he die, himself so often alone on a rock in Ulster? It is why I live apart from him in wartime, why I maintain my own rath far from Emain Macha. As if I would not think of him there." She shook her head. "But if we had a child, the Hound would go on. Our love would go on in the child. Even the child of Aoife I would raise to keep some piece of the Hound."

"But where is the child?"

"He lives with his mother on her warrior island between here and Alba. The Hound has never seen him."

"How old is the boy?"

"By now he would be some seven years."

It shames me now to think it, but my mind began to calculate, to number their married years. Emer watched me do so and she smiled.

"Friend, I will tell you directly. It was after he had wooed me and before we had wed. It was while he was studying at the warrior school of Scathach and before he had returned to me."

"This does not anger you."

"It should, I suppose, but perhaps I am like your mother in this. A bedding is a bedding. But the Hound's spirit is mine. From the first moment, we were spirit-bound, each to the other."

"And you bed others as well? Forgive the question, friend. Feel no obligation to answer. It is the question of Medb's daughter."

She laughed gaily.

"I do not, Finnabair. Your mother is more man, I think, than woman. What would we want with a man we did not love? Bedding such a one would be trouble only, so I think."

I smiled at her.

"So I think, too."

"Conchobar," we both said aloud at once, and we burst into laughter.

"Although I will tell you that there never would have been a child had it not been for my father."

"You spoke to Flavi of your father. I know well the meddling of parents, Emer. You are welcome to unburden it to me."

"My father was known as Forgall the Wily."

"Well, from that alone we learn much."

Again the burst of laughter. My burdens were much eased in Emer's presence and the days of this journey would be pleasant ones.

"Ah, Finnabair, if we knew when we were young the way the road would wind."

"My friend, we would fear to walk upon it."

"Perhaps we would. The Hound first came to me when we were young. We had only fourteen summers upon us, but he was looking for a wife. In fact, all of Ulster was looking for him, the men having decided that the women of Ulster were growing too fond of their boy hero. I lived then with my father at Luglochta Logo—the Gardens of Lugh. That is where I go still when the Hound is at war. That day, I was sitting in the green with all the women, practicing embroidery when Cuchulainn came among us. Still I remember it well, the way our eyes met only, for he did not see the women who surrounded me.

" 'May the road be blessed before you,' I said.

" 'May the apple of your eye see good alone,' he answered.

"Then he looked away toward the sky and the horizon; as if he were assessing the road, he said, 'I see a sweet country where I could rest my weapon.'

"I knew he spoke of me. 'No man will rest in that country,' I replied, 'who has not been a warrior at the ford.'

" 'In only that country will I rest my weapon,' he replied and he brought his gaze back to me.

"Isn't is strange, Finnabair, how love colors what we see? The Hound is not a handsome man, but his eyes were all I could see; in them I could not draw breath. But I am a woman of wit and I wished him to know it.

" 'No man will travel this country who has not done the salmon leap, bearing twice his weight in gold.'

" 'Still I would rest my sword on that fair plain.'

" 'None shall be permitted to rest in that country unless he can go without sleep from *Samhain* to *Imbolc*.'

"Then he met my eyes directly. 'How easy that will be then. For how should a man sleep elsewhere once he has seen the country of his dreams?'

"We should have married then were it not for my father. For he discovered from my women that I had been courted by the Hound. 'She shall not have the warped one,' he vowed."

She paused and shrugged. "Perhaps he only wished to protect me. The life of a warrior's woman is not an easy life. But it was too late for that. The Hound and I had recognized each other; from across the water we had returned, one to the other. Nothing could separate us."

"What did your father do?"

"He dressed as a Gaulish warrior and bore Gaulish wines and plates and cups to Conchobar. Can you imagine the boldness and the danger? Posing thus as a visitor, Forgall praised the warriors of Ulster. He pretended to be most taken by the Hound, told Conchobar of the warrior school of Scathach, on an island between Eriu and Alba. On and on he went on how the skills of the Hound would be enhanced by Scathach's training there. Conchobar determined to send Cuchulainn on the morrow.

"I suppose my father thought that Cuchulainn would be killed in training or that he would stay there at the school. Instead the Hound learned his lessons well—too well— for soon he surpassed his teacher. When war came between Scathach and her enemy, Aoife, it was Cuchulainn she sent forward to defend her, Cuchulainn who negotiated hostages and truce for Scathach. Aoife was much impressed with my boy warrior. She bedded him and did not tell him until just before his return to me that she was bearing him a son. I think she thought that the child would keep him bound to her. Instead, Cuchulainn gave her a ring for the finger of the boy and told her to send Con-

laech to him when the ring fit the finger. I cannot think
that Aoife holds him highly, no, nor me."

"But when the ring fits the lad, you may have a son to
raise."

"If she hasn't turned him against us."

"Then how did the Hound come to wed you?"

"My father's own plan defeated him. For Cuchulainn
returned, a warrior like none before. My father posted
guards outside his walls. Cuchulainn slew them all, those
that did not flee before him. Then he did the salmon's leap
into the center of the *rath*."

"That leap I have seen, for that is how I met him. It is a
most terrifying sight."

"It is that. So terrifying that my father ran from him
on the ramparts and fell to his death." She shook her
head. "The Hound would not have harmed him. He
spared my own three brothers and counts them as his
friends. He would have spared my father. Perhaps my father would have come to love him for the love he bears to
me."

"Stranger things have happened."

"And I consider myself most fortunate, for one thing
only could break my heart—if his spirit broke from
mine."

"That will never be."

"I pray that you are right, my friend."

Medb had aged, not enough to let my face betray it, but grey
strands threaded through her russet hair. Beside her eyes,
the little streams of age were deeper, longer, than before.

To her good fortune, Medb did not know it.

At her introduction to Emer, she shook her head, murmuring something about the poor boy not taking advantage of his opportunities. To her credit, Emer hid her
laughter behind her hand.

My mother called for Ailill. "Come, husband, and see

the grandchild our daughter has waited so long to bring to us."

I did not mention that the road between Ulster and Connacht traveled both east and west, for their delight in Tahar was palpable. Medb would have nothing but that he be sent home with his own horse—"a horse for a Connachtsman," she called it, far too big for a boy his size, but it would wait until his fourteenth year, and, of course, Ailill had to match her gift, so he brought my boy a brace of hounds.

No mention was made of revenge on Ulster, no whisperings of Connacht's discontent. The Maine actually came to see me, to fuss over my child, though they had given Medb and Ailill grandchildren by the dozen.

It was not until we were departing that Mathramail took me aside.

"Go with caution," he whispered. "She sends spies among you. Watch by land and shore."

"She has said nothing," I replied, surprised.

"'You are of Ulster now,' she says so often."

"How do you know this?"

"Do you remember the daughters of Calatin?"

"The wizard of Connacht? Cuchulainn slew him in the War of the Bull."

"And more than a dozen of his sons and grandsons."

"His daughters were the children of his later years, as I recall. They were children when last I saw them, little girls of some twelve years."

"They are women now and she has scattered them to the wind. One to Alba, one to Gaul, and one to Babylon."

"To what purpose?"

"To learn the dark arts."

"Why, Mahneemawra?"

"I can only think to practice them on Ulster. To take revenge on the Hound."

"I will speak to her."

"You dare not, Sister. She will know who has given you

intelligence. I will be cut from the councils. I will lose the chance to give you warning."

"But keep me posted, Brother."

"On that you can depend, Finnabair. There are many of us in Connacht who do not wish another war with Ulster. Among us Ailill and several of the Maine. Medb nurses all complaints against her as if their cause has always been the Hound. So much vengeance does she bear him."

Our mother bore down on us across the great hall of Cruachan Ai.

"She comes," I whispered.

"Only come to us more often," Mathramail said loudly. "And bring the boy, for Medb will dote upon him."

I was silent on the ride toward Ulster, puzzling my borders once again. What act would be disloyal to my mother? What words betray my brother? What omission would endanger Emer and the Hound, Rochad, Niniane, Flavius?

Emer broke the silence.

"Your parents are delightful, Finnabair."

Stunned, I turned toward her.

"Delightful? In all my life I have never heard them described thus. In Ulster or Connacht."

She tipped her head toward me.

"I know that your mother sold you in marriage to Rochad. Is that the source of your ill will?"

I let out a long, windy sigh.

"My mother is what she is, Emer. I came to terms with that long ago. It is when she threatens those I love that I am angry. Here is what you must know of Medb. She is hungry, always. To sate that hunger she will do anything, betray anyone. The Medb you see is beautiful, funny, so engaging. The Medb you do not see is dangerous."

"But was that in the past, Finnabair? Was that during the War of the Bull?"

I looked away toward the east. I had made my life in Ulster. Rochad and Tahar, Niniane and Flavi, they were my beloved family. The Hound and Emer were my friends. I let out a long, sad sigh.

"Emer," I said. "There is something I must tell you." I looked around at our outriders with a new and terrible suspicion. I whispered, "Away from all these ears and eyes."

21

Why is it that trouble, when it comes, comes not singly but in great flocks, like waves of migrating birds, as if, once the door is opened to sorrow, all of it must fly into the world at once? Or so it seemed to me in that, our seventh year of peace.

Ulster is difficult country, filled with hills and rivers, dense forest and bog. Conchobar garrisoned all of these against my mother, but no one came.

In the way of warriors, they had all grown anxious at the news, polished weapons, made a show of talking up their prowess against the warrior queen. When no great battles were forthcoming, they grew restless and then irritable. They began to fight among themselves. I blamed myself for bringing them the warning.

Conchobar had not been king for all his life without some wisdom won. He proposed a garrison by the sea where all the Royal Branch warriors would train and prepare for the eventual battle with Medb. So he took them to the beach at Tracht Esi, on the eastern sea, and there they set up camp—dwellings and practice fields, families following, and of course he would need his healers in case ancient Cathbad should develop the catarrh. The Hound was in his element, drilling the warriors and whirling up and down the beach in his chariot. Sometimes he allowed Tahar to ride with him and the shining excitement on his seven-year-old face tied my stomach into knots and filled my heart with worry, though Rochad called it "all good fun." Indeed, it all had the air of a great lark, of a holiday journey, were it not for the fact that all of them were so anxious for war.

But for the early part of summer, all was well in Conchobar's camp. For my part, I had decided that Tahar should learn the healing arts. In part, this was to keep him from the wild chariot rides with his uncle, the Hound. In part it was to keep him with me. Tahar had reached his seventh year; it was time for us to think of fosterage, to choose an uncle or an aunt who would raise him until his seventeenth year. Niniane had suggested my brother Mathramail who had taken to him a gentle wife. I knew that they would love my boy, but fosterage with them would mean that he would depart from Ulster, that even under my brother's watchful eye, he would be close to the plotting heart of his grandmother, Medb.

So I turned him toward healing, thinking that if he took to it, I could keep him close in Ulster. He stood beside Flavi each morning now, pounding at herbs with his pestle and mortar, his little body itching for his horses, for the sea. For two weeks I kept him to it, while he pestered Flavi ceaselessly.

"Grandfather, may I go now? The boys ride at horses. Grandfather, Cuchulainn needs my help with the chariot."

Flavi bent and hugged him close.

"Go along," he said. "And take a ride in the wind for your old grandfather."

"I will!" Tahar cried as he bolted through the door.

"You do not help me here, Flavi. I would have him learn the healing ways. I would have him stay in Ulster."

"You would have him choose any other but the warrior path. But the healing path is not his way."

I sighed and sat down hard on my little stool.

Flavi stopped at his pounding and crossed the room to sit on his sleeping bench. A fine sheen of sweat had broken out on his forehead and I watched it trickle into the tight curls, now all grey, that circled his bald pate.

"Are you well, Aither?"

"I have more than seventy years upon me now. I tire faster than I once did."

I stepped over to him, pressed my lips against his forehead, held my fingers on the pulsebeat at his throat.

"I do not like your color today. It seems a little grey."

He brought my hand away from his neck and kissed it gently.

"Finnabair, there is a favor I must ask you."

"Anything, Aither. You know that well."

"Do you remember long ago I told you that I sang a song for the Little Brother? The first song that I sang when he returned my voice to me?"

"I do."

"I would like for you to learn that song."

"Then I will do so. But now I must return to grinding up my herbs."

But he did not release my hand and when I looked into his eyes, they were filled with sorrow.

"Today, Finnabair," he said softly. "I would like you to learn it today."

We leaned against a rock where the stones ran down to the sand, the sand to the sea. The day was fine, with the wind moving from the east and high swirling clouds sweeping over us and away, into the west. Why did I not know at that moment how soon he would follow? He made me repeat the little song over and over in the tongue of Meroe:

> *I set my sails*
> *To traverse the wide river.*

With the wind I am going
Sailing to the farthest shore
With the light I am going.
Though I shall not see you more
Do not fear for me.
All of them await me
On the farther shore.

When I had learned it to his satisfaction, he seemed content to sit there in the sun beside me.

"Aither," I asked at last, "why did you sing this song for the Little Brother? For it seems to me that it is a song about dying."

He looked at me for a long time and then he smiled gently.

"It is the one he wanted to hear, Finnabair."

I did not ask how Flavi had known that to be so; his ways had always been the deep ways of listening, of knowing. He drew his arm around me and I leaned against his shoulder.

"No child was ever born to me, Finnabair," he said softly. "But all my losses vanished on the day they brought you from the river. We love you, Little Daughter, Niniane and I."

I kissed his grizzled cheek.

"Now you must bring her to me."

I ran for her, ran the way a child runs, with utter abandon. I found her in the forest choosing herbs and flowers. Wordless, I held her by the hand and dragged her with me all the way to the sea rock. She knew the moment she saw him. She climbed onto his lap and he drew his arms around her. I moved away, sat staring out to sea. From time to time, I turned to watch them, saw her curls, now almost thoroughly grey, bobbing in the wind to something he was saying.

At last she called to me. Though she did not move from the circle of his arms, I could see that his spirit had left the great body.

"Bring Rochad and Cuchulainn," she said softly. I knew there was no need to run.

To Conchobar's credit, he gave Flavi the burial of a great healer. He commanded a waking feast with salmon and leeks, venison and boar, honey cakes and mead. Musicians played the bodhrans and the pipes. He laid him out in all the finery of Eriu on a long trestle table between two torches. Rochad sat his head, the Hound his feet. At the turning hour, when the door is opened between this world and the next, I sang him into Tir Nàn Og with Little Brother's song. After that, all of the couples began to disappear and return from the lovemaking, the fierce dance of life to keep death at bay. Rochad loved me gently that night with all the tenderness he bore me, and he held me through the weeping that at last I could not contain. By first light, we buried Flavi in a cairn by the sea.

Niniane seemed listless for many weeks afterward. I would find her sitting on a log in the forest, her herb basket empty beside her or pressed against the rock where he had left us, staring out to sea, her arms drawn up around her legs like a little child. Nothing I said seemed to draw her out, though she would pat my hands with her tiny fingers, as if to reassure me. Finally, when almost a month was upon us, I found her at the sea rock and sat beside her in silence. For a long time, we said nothing, and then, at last, she spoke.

"I am old, Finnabair."

I would have protested that she had upon her fewer years than Flavi had when he had come to join us. But I knew that she spoke of her spirit as much as her body and I was silent.

"It seems I am lost in memory, for I think how far I have journeyed. I remember Egypt, the bright sails on the Nile, the curtains moving in my mother's room. I remember my mother, my brother, and my father, the terror I felt when I sailed away to Rome, when I came among my mother's Welisc people. Finnabair, do you remember that I told you long ago that twice in my life I had wished to die?"

"Now you have come to the third time," I said softly.

She looked at me and nodded and then the tears began to spill, rolling down her cheeks, trickling into the neck of her gown. I gathered her into my arms and held her, cradling her as though she were my own child until at last the weeping subsided into shuddering sobs.

"I remember something else you told me, Little Mother."

She looked up at me with swollen eyes.

"You said that each time something wonderful came to pass, something that you would have missed had you crossed the water."

A small, sad smile flickered on her lips.

"Ah, Finnabair, now here you are, pulling me from the river of my own tears."

That night I had a strange, sad dream. My daughter, Julia, came to me, standing at the far bank of the river, her chestnut hair swirling in the breeze. I did not dream her as often now as I did when first she left us, so my heart rejoiced to see her.

"Maither," she said softly, "I cannot come through the dream door for a time."

"Why not?" I asked in alarm. "Is all well with you? Sweeting, how I will miss you."

She waded into the river toward me and as she did so, she seemed to grow smaller.

"All is very well," she said, and she smiled.

When my courses did not come at the moon tide, I held the knowledge to me, not wishing to give false hope to those I loved, but already feasting myself upon its wings.

It was Tahar who bruited the news and the news of his own Bird-Sight at the selfsame moment. It was evening; all of us were taking the meal—Cuchulainn and Emer, Rochad, Niniane, and Tahar. I was walking among the company, the mead pitcher in my hand, when Tahar looked up in shock.

"She says that she will ride as hard and fast as I do! Tell me that will not be so!"

"Who says such a thing?" asked Rochad, laughing at Tahar's sudden outburst.

"That girl," he said, pointing at my belly. "The one who lives in there. Who says she is my sister."

All the tables stilled. My face and throat grew red and I looked at Rochad, made the tiniest of nods. He burst toward me, over the table in a single leap, swallowed me up in his arms.

"You have a sister!" he shouted to Tahar. "You are the warrior brother. You must care for her."

Hugging and back-clapping, tears and joy exploded around the table. When Emer ran to embrace me, I whispered in her ear, "I wish for you the selfsame joy," and she nodded in delight, sure that my long wait for a child would spill over onto her.

Niniane seemed thoughtful for a time and then she announced to all of us, "It is Flavi. He has sent her back across the water, so that we will not miss him overmuch."

It seemed so much to be his way, that all of us nodded agreement.

Tahar had the last word on the matter. "I choose the name," he said, "for I am the only one who can hear her. She calls herself Julia."

How I wish that our joy could have spilled onto Ulster. But the flock of sorrow birds had flown above our world and they were not finished with beating their wings.

Warriors without purpose are like children who are bored. The holiday atmosphere of the camp grew charged with restlessness. Their little warrior spats grew larger, their disagreements changed into fistfights and wrestling pairs. They were men hungry for battle, lusting for the excitement of war.

Perhaps that was what made them so spear-happy, so sure that the boy, when he came, came from Medb.

It was on one of those perfect days that the lookout saw his little boat coming across the sea. I was in the fourth month of my bearing, ministering to Cathbad, who had developed yet another of his wracking coughs; he was ancient then, more than eighty years upon him, his bones brittle, his skin very nearly transparent. I feared that he would not emerge from this illness and that Conchobar would hold against me and mine for his death.

So I was right among them all when the little boat came over the horizon, when the runner brought the news, when the boy and his giant companion hove into view. We gathered on the shore and watched them approach.

While the giant rowed the boat, the boy—who had much the same years upon him as my own Tahar—took up his slingshot and repeatedly brought down the seabirds that ringed around the little boat. Something about this puzzled me; it seemed familiar somehow, but I could not remember why. The warriors talked among themselves and decided that the boy must be a messenger from Medb. I wanted to argue that the queen of Connacht, the rough and stony country to the west, would hardly send a boy sailing from the east across the water. But I was a healer and it was surely not my place to speak in war council.

Among them they decided that they would send Condere mac Echach down to greet him because he had followed Fergus to Connacht and would know the accent of the boy. I thought it foolish to make so great a show of greeting a child, but that was what they chose to do.

We watched him converse at the water; he returned to us shaking his head.

"The giant is deaf and dumb and slow as well. He does not speak, but keeps his body always near the child. It is

obvious he has been sent to guard him. The child seems
far brighter and far older than his little years would say.
He speaks quite well but will not give his name. He said
there was only one among us who could hear it. His accent, though, has not the sound of Connacht nor of Ulster."

Cuchulainn shifted his stance.

"Well, I will go and greet him and get him to give away
his name."

"Perhaps we should first send Finnabair with her Bird-
Sight," said Conchobar and that is when the memory came
leaping back. The rock in the river of Ulster, my Bird-
Sight bringing to me this boy.

"My king," I said, "I have seen this boy in a vision,
many years ago."

It was a stupid thing to say, a dangerous thing. They all
began to talk at once. Conall Cearnach shouted that I had
seen it because Medb had told me he would come. So angered was the Hound at this insinuation that he lifted
Conall, who topped him by a head, into the air and threw
him to the ground.

Conall scrambled to his feet, shouting, "I will best the boy
if you will not." He ran toward the strand, waving his spear
above his head. The boy regarded this calmly, strung a stone
into his slingshot. With a single motion, he caught Conall
Cearnach in the forehead and brought him to the ground
where he lay stunned, rubbing the lump on his forehead.

I saw the battle rage begin upon the Hound, the eye that
bulged, the whirling dancing body. It was one thing for
Cuchulainn to drop Conall, another for a stranger—and a
child at that—to shame his warrior brother. The Hound
was defender of Ulster. He began to run toward the shore.
At the same time, I saw the boy clearly, the squat, barrel-
chested body, the calm slinging of the stone.

"Emer!" I cried. "Do not let him harm the boy. Stop
him. Stop the Hound. Make him see the boy truly. Do not
let the *riastradh* overtake him."

She ran toward me, followed my pointing hand. She

hurled herself behind him toward the child, screaming, "No, Cuchulainn, no. He is a child. A warrior boy. Think and do not let your rage become you!"

By now, Cuchulainn had the *gae bolga* in hand, had drawn back in the arch that would send it toward the boy, unstoppable as the sea.

Even through the fog that possessed him, the giant saw the spear coming. He stepped before the boy. The boy screamed out in terror.

"No, Ghilly, no. Do not stand in the way of the spear!"

The sound of the *gae bolga* split the air like thunder. The boy seemed to grow, to stretch. He leaped before the giant, heaving up from the water like a salmon swimming upstream, landing on his feet before the baffled giant, catching the spear in his own little side.

It was the salmon leap; I knew it well, as now I surely knew the boy.

I ran to the water, though the babe inside me protested. Cuchulainn was kneeling by the child, cradling him in his arms. He was weeping. "A child, Emer, a child. Never in all my battles have I hurt a child." She hushed him, stroked his wild hair. Oh, he did not know yet the true depth of his sorrow. They will say of him that he knew, that he challenged the child so he could not steal his power. I tell you now he did not know.

"Finnabair," he said, holding his free hand toward me. "Bring your healing arts; return the child to us whole."

I knelt beside the boy, examined the wound. It had creased the child's side, punctured the intestine. The barbed fishhooks of the *gae bolga* were lodged inside his organs. I shook my head. The little fellow saw my gesture, drew a shaking breath.

"She said I should not say my name until I saw the Hound of Ulster. I was doing as she told me."

"I am he," Cuchulainn said, "but who has told you such a thing? Is it Medb? For she has brought your death upon you."

"It was my mother, Aoife. I am her only son, Conlaech. She said that I should give you this."

He opened his hand and there upon his little thumb was the ring that the Hound had given Aoife those many years ago.

"I am sorry, Father," the little fellow whispered. "I would have liked to know you; I would have wished to live beside you here."

No *riastradh* overcame the Hound; he held himself to himself by sheer force of will.

"In these few moments I am your father; you are my beloved son."

He held the boy gently, rocking, rocking, until the little light remaining in him flickered out and died.

Then he handed the child into my arms and vanished from us at a run.

The big giant the child had called Ghilly began to howl and cry; nothing we could do would still his sorrow or ease his terror. At last I placed the child in his arms; he stilled his howling while he rocked the little body. "Connie," he whispered again and again. "Connie, now what should I do?"

Rochad and Laeg rode out to search for the Hound.

Between us, Emer and I managed to convince the befuddled giant to go with us to Niniane. She sang to him in Welisc; he quieted, and at last he slept. Niniane and I cleaned the boy and prepared him for burial; as we did, Emer began to weep over him. There was naught I could say to comfort her, so I let her purge her sorrow in her sobs.

22

Morning brought with it no surcease from sorrow. Rochad and Laeg did not return; just before dawn Cathbad took a turn for the worse. Conchobar sent his honor guard for me; when I arrived in his chambers, the king was seated by the bed, his head in his hands. Obviously, he had not left the bedside all through the night. He looked up at me through red-rimmed eyes.

"Finnabair, is there anything you can do?"

In his question the answer was already waiting.

I listened to the Druid's breathing, the wet rattle in his chest. I cooled his forehead and wrists with an herb poultice. Conchobar knew as well as I that we were only waiting, but at least I could wait with him.

Just before first light, I heard the death rattle.

"Ard Ri," I said softly, "if you have not done so, you should say your good-byes."

He nodded. I stood to leave, but he clutched at my wrist.

"Stay, Finnabair," he pleaded, and I knew that the fear of death was upon him.

Cathbad's spirit departed moments later. Conchobar looked lost, like a small child. He was dangerous and lustful, a king who had had too much power for too long, but my heart moved with pity for the child inside the man. I knelt before him and placed my hands over his clenched fists. Without lifting his head, he spoke to me.

"He was old and cantankerous; he was not a kind man, ever. What he did to my mother when she was young was cruel beyond belief. But I, too, have been a cruel man, more than once. He was my father; he never stopped watching over me, moving obstacles from my path. Can you understand?"

"Conchobar, I come from such a pair. How could I fail to understand?"

He smiled sadly.

"So you do, Finnabair."

He contemplated in silence for a few minutes, then raised his head.

"What I did to you those years ago . . . I frightened you. I had no right to do that. My . . . lust . . . gets the better of me, Finnabair. It is a lesson I should have learned long ago."

"I forgive you, Ard Ri. And I can offer you friendship; that is far more durable goods."

"Perhaps it is," he said. He stroked the ancient, withered hand of the Druid.

"Will all be well for him?"

My heart moved with pity.

"Will you trust me and do exactly as I say?"

He looked up, surprised.

"I will."

"Then press your forehead here, to mine, and do as I tell you to do."

He leaned his forehead against mine and I inhaled his essence—horse sweat and man sweat and the heat of power. I gestured and he inhaled mine. I kept him silent there until I could sense his spirit, long buried, rising toward his eyes. Then I lifted his hand and pressed his fingertips gently against my journey mark. His hand stayed still against my cheek for a long while and then he said, simply, "Oh."

I opened my eyes and drew back from him. His eyes were round and wide.

"Did my father know this, Finnabair?"

"In his life, he knew the future as it would be here in this world. My journey has taken me across the water."

"What I saw was . . . beautiful, peaceful."

I placed my palm against his cheek.

"Be not afraid, Ard Ri," I said softly.

And so we waked them together, the withered old man and the little child. Emer wept above the body of the boy. The king patted her shoulder awkwardly and tried to give comfort to all around him. Conall Cearnach, a huge lump on his head, blamed himself again and again, saying that if he had not challenged the boy, if the boy had not used the slingshot, the Hound would not have had to defend him. We all knew that Fate and Aoife had planned more deeply and more darkly than that.

We buried the little fellow next to Flavi, for Niniane said that he would await the boy across the water. She held the hand of the giant, Ghilly, who stood beside her like a child. And the Hound was nowhere to be found.

Rochad and Laeg returned after a week of searching separately and together. Rochad had ridden into Connacht, Laeg had gone among the Partraigi. There was no sign of the Hound.

"Was there a wolf? Anywhere? Waiting at the entrance to the Fid Duin?"

For the first time in my knowledge of him, Laeg grew angry. "Damn it, Finnabair, no wolf. Do you think I did not watch for her? And for ravens in the trees?"

For answer I closed his skinny frame in my arms.

"I am sorry," he whispered against my shoulder. "I have never feared for him so much as now."

I nodded my head. There was nothing else to say. Rochad and Laeg rode out again at first light.

Two weeks passed. Emer had ceased to eat or drink. Her weight fell from her rapidly and her skin, deprived of fluid, grew dessicated; it plucked up from her bones like withered leaves. Niniane and I tried everything, but we could plead her only toward a little tea. I finally suggested that she return to the Gardens of Lugh, where she dwelled when the Hound was at war, but she would not go.

"I cannot leave him now, Finnabair. He is not at war, except with his own spirit. I know my husband. He is a warrior. He does what he has been trained to do and thinks neither out far nor in deep. So his war deeds do not trouble him. This is different. He is at war with his own soul; he will lose all himself if we do not help him. But how to do that if we cannot find him? Oh, Finnabair, you are my truest friend. Do something, please, I cannot think what to do."

Near sunrise, I made my way to the river, admonishing Niniane to keep Emer busy, to say that I had gone to the forest for herbs. I meant to use my Bird-Sight and I knew that Emer's terror would prevent me from seeing anything.

I wore the buckskin braichs of the Partraigi, but the water on my lower legs was perilous cold. I carried Cuchulainn's cloak, high above my head. I had begun the wade out to the rock when I heard the horse behind me. Conchobar had been waiting in the forest, watching the river.

"I had thought that he might come here," he said. "I should not be surprised that it is you instead. Come, I will take you out on horseback."

For a moment I feared that this was the Conchobar of old, his lust guiding his movements. But he held out his arm and shook his head. "The water is too cold for you thus, with child. We are sore tried, friend. I shall leave you to your Bird-Sight and return for you at dusk. I pray that you will see him somewhere."

He deposited me on the rock and left bread and cheese and water from his saddlebag beside me, then rode away. I watched after him in astonishment, that the High King should be a source of hope in these trying days.

For a time, I sat on the rock and stilled my mind. When the wind inside me was calm, I stood. For a very long time, I simply turned and watched—north, then west, south, then east. I saw nothing: When the light moved past its zenith I ate the bread and cheese, grateful for the preparation of the king and then I stretched out against the rock. I drew Cuchulainn's cloak around me and dozed in the sunlight. I heard them in the trees beside the river; they could not see me, vanished thus beneath the cloak. They were talking, their voices smoky and deep, the ancient caw of the crow women. It was the Morrigu and her sisters, Badb and Nemain.

"He is nowhere. Nowhere in the world."

"I have traveled east and west."

"And I from northern sea to southern sea."

"And I have traversed all of Eriu between."

"He is nowhere, nowhere in the world."

I knew then that they were looking for their war boy. I remained still until I heard them fly the treetops, then I sat up. If they could not find him, he was not in the world. There were only two places he could be; either the Hound was dead or he had gone among the Other. I feared the one for the weight of his sorrow; the second I could traverse with Bird-Sight.

When the king arrived toward evening, I asked him for his help.

"Take me to the fairy mounds."

His eyes widened.

"He has gone among the Other?"

"I do not know, but the Morrigu cannot find him."

"You spoke to her?" His eyes filled with real terror.

"I overheard her speaking to her sisters."

He nodded.

"There is a *cnoc* full of *draiocht* north of Emain Macha."

"How do you know this hill of magic?"

"By avoidance, Finnabair. All the sensible people of Ulster stay far from it. But if it returns our Hound to us, then I will take you there. Ah, Finnabair, the worlds I did not know existed until your friendship came."

He sounded almost ebullient, but he was mindful of my condition; rather than whipping his horse into the frenzied ride I remembered, he kept her to a gentle walk as we picked our way north. At twilight we reached the fairy *cnoc*, at the blue hour between light and darkness. Conchobar helped me to dismount. I pointed toward the tree line behind us; without another word he rode into the forest, stationed himself silent with his mount among the trees.

I drew Cuchulainn's cloak around me and approached the hill, invisible and silent, rolling my feet against the ground and I had done in the Fid Duin. My heart was pounding. When I was within hailing distance of the hill, I stilled myself and opened the Bird-Sight. For a long time nothing happened, and then the door in the hill opened. It was exactly as I remembered it from childhood, not so much a door as a wall of water, viscous and multihued, less an opening than a view behind a curtain. Behind it was a world of beauty and song. A man approached the waterfall; he seemed familiar. When he reached the transparent curtain, he raised his hand.

"I see you, Finnabair," he said softly. *"Mo ghra."*

It was Froech.

I lifted back the hood on Cuchulainn's cloak, pushed my hand through the waterfall; his hand closed around mine.

A sob that I had been keeping for more than a decade rose up in me.

"Do not weep, sweeting," he said, softly. "Oh, do not weep."

"I am so sorry for what they did to you. I did not know."

"I know that. I knew they played me false when they asked me to go against the Hound. All of us here know about his powers. But I had no choice but to play it out; I had agreed to their task. There was no choice if I was to win you. Our chances were but small."

"I thought you had abandoned me."

"But you are wiser now; you know that I would never have left you of my own will."

"I do."

"You are with child again." He smiled at the four-month bulge of my belly. "This gives me joy."

His happiness for my state, his obvious watchfulness of me, pulled at my heart; I wished for him also to be happy.

"What of you? I would not wish for you to be alone."

"There is a hollowness to being human, Finnabair; my people call it the great alone. That is not the way of my people. And we do not need to hurry time for we have plenty of it." He smiled. "The girl child; you must teach her the tongue of the Welisc."

My hand went protectively to my belly.

"They will not take her from me."

"Neither your journey nor hers is over, Finnabair." He sighed. "I am glad for this time; I did not think to see you again so soon."

"So soon?" More than ten years had passed between us. "Why did I not find you before now?"

"You did not look." I examined this idea, knew it to be true.

"But you are here to search for the Hound of Ulster."

I nodded, though I felt ashamed. For this little time I had forgotten Cuchulainn, forgotten everything but my joy in seeing Froech again.

"We have searched for him everywhere. Either he is dead or he is among your people."

"He is with Fand, the woman of the sea. He is on her floating island. We have counseled her against keeping him, but she found him nearly dead with grief and she her-

self is . . . wounded. Long ago when the Hound was
wounded, she kept him for a month while he was healing.
She remembered him with fondness."

"Is her island in your country or in mine?"

"In my country, all of which is halfway between the human world and Tir Nàn Og. But Finnabair, I cannot bring
you to him; time does not pass among us as it does with
you; this you know."

I nodded.

"If I were to bring you here, your child would be born
among us. Years would pass but they would seem as days.
When you returned, all of those you knew would have
crossed the water. Your husband and your other child
would be gone."

The thought of such a loss filled me with terror.

"What's to be done?"

"We will send him to you. Go through your mother's
country to the first island in the western sea. Go on
Samhain. At the turning time when the door is thin, we
will open the curtain between the worlds."

"I will do as you have said."

"Finnabair, they must row you across the water and
leave you there alone." He slipped his hand through the
curtain and pressed his fingers on my journey mark. "You
are their only journeyer; you will not be trapped between
the worlds, nor will you be drawn across the water. We
will bring him to you. But be prepared, my sweeting. For
your Hound is sorely changed."

23

Autumn seemed to crawl toward *Samhain;* though it was only a little month away, I counted hours while the leaves turned gold, while the child grew in my womb.

All of them argued on how to proceed. Emer wished to accompany me; Rochad insisted that he would stay on the island. The king wanted to provision us all with warriors, horses, a moving tribe. I knew that the wisdom of Froech must prevail, that I must go alone.

I told no one what he had told me, told no one that it was Froech I had encountered at the door. The king had seen me talk to air; I said only that the Others had the Hound among them, that they would return him to me at *Samhain,* provided I was there alone.

At last they decided that Rochad and Laeg and a small contingent of warriors would ride me west. Emer and some of her women would go with us to the shore. I asked for Laeg to row me across the water; he was less likely to argue to remain than Rochad, especially if the return of the Hound depended upon my solitude. Tahar would stay with Niniane, though the king had to promise to take him riding.

I sent word to Mathramail that we would pass through

Connacht to the coast, that we would cross to the island of Fand; he sent word that Medb and her army were wintered in at Cruachan Ai, so that we could set our course to avoid that route. I did not tell him that we searched out the Hound; though my brother would tell no one, a slip of that intelligence would surely draw my warlike mother from her lair.

The late October wind was cold as we rode west. We kept our party small, Emer and two of her women, Rochad, Laeg, four warriors and me. Once we crossed from Ulster, we traveled light upon the land, built the smokeless fires of the Partraigi, rode by day in woodlands, spoke in whispers all the while. By the time we reached the sea, we were already nervous, always watching around us like owls in darkness, whether for my mother or for the Other was hard to say.

Not too far from shore, we could see the water breaking against the rock walls of Fand's island. Mathramail and some of his men had provided us a boat; a *curragh* pulled up on the shore between two rocks like a humped black beetle. It looked too small to brave the heaving waters. When we pulled it from between the rocks, a small fellow of some twelve years detached himself from the shore grasses and ran towards us. He held himself close against the cold, but looked at each of us until his eye fell on my journey mark.

"Finnabair?"

"I am she."

"Your brother sends you word. The harbor to the island is in its western lee. You must make your way around it to reach landfall."

"You have done well; now get you home to Cruachan Ai."

He shook his head.

"I will wait here for word; your brother wishes to know that you have returned from the water safely."

Emer stepped in then.

"Brave lad," she said. "Your maither and your aither must trust you well to let you take on such a mission for the Maine. For this good work, we will feed you well."

The lad's face brightened. "I have no parents," he answered. "I serve the Maine; Mathramail fosters me as his son. But, truly, I am hungry."

"And cold," said Emer, and she procured a cloak from one of our warriors. "We will see to that as well."

It was the first I had seen her come out of the shell of her terror since the death of the boy, Conlaech. I hoped that the Hound's return would not plunge her back to sorrow.

Samhain morning dawned crisp and cold with a light wind from the sea. For my part, I stuffed my bag with Cuchulainn's cloak, with flint for fire, with a skin of water. Rochad insisted I have two daggers, one inside my belt, the other hidden in my bag.

"What? Will you have me take to the knife some person of the Other?"

"It is an island, Finnabair. Anyone in this world can see it as well. *Samhain* is a dangerous night, as well you know."

Rochad would not hear of Laeg as my oarsman, insisted that he row me out to the island near dusk when the wind had settled. By the time we reached the windless lee where we would beach the small *curragh,* he was making snorting noises and shaking his head like a bull.

"You cannot stay with me, Rochad. I know what you are thinking."

"No good can come of leaving you alone."

"The place is thin; the night is thinner. He said that I must be alone."

"Who said?"

"He of the Other who spoke to me."

I shifted my eyes when I said it; I knew I did so. Rochad was not a stupid man.

"It was Froech who spoke to you."

"It was and he is well, I thank the gods, the Hound and Laeg."

"I will not leave you alone with him."

"He cannot come into this world. To do so would be certain death, for here he was wounded by the Hound."

"But you could go into his world."

"And leave you? Leave our son? Deprive you of this un-born child? What must you think of me to say so cruel a thing?"

He heaved a deep sigh.

"When first we met you spoke of him so often."

"When first we met, he was my first love. Now I have another, here in this world."

He smiled at me as he tugged on the oars.

"I am a great fool, Finnabair."

"You are a great fool who loves me; my heart does not forget that, husband."

In the end, he knew the choice that he must make to save his friend.

He left me wrapped in the cloak of Cuchulainn beside a snug fire, plenty of wood by my side. I knew that the Oth-ers could see me well, but I did not tell Rochad that the cloak would provide no cover. It was all that I could do to get him off the island before the turning time; I was glad there was a moon for him to row by. After he departed, I watched the sparks from the fire rise and shift away to-ward starlight. An island seems to me a protected place, surrounded as it is by water, peopled by so few human be-ings. I felt safe on this rock in the sea just as I liked the river rock of the Hound.

I knew they were with me first by smell—pine pitch, spring lilacs, a strange, sulphurous, smoky smell. The songs began soon after, some of them whispering light, like water over stone, others the terrifying *na caoine* of the *bain sidhe*. My little Julia whirled and turned inside me, though I could not tell for fear or joy. I clenched my hands together, breathed and stilled, breathed and stilled. The Finnabair of long ago would have been swallowed by her fear, would have been too filled with fear to stand vigil for a friend. The Finnabair of long ago was friendless. I thought of the Hound, of Emer, of Rochad and Tahar, of Flavi, even of Conchobar the king. I spoke aloud.

"People of the Other, I am Finnabair, friend of the Hound. I am here that I may bring him home to Tir Inna m'Beo, the land of the living."

The stars in the bowl of the sky that surrounded me grew thick like honey; they ran down the world, slow and heavy.

The door between the worlds was open.

I do not know when they pushed the Hound through, but when I looked down he was stretched at my feet, on his face a look of deep repose. He turned his head toward me; no recognition was in his eyes. He did not rise. Fear moved through me, deep and cold. I leaned above him.

"Dog-Boy, it is Finnabair, your friend. I have come to take you home."

He smiled languorously.

"You are lovely, Finnabair, all that cloud of hair."

He reached his hand out, twined it through my hair.

"It is very long."

"It would be longer were it not for you."

I watched for a flash of the old humor, for the quick-witted barb in return. I was baiting him deliberately; there was no response.

He shook his head, the way a dog shakes off water.

"Where is Fand?"

"I do not know this one."

"Surely she came with me."

My stomach lurched. I looked around. She was standing directly behind me, silent as the stars. I gasped and scrabbled backwards toward the Hound, like a crab.

"Who are you? Why do you stand behind me so silent?"

I regarded her closely. I have lived long, but I have

never seen a woman more beautiful than Fand. Her hair was as black as the night sea. Down the long length of one side ran a thick silver streak that seemed almost luminescent. Her skin was flawless milk, her eyes a light grey, visible even in the firelight. She was lissome and tall, her white bosom rising gently above a flowing tunic of midnight blue, woven through with sparkling silver strands. She let me watch, knowing full well what I would conclude. At last she spoke.

"I am Fand, wife of. . . . I am Fand, woman of the Other."

"Why are you here? Why is the Hound with you? He seems not well at all. What has been done to him?"

"You ask many questions for a human."

"Humans ask many questions; that is what we do."

A small smile creased her lips.

"They have told me of you; they say you are a journeyer."

"Who has told you?"

"My people. They have forced me to return him to you."

"Forced? The Hound is of us; why would the Other keep him in your world?"

"In some ways, he is of us also."

"Who among the Other wishes to keep him?"

"Not the Other. I. I would keep him, for I love him well."

Like a drunken man too full of mead, the Hound spoke from the ground.

"That you do."

He lifted a hand toward her. She descended toward him like stars falling, like a great bird wafting in. She knelt over him stroking and kissing, murmuring his name, deliberately oblivious to my presence. I knew that she was boasting to me—vaunting her control of him, his full dependence on her. I am the daughter of Medb; I know how to turn a horse's head.

"Hound, your true wife waits for you. Emer is but a little way across the water."

He sat up suddenly, his arm around the woman on his lap. I watched as he came to life behind his eyes.

"Emer? Is she well? How does my beloved?"

Relief was so strong in me that I sagged with it. Here he was, my friend the Hound. I had feared that only this slow and languorous shell remained to him.

Fand looked up at me; I did not veil my look of triumph. She disentangled herself and stood before me.

"What do you think you have won, Finnabair? What you see before you is so much more than what I found."

"Speak to me, *bain sidhe*. If you are the source of any healing, then I thank you."

"I found him near the giant's causeway. He was lying by the water, covered in bloody wounds. I thought some terrible enemy had fought with him and won. But while I watched, he stabbed himself again and yet again. He was moving perilous close to his own heart. He saw me watching, but he did not cease his work. 'Are you of the Other?' he asked. I said that I was. 'Cease your weeping,' he commanded, 'and tell me where it is that I will find my soul. For I am trying to root it out and kill it. It is an evil thing and foul.' "

She spread her hands.

"That is what I found."

"Why were you weeping?"

A slow flame crept up her cheeks.

"You listen deeply for a human, Finnabair."

I remained silent.

"I was once the wife of the King of the Sea."

"Manannan Mac Lir?"

She inclined her head.

"Once, you said."

She waved her hand, tossed the magnificent hair. Sparks of lightning cascaded from her hair; thunder cracked from the hand. I knew her now, Fand, wife of the sea, Queen of Storms.

"I do say. For he has left me for another, proclaimed himself besotted for her."

"Then he is a great fool. For you are more beautiful than any woman I have ever seen, in this world or the next. But surely he is proof that men are fools in this world and the Other."

Now she laughed.

"Well, you make the burden lighter with your wit."

"I am a woman who lives by my wit, being not graced with beauty nor fraught with power."

She shook her head. "Perhaps it is a way that I should learn."

"It is not your wit that you have used on the Hound. Has your bedding him worked good vengeance on Mac Lir?"

She regarded me thoughtfully.

"I will speak truth to you, Finnabair. At first it was that. All the Other know of the Hound; he possesses qualities we recognize. And I did hear that Manannan was angry with me for trysting with him. Though not angry enough to give up his paramour. I have always known how to trap a man in the weather I create; the Hound will forever long for me when it is raining, when the smell of lightning moves the air. Manannan made me question whether I still had that power; I proved it on the Hound. But Finnabair, I tell you now that something more has grown in me."

She lowered her voice, took my hand and drew me away from the Hound. I could feel the electricity pulse from her fingers to mine.

"He never speaks of the boy, though, of course, all of us know. Nor did he ever speak of Emer—not once, Finnabair, though I am no fool. I saw his soul leap up tonight when you spoke her name. Somewhere in the course of things, I saw that the trysting healed him some, that he grew docile in the mating, that it somehow eased his pain. I pitied him then and pity turned to love."

"You are his soporific, Fand; you are the herb that brings the waking sleep. But now I speak as his friend; once before I saw him sick with sorrow; he converted grief to rage. This is a deeper sickness for it has put out some light that always shined within him. If your ministrations bring him comfort; if they still his sorrow for a time, then it is true that you have helped to heal him. I do not know if any of us will ever be able to relight his little flame."

"You are wise, Finnabair, so I will tell you one truth more. The Hound is not finished with me. You can take him back into your world, but the space in him that is hollow with grief and longing will still call out my name. He will look for me and I will come."

The stars behind her grew thick and viscous; she was there and she was gone.

I sat down beside the Hound. He opened his eyes and regarded me.

"Where is Fand?" he asked. "I need her."

"She has returned to the country of the Other."

Panic moved over him.

"She has left me."

"I am here. I am Finnabair, your friend."

"I am afraid."

In all my life, I had never expected to hear those words from the Hound. Pity moved in me. I unpinned his great cloak and opened my arms.

"Come here, friend," I said.

He curled in against me like a child and I drew the cloak around us both. I cradled him against me and rocked him, rocked him. He made no sound at all. Just before dawn when the light began to pearl, he said my name.

"Finnabair?"

"Yes, Cuchulainn."

"If I had had a boy child, I would have rocked him just so. Just like this."

I blinked hard at the tears which stung my eyes.

"Yes," I said, "you would have done just this."

When Rochad arrived, he ran toward us in delight,

though my arms were still wrapped tightly around the Hound.

"Old friend!" he cried. "You have returned to us."

The Hound did not move from the circle of my arms. He looked up at Rochad and looked away.

"Rock me, Finnabair," he whispered. And I held him in my arms and went on rocking.

24

We carried him back to Ulster in a litter, fed him meals like a yearling child. He did at least rouse up when he first saw Emer, his eyes lighting, his hands reaching toward her.

"*Mo ghra,*" he said, "you are well."

But as soon as he looked away from her, he seemed to forget that she was there. For months she had lived with fear and now it was not abated. The Hound was not the Hound.

"The tether that bound us is severed," she said. We rode well behind the litter and she spoke of her fear for the first time since we brought him back. "We were always bound to each other, soul to soul. I thought that no distance could sever that bond. But Finnabair, it is gone. What was done to him among the Other?"

I did not wish to make her burden heavier. I spoke not of Fand, but of the Hound.

"It is not the Other who have made him thus, friend. He does not know himself. The man he knew himself to be would not have killed his boy, would have known the child, would have slowed his spear arm. We all tell our-selves a story of ourselves, Emer. The Hound is a warrior;

to do what he must do, he told himself a story with borders of honor. The death of the boy crossed those borders; he cannot return to himself because that man is dead."

"You are wise, Finnabair, but tell me this. Will he ever return?"

"I know not," I answered, but it was not wholly true. I feared that the Hound we had known would never again be quite the same.

In Ulster, as always, there were rumors of war. Cuchulainn returned to health among us. He rode his horse by the river with Rochad and Conchobar. He practiced at weapons; he did the salmon leap from the river rock to the shore. He never laughed at the bawdy jokes of the warriors, never teased me at all. He never met my eyes. I did not know if it was shame at his weakness that drove him from me or the knowledge of Fand that I carried in silence.

Emer spoke to me in desperation.

"I love him as I always did. I pour my body and my spirit over him, Finnabair. His lust responds but his spirit is not present. Only I am there."

I listened quietly, did not speak of Fand. I hoped that he had begun to forget her.

It was a cloudy day, coming on toward *Imbolc*. The winter had been warmer than usual and the heavy sky hinted at rain. The weight of it pressed against the temples. Thunder rumbled in the far distance. Now and then a pool of lightning lit the underbelly of the pregnant clouds. I ran my hands across my six-month belly as I walked through our little *rath*. Beside the hut of the Hound, I saw Laeg polishing the chariot fittings to a high sheen. Hope sprang up in me.

"Friend Laeg, you and the Hound will journey?"

"The Hound will journey, Finnabair, for I am forbid to accompany him."

"He will journey by chariot without his driver?"

"So he says." Laeg seemed clearly angry.

"You do not wish him to go."

"He has always come and gone as he wished on horseback or on foot. But in the chariot, I drive him."

"Where does he propose to go?"

"To Baile Cinn Trachta, the Strand of the Yew by the northern shore of the sea. But this I had to nearly beat from him. Nor will he say why. He confides nothing in me now; our long friendship is a memory only."

I nodded sadly.

"His absence among us is a thing we all know well."

It was not until dusk was falling, until the deep pregnant bellies of the clouds were red with lightning that I remembered the words of Fand.

"The Hound will forever long for me when it is raining, when the smell of lightning moves the air."

I knew then where he was going and why. And I knew that we must stop him, that the time for gentle loving-kindness was past.

We made a strange procession, sweeping north, Laeg driving the chariot in which I rode, pregnant as a sow, Rochad on horseback, Emer behind him with so many of the women of her retinue that their numbers alone would frighten the *bain sidhe*.

How I had loathed to tell Emer.

"I think of you as my sister. This you know." She nodded, her eyes wide. "What I will say now will hurt you. Please do not turn away from me for the message I will bring."

"You will say that there was a woman among the Other."

I gasped.

"Why do you think that I did not ask? Who kept him all that time? What was his abode? A woman knows, Finnabair; a man is present with her or he is gone. The Hound is gone."

"She is Fand, the wife of Manannan mac Lir. He is drugged with her, Emer. She is his sleeping draught, his mead. I think she keeps his pain submerged."

"What shall we do?"

"I do not know. Only that while she calls to him, he will never return to Ulster."

"Oh, break my heart. I do not know if I should weep, or better, kill him with this little knife." She tucked her woman's dagger into her belt.

I smiled sadly. "I think he would welcome the dagger, friend."

We found them in the grove of yews by the sea. Huge waves thundered up on the shore beyond them; thunder and lightning rumbled over the water. They were twined together in a deep embrace. The Hound pressed kisses to Fand's lips, her neck. She wore a velvet gown of deepest green; it shifted in the wind like undersea grasses. Her ebony hair sparked fire in the burgeoning of the rain. My heart ached for Emer that she should see her beloved so. He did not hear us coming above the thunder, but I did not think he would have heard us in silence, either. Whatever remaining sense he had to him had fled in the presence of Fand. I knew that he could not see me, for I wore the cloak of Tir Tairngire, but my pregnancy had made me slow; I did not reach them first.

Emer leaped from the saddle, ran between them. Her little dagger was out before I could say her nay. She pressed it at the throat of Fand.

Fand leaned back.

"Who is this one?"

"This is Emer, wife of the Hound," I said.

She looked around at all of us.

"Ah, Finnabair. All of these you bring to welcome me."

She touched her fingers to Emer's little blade, I saw the lightning jump from her hand to the blade, spark down the blade to the hand of Emer. Emer dropped the dagger, clutched her hand in pain.

"No welcome, *Bain Sidhe*. The Hound will never return to us while you drowse in his memory."

"I told you it would be thus."

The burning hand fueled Emer's anger. She closed her fist and hit the Hound hard below the eye, then struck him open-handed again and yet again. She cried aloud, "What have I done to you, Hound of Ulster, that you would shame me so before all the women of Ulster?"

He came up then from the deep pool below his eyes.

"Shame you? I do not seek to shame you, wife."

"Am I no longer pleasing?"

The question sounded small and broken, all the weight of deep sorrow behind it.

"You are my true wife, beloved of my heart. Of course you please me."

Her anger returned.

"Well, you do not please me. She is the queen of the Other, new and dazzling to your eyes. I am old and comfortable, ordinary. She excites you!"

I knew that was not truly the way of it. The Hound was past exciting; the fire in him had gone out. Fand calmed him; she lulled him into forgetfulness. For the little time that he was mating with her, he did not think of the boy. But I saw with the eyes of a friend; Emer saw with the eyes of a wife. The betrayal was beyond bearing.

"Have her then!" she cried. "Mate with her as often as you like. But you have spent your last day, your last hour, with me."

For the first time since the death of the boy, the Hound appeared. I saw his eyes take fire. One began to bulge. I prayed for the *riastradh*, for the cleansing pain of great anger. He whirled his body from the tree.

"Emer!" he cried. "No! Do not forsake me. You are the wife of my heart!"

Fand's face opened wide with shock and surprise. She turned toward me.

"Finnabair," she said. "It seems that he truly loves her."

"That I told you, *Bain Sidhe*. And she him. You cannot say the same on either scale."

The Hound had begun to spin and whirl. His voice grew low and stony. The *riastradh* was upon him.

"Emer," he shouted. "Emer."

Rochad and Laeg moved in to hold him; it was all they could do between them to rein him in; I knew that their control would not last long.

"Emer!" I cried. "The *riastradh*. It comes upon him; you must calm him now."

"I shall not," she said. "I am no longer his, nor is he mine."

A huge wave broke from the sea. It seemed that a man rode out of the wave, his great white horse foaming sea froth from its mane. The man's hair streamed behind him, midnight black braided through with silver. He rode straight for us with no slowing, hauled the horse up so short that it whirled in the air, hooves still running in the wind. He was handsome as darkness, handsome as sea-storm. Fand turned toward him, dropped her eyes.

"Manannan," she said, her voice dismissive and cold.

"I have said you shall return to me." His voice was deep thunder.

"I have said that I shall not."

The Hound had broken away from Rochad and Laeg. He was spinning and whirling, his vast anger sending sparks from his hair, his very mouth.

The Sea-King pointed a great hand at me.

"Girl, give me the cloak of Cuchulainn."

I complied, unpinning the cloak of invisibility with shaking fingers. Did not all know the wrath of the sea when Manannan was aroused? I threw it to him; he caught it in midair. Over his head he whirled it again and again. I saw stars whip through its fabric; I saw the foam upon the sea.

"Stand back," he called to Rochad and Laeg. They complied, stepping away from the Hound. The cloak spun through the air, singing a windy song. It settled over the Hound, collapsed to the ground.

"Where have you taken him?" Emer and Fand asked as one.

"I have sent him to the mountains of Tara Luachra. There may he fend for himself without the help of women."

In truth, I thought this a fine idea, so I said nothing.

Manannan turned toward Fand.

"I have purged her from me; I wish only you."

"I do not wish you, so find another."

"He has played you false?" asked Emer.

"He has. He spurned me for another, I who was his true wife."

Emer swept her little dagger up from the grass, advanced on the Sea King.

"Are you blind or daft?" she asked. "Can you not see her beauty?"

I stood stock-still, said nothing. How strange the scene, that Emer would defend the woman of the Other! Behind me I could see Rochad and Laeg edging away, sensing some deep female danger.

Emer turned to Fand.

"How weak are these men who cannot rule their cocks to save their kingdom!"

The huge king looked down from his horse at the scene below him; his eyes met mine in amusement. I lowered my eyes toward the ground. Best here to be Finnabair the Mouse.

Fand looked ashamed.

"I was sore wounded when I took your husband to me."

"You are welcome to him; I do not want him longer."

"He loves you; the man I saw in his eyes is not a one that I have ever seen. The terror that he might lose you; it was real."

"As is the memory of you, Queen of Storms. I do not wish a man who remembers another with longing."

From high atop the horse, Manannan saw his opportunity.

"I am filled with the longing of memory, for I remember only the mouth, the hands, the voice, the loins of Fand."

I kept my eyes lowered. Behind me I heard Laeg clear his throat. I willed his caustic voice to silence. Let the Sea-King's magic work.

"Is this true?"

"I have been a great fool. I have let the sea tides carry me far from you, my true shore."

I thought this also a bit overdone, but Fand seemed glad of his saying it. Everything about her began to spark and dazzle. I saw the Sea-King draw in breath as he watched her, saw the desire come up in his eyes. I wished them well of each other, for surely they were a stormy and well-mated pair. He held out his hand. When her hand touched his, there was lightning. He lifted her behind his saddle in a single sweep of his arm. From high in the saddle, he looked down upon us.

"I shall hide the door between the sea world and this world. Neither the Hound nor Fand shall ever cross again."

He turned and rode straight for the water.

For a moment we were all still, not trusting all that we had seen and heard.

I gathered the empty cloak from the ground, stuffed it into my pack in favor of my ordinary cloak. What need had I of invisibility after what we had witnessed?

Laeg pulled the chariot around, steadied the Hound's Black and Grey of Macha. He gestured to me. Emer mounted her horse, her serving women gathering around her. Rochad came up behind me, slid his arms around me, pressed his hands against my bulging belly.

"We are most fortunate, wife," he whispered, soft and low. I could only nod.

"Come," said Laeg. "We will go to the mountains to find him."

"You will go," said Emer. "I will take no man who bears another woman in his memory."

In the end, I returned with Emer to our *rath*. Rochad and Laeg went to search for the Hound in the mountains. I did not think our state would improve when they returned him; Emer had quaffed bitter wine and her spirit was drunk with anger.

When at last they brought him home, he was pitifully thin. His skin was stretched perilously tight on the barrel frame. He had dark purple circles beneath his eyes. Though Emer did not go south to the Gardens of Lugh, neither did she take him in. He dressed himself in his finest cloak and tunic and went before her; she went about the business of her house as if he were not there. If his memory longed for Fand, he did not say so to me.

I was glad he had returned. Even thin and pale, he was once again our Hound, the eyes alive and full of sorrow. I was hopeful that his path of grief was ending.

But Emer could not stop the thought of Fand. It came at her like bees, buzzing at her ears, her eyes, until at last it stung her. With me, she spoke often of Fand, her hair, her dress, her beauty; the *bain sidhe* was her mirror, her whipping cord. To the Hound she said nothing. When he had been home for a fortnight, she came to me.

"He thinks of her," she said.

"How do you know this? You spend no time beside him. I think that he does not, for it is our own Cuchulainn that I see behind his eyes."

"I know. A woman always knows."

There was nothing I could say to this.

"I wish for a potion, Finnabair."

"There is no potion for a heart that has been broken."

"I do not speak of my heart."

"Nor do I. You forget in your anger over Fand that the wellsource of this river of sorrows was the death of the boy, Conlaech. At the hand of the Hound."

"That is why I wish the potion."

"I do not understand."

"I am asking for forgetfulness. Something that will reach into his mind and take away the boy, his dying, the woman of the Other, his bedding of her."

"No such thing exists."

"It does; the Druids work a spell of forgetting."

"No, it is not a spell. They chant the mind into its deepest state; they command it to forget. It is temporary only."

"I will have it."

"I cannot give it to you."

"I will find those who can."

"Hear me, friend. Emer. Listen to me. We cannot turn back time, undo what has befallen, any more than we can stop the sun from rising. Grief is a journey; it begins as a wide path and it narrows, but so slowly. To reach the narrows, everyone must walk the path. It is the only way."

"I wish for him to forget her."

"No! You wish to forget her! You wish never to see in your memory his lips on hers. But no potion of forgetting for the Hound will take that memory from you. You must choose to forgive it; you must burn it from your memory with a fire made of love."

"I cannot."

"I cannot blame you, friend. But hear this well. Though the Hound forget her utterly, you never will."

But she would not listen. She went to Conchobar's Druids. She pleaded for the memory spell. To force the Hound to submit to them, she whispered that perhaps she would reclaim him. He went with her to the oak grove; the

Druids murmured, murmured, until his arms went heavy, until he found the waking sleep. Then they whispered Conlaech and Fand into oblivion. The Hound returned to us, a blankness in his eyes, no joy upon him, but with the woman and the boy purged from him and gone.

Oh, I feared it; I know the mind. It is a garden; even in the darkness, things are growing in the soil.

Emer took him back into her hut. She bedded him; they did not twine their arms about each other as they had before when they had mated well. They did not tease each other with their veiled and lustful wit. In company, Emer sent verbal barbs in his direction, veiled comments on his prowess, flirtations with the other warriors of Ulster. It was most horrible to watch; Rochad and I would speak of it each night with sorrow.

Six weeks passed. The Hound began to dream. Emer called me to her one night three hours before the dawning.

The Hound was thrashing on his platform, drenched with sweat, his spear arm convulsing. He opened his eyes and they rolled backwards into his head. His whole body began to spin and thrash.

"What is it?" Emer cried. "Is he dying?"

"I know not. I have never seen this sickness. Send for Niniane."

My mother-in-law came running in her sleeping gown, barefoot, her medicine bag bouncing on her hip. She took one look at the Hound. She slapped him hard, three times, open-handed.

He sat up. He began to sob.

"I had a child, a child. My own arm killed him. I have dwelt in forgetfulness, like a coward. He comes to me in dreams."

Niniane turned on Emer. Open-handed, she struck her hard. I gasped and stepped back. I had never seen my little mother-in-law do such a thing.

"Do you see what you have done with your Druids and your forgetting spells? Now his grief is as fresh to him as when it happened. You have done to him just what Fand did; she let him bury his memory of sorrow in her thighs; you have let him bury his memory of sorrow in a Druid's chant. He will never walk the path of healing until he can remember and go on. Nor will you. And why, Emer? So that you would not sorrow. So that you would hide your own wound and never walk the path."

Emer hung her head.

"The Hound killed his child. He broke your spirit bond with Fand. His heart is broken. Your heart is broken. Either you will walk the grief path together or you will walk it apart. But you will both walk it. That is all."

She stalked out of the hut.

Emer began to cry, the deep sobs of betrayal that she had never released once in all the months since Conlaech, all the months of Fand. I wanted to go to her, wanted to put my arms around my friend, but I saw the face of the Hound. He was looking up at her, fully there, his face full of pity and sorrow and remorse.

"Beloved," he said. "Come weep, and let me comfort you." She ran to the platform where he was sitting, folded herself like a child into his arms. He began to weep as well. I backed out the door of the hut; my last glimpse was of the two of them, rocking and weeping together.

25

"Where are my warrior boy and my baby girl?"

The Hound came bellowing through the door of my dwelling, Rochad close upon his heels. I was breast-feeding six-month Julia, her little head of curls in the crook of my arm while she made slurping, sighing noises.

I looked up in mock irritation.

"Hound, is there no privacy wherever you go?"

From where she sat beside my bed, Emer responded. "You know that there is not; he moves all alone like an army." She smiled in the Hound's direction.

From the doorway Cuchulainn rubbed his hands together in delight.

"The baby and the breasts of Finnabair. Have we not timed this well, friend?" He punched Rochad on the arm. My husband shook his head in my direction; his face was full of laughter.

From the floor, Tahar spoke up. He had been playing at stones, but now he regarded the warriors.

"Have you come to take me riding?"

"We have!" the Hound proclaimed.

"But get your cloak," said Rochad. "The morning is chill for summer."

Tahar scrambled for his cloak, his leather shoes. He ran to my sleeping platform, placed his little hand on Julia's curls.

"Don't worry, Little Sister. I'll teach you to ride another day." I blinked my eyes at the sweetness of the gesture. The Hound leaned over the bed and kissed me on the cheek. He pressed his palm against my journey mark.

What matter that his eyes when they met mine were remorseful and replete with sorrow. What matter that when Emer lifted Julia from me, her eyes above her smile were deep with longing. They had returned to us, sadder, wiser, but whole and loving, gentle with each other.

I feared only that Medb would take from us our fragile peace.

Mathramail came to us at nightfall two weeks later, hiding his passage among us. I knew then that Medb's retribution had begun.

"What has she done?"

"She has gathered to her all who lost their loved ones in the War of the Bull. She blames their losses on the Hound. To each of them, she gives a division of the army, land, and honors. Lugaid leads a troop; the Hound killed his father, Curoi, king of Munster; he leads the men of Munster. Likewise, Erc, son of the king of Leinster, who fell at the hands of the Hound."

"We must stop it, Mahneemawra."

"It is too late, little sister. The daughters of Calatin have returned from across the water. They bring dark knowledge with them, magic we have not seen before. The darkest of our Druids gather round them, anxious for the power that their knowledge will impart. They go out in darkness, bearing torches, return in darkness with the wind around them. What ceremonies they perform I do not know, but they bode ill for Ulster and for you. It begins, Sister; I cannot say how it will end."

"I fear it, Brother."

"As do I."

"My heart forbodes this darkness. I shall take the news to the Hound."

"Sister, I believe the daughters of Calatin will come among you first; she will use them to draw forth the Hound."

"She is evil, Mahneemawra. Not a mother or a woman."

"She is Medb, Finnabair. She is what she is. In Connacht, they whisper that the War of the Bull took away their loved ones. They blame her. This is how she deflects that anger; as strategy, it is not wrong. She has chosen a scapegoat; soon they will believe that all their losses were visited upon them by the Hound. They will purge their loss on him and on Ulster. Medb will keep her position and her power."

"Does she not care that he is my beloved friend, that she puts my husband, father of her grandchildren, in mortal danger?"

"She thinks not of you. She is queen of Connacht; it is that position she considers, its safety, its consolidation. Yours is a human consideration; hers is one of politics."

I shook my head.

"How can you accept her so?"

"I do not accept her, Sister. I see her clearly."

He gathered his cloak. I called for Rochad, who brought Tahar and Julia that their uncle might embrace them.

"Journey safely, Brother," I said as he was leaving. "I would have no harm come upon you." He hugged me, clasped arms with Rochad.

"Fight well, Rochad," he said to my husband. "For my little sister loves you."

We found the Hound on the rock at Ferdiad's Ford, staring across the water toward Connacht.

"It begins, does it not?" he called before we had even dismounted. He made the great salmon leap toward us, stood on the bank beside us.

"How did you know?"

He pointed toward the woods line. The she-wolf sat there, yellow eyes ablaze, the wind ruffling her fur.

"She smells the scent of war. She is hungry for it after so long a peace. How will your mother come this time, Finnabair?"

"You will not like my answer, friends, for this time, I think that she will come against the Hound en masse, whole troops against him. If the Ulstermen are plunged into their cursing, he will be alone."

"He will not," said Rochad. "For the warriors of Rigdonn will stand beside him."

"A small enough army against the weight that Medb will gather, husband."

"Finnabair is right," said the Hound.

"Then we must go to Conchobar," Rochad answered.

At the hill of Emain Macha, the war council of Conchobar exploded with opposing viewpoints. Some favored sending the Hound alone to his rock in the river. Others favored sending him away, perhaps to Alba, where the armies of Medb could not find him. As always, when they were called upon, some of the Ulstermen had conveniently fallen into their curse, a handful already writhing in pain. I carried Julia with me to remind them that women survived such pain again and yet again and went on with the business of Ulster. Being men, they made no connection with their suffering and the babe upon my shoulder. It became clear soon enough that no plan would emerge from their debating and I thought it unlikely that the war would start today. More fool I.

Emer and I retreated across the great hill to the *grianan,* the sun-house of the women. There, among the women of Ulster, I fed my child. We chattered of the weather, of our husbands and our children. I took comfort in their presence, like birds in winter trees singing of simple things, flittering about, deliberately unaware of danger.

How cruel then, that when danger came first among us, it came among the women. And how wrong I had been about Medb's mode of attack! I had just lifted Julia from my breast when, in the distance, we heard a sound as of a great wind.

"Does a storm arise?" asked Emer. No sooner had the question left her when we heard horses' hooves, hundreds of them, thundering, warlike, toward the stronghold.

In the *grianan,* momentary silence fell. White-faced with terror, the women of Ulster regarded each other, silenced the children who still ran about in play. The hall grew absolutely still.

The thundering of the hooves grew louder. With it came the sound of chariots, the clang of arms.

"By the gods!" cried Emer. "The armies of Medb come upon us, here in the women's hall. They have taken us by surprise! Oh, gods, the children!"

In the *grianan,* women began to scream. Some few sank to the floor unconscious. Others called the names of their children or ran, pell mell, holding their little ones to their breasts, no place of safety open to them.

Emer ran toward me, her plaid in her hands. She wound it around me, binding Julia deep into the fabric, pressed against my body.

"We must save our little girl!" she cried.

"Tahar!" I cried. "Oh, gods! Emer, we must find Tahar!"

We linked our arms together, ran toward the doorway, prepared to fight our way among the horses. In the yard before us stood three women. No armies, no weapons of war, no horses of Connacht. We stopped, perplexed, the running mothers of Ulster gathering around us while their screams died down. Around us, the hill and all of the surrounding plains were still and silent, peaceful in the dappling sunlight, just as they had been before we entered the *grianan.*

Dressed all in black from head to foot, the three women

stood with their hands upraised and linked. Around them swirled a wind, carrying with it a small vortex of puff-balls and thistles, grasses and withered leaves. From that vortex came the sounds of war, thundering horses' hooves, the clash of arms. Out of the mouths of two of the threesome came a strange, sustained humming sound.

From the far side of the hill, Cuchulainn and Rochad burst from the Craobh Rioga, the warriors of Rigdonn behind them, strapping on their arms. The *riastradh* was upon the Hound already; he began to bulge with transformation. The warriors stood dumbfounded on the hill, looking from side to side, no enemy there to call them forth. The Hound writhed in agony, trapped halfway between his human self and his war god. In the trees above him, the Morrigu and her sisters cawed in anticipation.

For a moment I stood perplexed before the wind women and then I understood.

"Daughters of Calatin!" I commanded. "Cease this racket now!"

Immediately, the sound subsided, though the vortex continued to spin around them. The two who had been humming were silent.

The girl at the center of the threesome stepped forward. She was spectacularly ugly, her features twisted and mis-shapen, her nose overlong, her teeth gapped and yellow. She was short, her gait uneven. Her dress seemed to be spun of dark cobwebs. Her hair was thin and yellow; I could see her reddened scalp through the withered tresses. Her sisters stood behind her, their hands still linked to hers, silent. They were twins, quite lovely but for the burning coals of their eyes and the twist of their lips.

"People of Ulster, hear me," the central sister cried. "This is the curse we lay upon you. War will not come as it came before. It may come among your women; it may steal your children from you. You will never know. You have taken from us our sons and our fathers. This is our retribution."

She turned toward the Hound.

"Hound of Ulster, prepare yourself for battle. The *ri-astradh* will come upon you again and yet again. But no enemy will accost you; we curse you with weariness unto death."

She began to laugh, delighted with the possibilities. The Hound rushed at the vortex; it seemed to slip away from him like water, reassembling itself further away on the hill. He stood where they had been, surprised.

"It is sorcery only, husband," Emer called to him, but the war god who dwelled inside him wanted action.

I handed Julia to Emer, walked toward the spinning vortex.

"Daughters of Calatin," I said. "Hear me now. You have learned the dark arts; you have not yet met the darkness. Heed what I say. You are a doorway only; what you will unleash into the world will destroy you as well. You will win nothing for yourselves, nothing for Connacht. Darkness will feed on you to grow."

The speaking sister inclined her head before me.

"Finnabair, daughter of Medb, your mother sends you greetings."

"If she has chosen the path of war, I do not wish her greetings. Nor will we accept yours."

The journey mark on my face grew warm; it began to pulse. My Bird-Sight opened wide and I could see their doorway, the place where they were vulnerable. I walked toward the vortex, stepped through it. They gasped and shrunk from me but they had nowhere else to go. Inside, it was dark; the threesome looked out from this interior blackness toward the light on the hill. It was too late for them, then; they had gathered the darkness around them. Still, I grabbed the clawlike hand of the speaking sister, pressed it against my journey-mark. Her eyes grew wider and wider; she began to scream. Still I did not release the hand.

I pressed my lips to her ear.

"Each journey is a choice of darkness and light. Turn away from this journey of darkness."

In answer, she dragged her hand from my cheek.

"This darkness gives me power," she said. "How else do you think that such a one as I will attain it?"

"Power is not everything."

"If you believe that, you are not the daughter of Medb."

The vortex began to spin and whirl around me. From inside its darkness I could see the outside world as flashes of light, green and blue. Then, suddenly, the vortex shrunk to a small dark cone. With a sound almost like a sigh, it disappeared. I was left sitting on the hill alone, my hair and tunic looking as though I had been blown down from the trees.

By evening, whole families had packed their belongings, had disappeared with their children to the north, to the east, to Alba across the sea. The warriors remained, arguing among themselves for how they should proceed, how they should keep the sisters at bay until all of Ulster had made ready for war, until all of the warriors were free of their cursing.

I had underestimated Medb. She had played against not their armies but their minds. They were terrorized, afraid of light and shadows, afraid of noise. It struck me that this was more formidable than war itself, this game of minds. How to proceed against an enemy that would terrorize women and children, that would bring a cone of darkness into our safest fortress? And on so beautiful a day. I hugged my children to me and tried to hold back my own terror with reason. Medb was neither a brilliant strategist, nor were her armies invincible. She had been lucky this once; she had caught us sleeping, too sanguine with our years of peace, not believing that she would come against us once again.

It was Conchobar himself who remembered Glen na

Bodhar, the Valley of the Deaf, where no sound could enter or leave. "There the Hound will be free of their cursing, for there the sounds of war cannot reach him." He pointed at Rochad and Laeg. "You must take him there. Finnabair and Emer, I shall send my druids with you that their magic will protect you all."

I doubted that the Druids of Conchobar possessed the kind of magic that would protect us from evil; once unleashed into the world, evil is a juggernaut of its own. It feeds on fear and uncertainty.

All of us had decided that Julia and Tahar must be removed to safety, but where to go? We could not send them to Connacht; their own grandmother was the agent of war. We knew no one well across the water.

In the dark of our dwelling, the five of us sat circled around the fire. The children slept, oblivious to danger. Behind us, Niniane was gathering her herbs and medicines, packing them into her traveling bag. She moved quickly, her six decades of life not evident in her hurry.

Now and then she pointed to Ghilly, who assembled things for her without speaking, his months with her making him competent and sure.

It was Niniane who decided for us, plunking her bag down in our midst and sitting cross-legged.

"The Partraigi," she said softly. "The children must vanish into the Fid Duin. And I must take them."

The Hound nodded.

"Most wise. The Ghilly will accompany you and two of Rochad's warriors. Emer and Finnabair will go with you as well."

Emer shook her head.

"We have been ordered by the king to go with you to Glen na Bodhar. Only I can calm your *riastradh*. And even if that were not so, I would not leave you. I will not be parted from you again."

"Finnabair will go with Niniane," Rochad said.

"She cannot," said Niniane. "She is the healer of Ulster.
There will be wounds of war and I will not be here to bind
them. More than that, she will bring danger to your children. The daughters of Calatin know her; they will follow
her movements, trail her scent like hounds of war. Where
she is, your children should not be."

Rochad and I regarded each other across the fire, our
eyes locked. She was right and we were terrified.

"When will you go?" I whispered.

"Now," she answered. "I will not wait for first light, will
not give them time to call their strength together. You
weakened them when you breached the walls of their vortex; you surprised them and made them fearful. I think
that they will return stronger than before. Surely the
armies of Connacht will follow."

"My mother does this to her daughter, to her grandchildren, to all of you!" I burst out. "Forgive me, friends."

"Finnabair, we all passed that point long ago," the
Hound said simply. "We will do what we must do now."

We bundled the children into warm cloaks. Julia did not
awake at all. Tahar came up from sleeping with a single
question, "Papa, will you take me riding now?"

Rochad closed him in his arms, holding to him tightly.

"Niniane will take you to the magical forest. And when
I come for you there we will go riding. I will bring you a
pony your own size and we will tie it at the edge of the forest. How will that be?"

He nodded in delight and anticipation. For him, it was
all an adventure. I knelt and swallowed him up in my
arms, kissed his little face.

"Mama," he protested. "I am too big a boy for kisses."

"No boy is ever too big for kisses," said the Hound.

"Is that true?" Tahar asked solemnly.

"It is," Cuchulainn answered. Tahar took my face between his little hands and kissed my cheeks. I blinked and
blinked, keeping at bay the tears that would frighten him.

"Hear me now," I whispered. "I cannot kiss your sister for I would awaken her. You must kiss her for me. You must care for her until I come. Will you do that?"

"I will," he said.

"There is a story I must tell you before going. It was told to me long ago by Flavi."

When I had finished, he put his hand in mine.

"It has no ending," he said, "for we do not know what happened to that boy of long ago."

"That is so."

"But I will remember in case I learn it on my journey."

"You are our warrior boy," said Rochad. "You know the ways of Eriu. Warriors must watch for women and children."

Tahar nodded solemnly.

"Then I shall care for Julia and Ghilly. And for Niniane too."

And then they were gone, the warriors of Rochad taking up beside them at the tree line. I clung to Rochad's arm, my legs turning to water as I watched them vanish in the darkness.

We had been at Glen na Bodhar almost a month when the sisters came again. In truth I had thought us safe enough, for the little glen was surrounded by dense forest, rich with autumn gold, and high hills. A clear, cold stream flowed through it, but even its water made no sound. Sound did not enter Glen na Bodhar. Even when we spoke to each other, the words came out thin and whispery, the sound flat and devoid of echo. Conchobar's choice seemed wise; here the Hound would not hear the sounds of war conjured up by sorcery. He could not be driven into his *riastradh* by what he could not hear. They would not wear him out before the war began.

Three of Conchobar's Druids accompanied us to the Glen; each morning they consulted their yew sticks, prayed in their oak grove. Even they could not keep the daughters of Calatin from us when they came.

What we had forgotten was that the body has five portals to the world; sound is not the only doorway. The sisters knew it well; instead of sound, they conjured the sight of war. We emerged from our little dwelling to see the plains afire, to see women running, their children clutched against them. Never mind that no one else was in our little glen. Never mind that we knew that. The mind sees what it believes. The Hound was trained for war. He ran toward it all, the *gae bolga* in his hand. The *riastradh* came over him and he grew to twice his size, the flames of battle leaping from him as he ran. It was not until he cast his spear and it fell through the air to nothing that we ourselves knew it was a trick.

"Sorcery," cried the Druids of Conchobar, but by then we all knew it well. Across the plain Cuchulainn ran, chasing this fire and that warrior on horseback, wearing himself out for pictures in the air.

"Mount your horse!" I cried to Rochad. "Ride him into the water. Force him toward us."

Emer and I ran to the stream, stood knee-deep in the water. Between us we stretched a length of rope. Rochad rode behind him, the Hound coming toward us, the fury of war upon him. It was all I could do to make myself stand still to watch his oncoming fury, the wrath of war driving him at us like a singular army. We tripped him with the rope and he fell flat and hard into the water, face down.

"Straddle him," Emer cried. "Hold him where he cannot see or hear."

It took all of us, even the Druids of Conchobar, to hold him down, until at last the cold water, the absence of the sight of war drew the *riastradh* away from him. We released him cold and sputtering to gaze around the Glen in amazement.

"There were no fires," he said.

"No, nor men nor horses."

"I will stay at the water. When they come to us again, push me below the water. If I cannot see or hear, my war god will not overtake me. Soon enough they will tire of their game."

Three more times over as many days the daughters of Calatin showed us the fires of war, the blood and gore of slaughter. But we did as the Hound had told us and at last, they disappeared.

"They will try something else," said Emer. "They require only the time to think what they will do."

I nodded. "They mirror for us the times that are to come."

"Conchobar will send us word soon," said Rochad. "To tell us that the warriors of Ulster have risen from the cursing just as they did before. We cannot stand this sorcery much longer."

What he said was true. For the Hound slept all night and most of each day while the war spasm left him. And the rest of us kept vigil, sleeping not at all.

When a fortnight had passed, Fand came among us. She stood at the far side of the stream at twilight and called to us across the water.

"Hound of Ulster, it is I, the woman of the Other."

We emerged from our dwelling and started toward her.

"Stay back," she called and we stopped in our progress.

She was not as beautiful as I remembered her; her hair had no spark of electricity in it. But then her mien was solemn, her news tragic.

"I come among you with sorrow," she said. "For all of Ulster is ravaged, Muirthemne has been destroyed. Rigdonn is no more; its *rath* burned to the ground." She turned and walked away, her black skirts swirling around her.

How we clung to each other then; how we sorrowed.

"While we were here in hiding, Medb has bested us after all!" the Hound cried out. "This was her strategy, to force us to where we could not protect them, to destroy all of Ulster while they were in their cursing."

"Friends, forgive me," I cried. "Always before she has

fought as a warrior fights. This is a war of darkness and deception."

"Saddle the chariot, Laeg," Cuchulainn called. "We must return to Ulster. We must bind up what can be bound."

But the grey of Macha, Cuchulainn's faithful horse, refused to be put in the traces, skittering away, stamping his feet upon the ground and shaking his mane. It took all of us to hold him and he kept turning wild eyes in the direction of the river.

We rode hard from Glen na Bodhar, back toward Ulster. Toward morning, we dismounted by the side of the road. All of us passed water and ate jerky from Laeg's pouch of provisions. The light was just beginning to come up when we saw a woman walking toward us from the west. She was carrying a silver cup in her hand. The Hound stood and shaded his eyes.

"Maither?"

The woman stepped closer, ghostly and silent.

"Dechtine?"

"His mother is alive?" I whispered to Emer. She shook her head, her look transfixed on the woman. She had reached us now, held forth the cup to Cuchulainn.

"This is his mother?" I whispered. Emer nodded.

He took the cup from her hands, lifted it to drink.

"Remember the daughters of Calatin," I cried. He looked into the cup. He threw it from him. It landed in the dust of the road and its contents spilled everywhere onto the ground. It was filled with blood.

We were almost to Ulster when we came upon an old woman. She was washing clothes outside a little bothy, in a steaming tub of water. Beside her cauldron, a suit of armor was hung neatly on the branches of a tree.

"Is this the armor of a slain warrior of Ulster?" Rochad asked her.

"It is," she said softly. "One of the greatest warriors among them."

"Speak his name," Rochad commanded.

"He was called Cuchulainn," the old woman answered.

Before we could make a response, riders approached us on the road in a cloud of dust, a contingent of Conchobar's soldiers, wrapped in the plaid of Ulster. By now we did not trust our senses. I stepped forward to touch them when they dismounted before us, to be sure that they were flesh and bone. The Hound embraced them, clapping their shoulders.

"I am glad you have survived," he said. "But tell us all. For though we ride into destruction, we will do what we can to bind the wounds of Ulster."

"Destruction?" said the warrior. "There has been no destruction. We bring you good news from Ulster. Our warriors are free of their cursing. They are ready to fight beside you; Ulster is ready to defeat the forces of Connacht!"

Now Cuchulainn and Rochad were delirious with relief, glad to be back in the real world of men, hot with the lust of war. But Emer and I regarded each other silently.

"It was not Fand," said Emer.

"It was not," I answered. "But just so did they draw us out. In the place where we were weak. We should have known; Manannan closed the door."

"Finnabair. . . . First Fand. Then his mother. . . . Now the old woman. . . ."

I made no answer. I knew what she was thinking and I, too, feared it. "We ride toward his death," she said. "We ride toward the death of Cuchulainn."

26

In the end, it was not their sorcery that killed him. In the end, they killed him with his honor.

So little time we have together in this world. So little joy.

The Hound had insisted that Emer be sent to the Gardens of Lugh. She protested and fought, but he would not relent. He knew that he walked toward death; he would not have her see it. I held her hard at her departure, both of us weeping.

"Rochad will come for you," I whispered. "I will send him." It was little enough comfort, all I could offer.

"Do what you can to heal him," she whispered.

"So I shall."

I stayed away from the battle, worked in my hut, stitched and cleaned and splinted those who were brought to me. In the second week, Rochad came to me just before dawn. I felt his hands upon my face, startled awake on my sleeping platform.

"Hush," he whispered. "The Hound is sorely wounded. I have come to fetch you to his side."

I slung my bag across my shoulder. Rochad drew out the cloak of Tir Tairngire.

"You will need this," he said. "You will walk among the armies."

I nodded, drew it around me and over my pack with the hood pushed back.

"Speak to me of how he was wounded."

"The daughters of Calatin sent Druids among us, old men, gashed and bloody, weaponless in the fray. One by one they called to Cuchulainn, begged spears of him that they could defend themselves. He answered. Druids should be neutral; they were aged men in the white of their office. None would ever decline the request of a Druid. Why should the Hound think that they were the servants of darkness? A priest should never serve the darkness. He threw them his swords, full with his own power, the power of his war god.

"Oh, Finnabair. His generosity of spirit, the honor that he bore throughout his life. It killed him! For the druids passed the spears along. Erc of Leinster took the first; with it he wounded the Grey of Macha. How was Laeg to drive with the great horse wounded? The chariot spun in circles on the battlefield. Lugaid, son of Curoi, came running with the second spear. With it he killed Laeg mac Riangabra."

"No, oh no! Our Laeg is dead! Our water-reed."

"The Hound threw himself from the chariot. He called Laeg's name again and again. 'King of Chariot Drivers,' he screamed. 'Oh, friend Laeg.' He ran at Lugaid; the battle rage was upon him. He would have killed him, Finnabair, but Erc returned, the third spear of the Hound tight in his fist. Erc wounded him sorely; his guts are spilling from him."

"But he lives?"

"Barely. He has gone to the river. He has tied himself to the pillar stone; he says that he will die standing. The grey of Macha, wounded, is beside him. He defends the Hound with hooves and teeth. All around him are the armies of

Ulster and Connacht. None will approach him for they fear his battle rage."

"Come then," I said. "We will go."

Dawn light was grey and shadowy on the water. I left Rochad at the tree line, walked among them, silent as I moved in the Fid Duin, invisible, Finnabair in the cloak of the Hound. I entered the water; the cold of late autumn sluiced against my ankles. I moved in it slowly so that I would not much disturb it, so that the armies could not see my passage. The huge horse snorted and tossed his mane when I approached; his eyes were wide and wild. His nostrils dilated; at my familiar smell, he calmed.

"Finnabair," Cuchulainn said when I reached him. So he could see me in the cloak. I shook my head. He grinned. It was the smile I remembered from our first day in the field. "So now you will smell up my cloak, too, Stinkweed."

"This cloak has been all over Eriu, Dog-Boy. It stunk long before today."

"Has it?" he said. "I forgot that we gave it to you."

"Of course you did."

"Finnabair, Laeg is gone."

"Rochad has told me."

"Is there aught you can do for my horse?" He gestured at the grey.

"I would look at your wound first, friend."

His eyes shifted toward the shore, toward the amassed armies.

"They cannot see me talking to anyone; they will think I have lost my mind."

"They will think that the Other have come to talk to you."

"Will they come, Finnabair?"

"I will need to see the wound, old friend."

"I will be ashamed to have you see it."

"You have been my true friend, Dog-Boy. When I was young and afraid, you taught me not to fear. Let me return the gift to you."

He lifted away his cloak. His intestines were spilling

into his hands in a twisting, glistening, bloody rope. I drew in my breath, closed my eyes.

"I am thirsty, Finnabair," he said softly.

"Of course you are."

I cupped my hands into the river, lifted the cool water to his lips. He drank.

"Do not let them take me," he said, his eyes blinking upward toward the trees, where the crows were waiting, leaning over the water. "Nor them." He flicked his eyes toward the warriors of Connacht. "I must go to Emer."

My throat closed; I nodded my head.

"Finnabair?"

"Yes, old friend."

"The boy Conlaech, my son."

"He will be waiting on the far side of the water, Hound. His arms will be outstretched."

He smiled then, the full and guileless smile I remembered from the boy that I had known.

"I shall be glad to see him."

I could only nod.

"Go back now, Finnabair. Before I go. Before they all think to have me. While you are still safe. Tell Emer I will love her always."

"Beloved friend, I shall."

By the time I reached the shore his head had tipped to his shoulder. The light that had illuminated the Hound was gone; his form was still and grey. The largest of the crows flew down from the trees. She began to peck at the eyes of her war boy. None of them would move until they saw her on his shoulder. Only then did they know that he was gone. Cowards all, they raced for the river after his spirit had left his body—the men of Connacht thinking to take his head, to parade it as a trophy of war, the men of Ulster thinking to preserve it.

Lugaid reached him first. I heard the thunk of the

sword, the splash into the water. I heard the cry of victory from Connacht. I stopped when I reached Conall Cearnach. I threw back my hood. He started back in terror. I put my hand on the center of his forehead, on the place where the great lump of Conlaech had been.

"His spirit must not go to Connacht," I said. "There are others who await it."

He gave a great cry, a huge sobbing scream. He raced toward the water. The warriors of Ulster followed. Rochad streamed past me in a blur. I kept moving to the tree line. When I had reached the forest, I drew the hood back over my face. I lay down on the ground under the cloak of the Hound and wept like a little girl.

We wrapped his severed head in silks and cradled it in his own plaid.

"Here his spirit resided," I said to Rochad. "Just so, he must go to Emer."

"My warriors will take you to the children."

"The war is ended, Rochad. I will go at the first light; we will have this night together."

He held me hard against him.

"Finnabair, this is the end of Ulster."

Hot anger flooded up through me. I drew back from him.

"I care not for Ulster! No, nor for Connacht! I care not at all for war. This is what war has brought us!" I thrust my hand toward the bag with its grisly contents.

He drew his arms around me again, pressed his lips against my forehead.

"Finnabair," he said. "I am a warrior, born and raised. But I am not a fool. Know this now. What is between us, this love, the children we have brought across the water . . . this is the only sacred thing; never forget that I know it well."

"I will remember."

I lifted my face to his, twined myself into him, comforted him from sorrow, strengthened him for our coming separation. The night passed all too swiftly.

At first light I gave him the cloak of the Hound.

"What is this? You will wear this; you may need it."

"I go to the Fid Duin. There, of all places, I will not need to be invisible to danger. But you will make a journey in a country that is ravaged after war. You carry with you a prize that many wish to have. Hide yourself inside the cloak. Keep safe and with you keep our friend the Hound."

Tears flooded his eyes.

"He had only twenty-seven years upon him, Finnabair."

"He told me once that he stood on the rock in Ulster to defend those who could not defend themselves."

"Then this last time, I will defend him well."

He pressed his lips against mine, touched his fingers to my journey mark.

"What a gift they gave me, Finnabair, when they gave me you."

"Return to us swiftly, husband," I said.

I watched as he swung the bag across his shoulder, watched as the cloak of Tir Tairngire descended over his shoulders. For a moment I could see his face. Then he lifted the hood forward and my Rochad disappeared.

Sorrow had reached even into the Fid Duin. Jigahnsa had crossed the sky bridge into First World. Ahweho, the new clan mother, welcomed me, but I longed for my old friend, who had also known and loved the Hound.

Niniane's relief at seeing me was palpable. She raced the children into my arms and I smothered them with kisses, drawing in their scent and holding their little bodies to me tightly. Tahar drew himself up before me proudly.

"I took care of Julia and Niniane, Maither," he said. "Aither will be proud of me when he returns!"

Niniane folded me into her arms and held me hard when

I told her of the passing of the Hound. Though her eyes filled with tears, she nodded her head, her curls bobbing.

"This was how he would wish his life to end, defending Ulster."

"Rochad will return to us when he has taken the Hound to Emer. If he can, he will convince her to come with him."

"I do not think she will come."

"Nor do I. I do not know where we will go now, Niniane. Ulster lies in ruins; all its power is broken with the death of the Hound. And I will never go again into Connacht. I hate them, Niniane!" It burst from me in a hot stream. "Medb and Ailill and their stupid wars. Look what they have cost us all. By the gods, how I hate them."

For once, she did not caution me to kindness, only bent her head against mine, heavy, too, with sorrow.

"I know only that I shall be glad when Rochad returns, when we are all together."

We worked on our herbs and medicines, gathered riches from the forest floor. Julia took her first unsteady steps. Tahar was already restless with the forest, asking every day about his father, about the pony Rochad had promised him.

Two months passed.

The forest moved into deep winter, the trees cracking with frost. Sometimes in the mornings, a dusting of snow coated the silent ground.

I began to worry, watching the paths at morning, listening for movements in the dark of night. I could tell that Niniane worried as well, but she said nothing, knowing that she would only increase my fear.

We were bringing roots up from beneath the snow when I sensed movements on the path. I turned and looked along its length. No one walked it. I sniffed the air; there was a familiar smell, redolent and sweet. I stood and watched to where the forest curved away. Still I saw no one, but a sound moved against the forest floor, the crack of a twig. On the path, space shimmered and shifted. For a moment I was reminded of Fand, of the honeyed stars when she opened the door of the Other world. I shifted Julia in her sling of plaid against my back, hushed Tahar.

"Show yourself!" I commanded.

Niniane stood and turned in the direction I was facing.

Slowly the face of Emer appeared in the shadows, lifting the hood of Cuchulainn's cloak away from her moon-white face.

"Emer!" I ran to her, enfolded her in my arms. Niniane and Tahar followed, embracing her.

She was pitifully thin, her eyes far too large and round for the pinched pale face. She did not smile.

She unpinned the cloak of Tir Tairngire, shrugged it from her shoulders. It fell, a drift of white against the snow. Over her shoulder was slung a huge traveling bag, unwieldy and lumpy. It banged against her hip as she moved.

"Where is Rochad?" I asked, staring behind her on the path.

"I have brought him to you."

"Where?"

She swallowed once, hard.

"They were roaming Ulster, Finnabair."

"Who? Speak clearly, friend."

"Erc and Lugaid. Other warriors of Connacht. Looking for this bounty." She pointed at the bag slung across her hip. "Looking for the head of the Hound."

I looked at the bag, blinked away.

"Rochad brought him to me. He was bringing us to you. He had hidden me beneath the cloak. It was Erc who came upon us. He fell on Rochad from behind. But do not worry, friend. I did not let them take Rochad's spirit. No, nor the Hound's. Inside the cloak, I had my woman's dagger." She lifted it from her belt. "I killed him; Erc is dead. I brought Rochad home to you, here, as always, beside the Hound." She gestured at the bag.

My eyes traveled down to it; I could not look away. Behind me I heard Niniane begin to moan, a high keening. I looked around to see why my mother-in-law was making so strange a sound.

For the first time since the day I had met the Hound at the river, I felt the blackness begin to come up at the sides of my eyes, to close around me. I welcomed it, hurried it toward me. It plunged me into darkness, carried me mercifully to the forest floor.

27

We lived for ten years in the forest; most of the early years are a blur of pain. We were like the trees, we three, our roots entwined in the darkness, our bodies soughing in the passing wind. When one of us would fall into darkness, the other two would comfort her, hold her in the darkness, feed the children, bank the fire.

Mathramail came to us when only three months had passed.

"We have heard of this in Ulster," he said. "Medb is beside herself with anger. She has executed Lugaid and others for his part in roaming the countryside of Ulster. She blames herself for the death of Rochad."

"All of them are upon her," I said. "All the dead of Ulster. She has taken a father from her own grandchildren. All of it is upon her. And still her blame will not return them to us. Rochad or the Hound."

"That is partly why I have come," said Mathramail. "Let me foster Tahar for you. He is of the age and he will need a father. I will give him all the love and guidance Rochad would have offered. I will teach him to hunt and ride, the skills that a man can teach him."

"I would not have him in Connacht where she could reach him."

"That is what I thought that you would say, so I have made arrangements. We will raise him up in Alba."

"And what of your wife, of your foster-boy?"

"They are with me, Sister. Let us do this for you; we will not fail you or your son."

"I know that you would not," I said. "You never failed me as a child. Only that I do not think that I can let him go. I have so little left of Rochad."

"Think upon it," he said. "I will return in six months' time."

Tahar had eight years upon him. He chafed at the quiet of the forest life. He longed to hunt and ride. Niniane convinced me to foster him with Mathramail.

"Look upon us here," she said. "This is no fit training for a child. Among the three of us, we contain all the sorrow in the forest."

In the end, it was not so much that argument but the knowledge that he would be across the water, far from Medb, that convinced me to let him go.

When Mathramail returned, Tahar was waiting, his traveling bag packed and ready, his excitement ill-contained.

"I will ride a pony?"

"You will have your own pony; it is tethered at the forest edge."

"My father sent it for me?"

"He did."

I turned my head away, clenched my hands together.

"Maither says we will sail the waters."

"So we will. On a ship with winged sails."

He hugged Niniane and Emer, squirming to go. He placed his little hands against my cheeks.

"Don't be afraid, Mama," he said. "Remember that I have the Bird-Sight. I can see across the water and back."

I nodded my head, held him hard against me.

"Make your father proud," I whispered.

"Keep him safe," I said as I hugged my brother.

"As if he were my own. When I can, I will bring him here to visit."

I thought that would be never, but I nodded my head.

"Finnabair," he said. "Medb . . . our mother."

"Yours."

"She is so sorrowful for the death of Rochad. The guilt of it has changed her."

"Even that will not return him. Go and keep my child safely from her."

In our third year in the forest, Emer mated with a man of the Partraigi. I did not think I would ever mate again. Though I had but thirty years upon me, I had been graced with two men who had loved me; that was enough for a lifetime. I had no desire for more.

Though Emer did not call her man a love match, they were kind to one another. The mating eased her sorrow. It brought some color to her cheeks, a lightness to her step. It also produced a girl child whom we named Jigahnsa. At five years old, Julia was the little mother, all wild Niniane curls and old, grey eyes. She believed the child to be her sister, called her "my Jigahnsa." She was ever tender with the baby. Julia's loving kindness and the sweet new life among us softened out the edges of our sorrow. Niniane began to teach Julia the Welisc language, as Froech had told us to do so long ago. We began to laugh again, to play with our children with our hearts in the game.

It was while we were out among the trees, playing at hide and seek, that Medb came among us. Two men of the Partraigi accompanied her; they had forced her to leave her own guard, bristling with weapons, at the edge of the forest. She was white-lipped with anger at being weapon-less, but still she came.

I was dashing across the path in pursuit of Julia when I saw her. I stopped and stared, not certain that I was seeing something real. Julia returned to me at a dash. She stared at the approaching stranger.

"Mama, who is that woman?"

I could not speak. Niniane came up behind us.

"That is your other grandmother. She is called Medb."

"I have another grandmother?" She dashed toward her, her hand outstretched. "Have you come to play seek and hide?"

Medb knelt and stretched out her hand, her face alight.

"If you like."

I turned and began to walk away.

"Mama, where are you going?"

"Back to the village. Come with me now."

She came, dragging Medb by the hand. I would not take her inside our dwelling, but stood instead before the door. Niniane took matters in hand, moving me aside, emerging with two stools. She sat them opposite each other in the sunlight. She made to leave, but I pleaded with her.

"Stay with me, Little Mother." And so she came behind me and put her hand on my shoulder. I clutched it like a drowning woman, the wave of bitterness and anger threatening to take me down with it. I said nothing.

Medb's face moved through a series of emotions. It lighted on Julia, went sorrowful when it regarded Niniane and me, opened wide in disbelief at our forest life. She looked around the village. That was when I knew what to say.

"These are good and gentle people. They do not make war. They have nothing you want, nothing you need. If you ever come among them again, I will kill you and everything that is dear to you with this little hand. Do you hear me well?"

"Mama!" said Julia on a gasp. In her five years, she had seen me weep, but she had never heard me angry.

But Medb simply nodded her head.

"Nor me nor any of mine shall ever come among them. From me none shall know where they are or even that they are here. You have my word as a warrior."

I made a sound, half laugh, half snort.

"Finnabair," she said softly. "Your Rochad. Never would I have taken him from you, nor the father of this child, my granddaughter, nor this woman's son."

"And yet you did. And also the Hound."

"The Hound was the lightning rod of Ulster. He knew this well. He knew the way that he would die. All the power of Ulster rested in him. To have rid Ulster of him has returned all my power to me." She nodded her head. "But Rochad was an accident of war. Erc and Lugaid were to kill the Hound. I did not sanction their search for booty. Both of them have paid the price of their lives."

"Much comfort, Queen of Connacht."

She had the grace to drop her head in shame.

"Did this child know her father?"

"She had little more than nine moons upon her."

She turned toward Julia.

"I knew your father. He was a great, handsome warrior who loved your mother well. He bargained hard to have her years ago."

"My mother weeps for him," said Julia. "We keep his spirit in our dwelling and I ask him often to help her not to cry."

Hot color flamed up in Medb's cheeks.

"Oh, you gods," she whispered. "I have brought this on my child."

She looked at me directly.

"Tell me what I can do. Name anything. Finnabair, please. I have lost two of my sons and Mathramail is far from me. I do not wish to lose you. I know that I have wounded you. Tell me anything that will bring you surcease from sorrow."

"My pain would ease if you were dead."

It was the cruelest thing I have ever said. Behind me Niniane gasped and pressed her hand into my shoulder. All the color drained from Medb's face. She stood.

Emer came down the path toward our dwelling, Jigahnsa in her arms. She stopped when she saw the tableau before her. Medb turned in her direction. Niniane spoke.

"This is Emer, wife of the Hound of Ulster, and her daughter Jigahnsa."

I watched Medb's face light on the child, watched her mentally add and subtract the years.

"This is not the child of the Hound." It was a statement.

"It is not," I said. "So it is of no interest to you. And you will not need to kill this child. Ever."

She turned her face back toward me. She looked old, haggard. She pressed her hands together, unclenched them.

"I understand you well, Finnabair. I tell you this. You and all of yours are under my protection from now until the time I die. None of these will ever be harmed. It is all I can offer."

"It is little enough and late," I said.

She turned and made her way through the forest. In all our years in the Fid Duin, I never saw or heard from her again. In our fifth year, when Ahweho the Clan Mother died, the people came to me with the traveling feather to ask if I would be Clan Mother. I declined. The hearts of Jigahnsa and Ahweho had been pure for traveling. Mine was not. In the place where I thought of Medb of Connacht, there was a twisting, hard black knot.

Mathramail brought Tahar to see us when Julia was eight years old. Tahar was fifteen then and full of stories. He talked of Alba, of lakes and mountains, of the shaggy ponies of the hills, of the clans of the Highlands. He was shocked when his little sister spoke the Welisc language of the coastal people. He tousled at her curls and proclaimed her brilliant. She preened in his praise and when he left us, she was full of questions, hundreds of them, about the world outside the Fid Duin. For days, we heard her telling four-year-old Jigahnsa about Alba, Ulster, and Connacht.

Conchobar called for us when Julia was nine, Jigahnsa five. He was ill, in fear of dying, an old man in need of the only healers he had ever trusted.

Niniane snorted at the message from the king.

"Old," she said. "The old fool is no older than I am."

Emer and I burst into laughter at her judgment, for Niniane had two and seventy years upon her. The only difference between our little mother and the old king was that Niniane did not know her age. She bustled about the forest with her basket, herded her grandchildren with high energy and laughter, pounded at her herbs with all the power in her tiny body.

"Well," I said, "no matter. Of course we will not go."

Niniane stood still at her grinding.

"I think we shall," she said.

Both Emer and I stopped, still.

"No," we said in unison.

"We do not wish to return to the world of Ulster," I said, speaking for both of us. Emer nodded her head.

"And so you think also to speak for your daughters, to keep them here in the forest forever."

"This is a good life, a life of peace and solitude."

"It is a good life for three women who lived far and wide when they were young, who loved and lost. You have two curious young daughters who know only that there is a world beyond this forest. Will you deny them all the world for your fear and your loss?"

I looked out at the clearing before our dwelling to where Julia and Jigahnsa were playing in the dappling light. I turned toward Emer. She held out her hand.

"It is time for a walk in the forest," she said.

*   *   *

Ulster had changed and not for the better. The hill of Emain Macha seemed shabby to me, the *grianan* sagging with age, the Craobh Rioga with its twinkling hoard weary and unpolished.

Not so to Julia and Jigahnsa, who oohed and aahed at every new sight and sound.

Conchobar did indeed seem older by far than Niniane, his face a pasty shade of grey, his pate bald and shining. The wasting sickness was upon him and though he knew it well, he wanted only confirmation and the comforting presence of old faces and old friends.

"I long for the old days of Ulster," he lamented. "When the Hound was at his rock in the river and Rochad and the warriors of Rigdonn would ride to our defense. Those were the great days of Ulster!"

Emer and I said nothing, tending to the king in silence.

I longed for nothing; all longing had burned away from me when Rochad died and I thought it likely that I would never feel fire again.

The old king died in the spring of the year and the people of Ulster elected his son Finnchad the new king. Though he was much upon my own forty years, he seemed to me but a boy. He had the odd and silly habit of wearing on his head a Lochland helmet made of two great silver horns. For that habit, he earned himself the nickname Finnchad the Horned. He surely lacked the fire his father had once possessed; he ruled in name only for he was possessed of no force of personality.

He knew neither Emer nor I, knew nothing of the warriors we had loved or the great war we had fought. To him, and to the new court of Emain Macha, we were simply two healer women of middle age, strange and reclusive creatures of the forest, irrelevant unless an illness fell upon them. Together with Niniane, we three were our own triune oddity, three women silent and alone, tending to our herbs, our daughters. We were more isolated than we had ever been among the Partraigi. I began to feel a constant strange vagueness, as though my time of life had passed. I was weary all the time.

And then Tahar returned to us from Alba. He was nineteen years old, tall and sure, swift of foot and strong on horseback. How he reminded me of Rochad! Julia and Jigahnsa were smitten by him, trailing him everywhere, plaguing him with questions and demanding stories. I was so proud of his patience with them, as he taught them to ride and swim. Their faces shining up at him made me glad that we had returned to Ulster, hopeful that perhaps, with time, we could emerge from our self-imposed exile.

As ever, I was a fool to believe in any promise of joy.

28

"Raiders from the sea! Slave raiders! Mothers, they have taken our girls!"

Tahar burst in upon us, his face a mottled mess, blood running from his forehead and his arm.

He awakened me from the long afternoon naps I now took each day. I stared up at him through heavy-lidded eyes.

"You are bleeding," I said.

He clutched me at my upper arms, lifted me to my feet from my sleeping platform.

"Hear me now. Slave raiders have come from the sea. Men who spoke the Welisc tongue. They have stolen dozens of our people from Tracht Esi by the sea."

"That is where the Hound killed Conlaech," said Emer, her back to us where she worked quietly among the herbs so as not to wake me.

Tahar ran to her; he caught her by her hair and yanked her toward him. She gasped, slapped at him with both her hands.

"Tahar, what lack of respect is this?"

"Hear me, both of you. Come into this world; you dwell, both of you, in the past. Stop hiding in your forest and your herbs. I need you now; the girls will need you. I tell you they have taken our girls! Not just any girls of Ulster. They have taken Julia and Jigahnsa."

I awoke clearly to what he was saying.

"No! Oh no! Not my child; she promised me she would not harm my child. She swore it on her honor as a warrior."

"Not she. Slave traders of the Welisc. Of whom do you speak?"

"Julia! Jigahnsa! Tahar, what shall we do? Oh, Finnabair." Emer clutched at my hands, the story now clear to her as well. "Not our children. They are all we have!"

"I tried to stop them," Tahar said. "We were riding. They came up from the sea. So many of us, more than twenty of our people. They took them all. There were so few warriors to fight them. They knocked me unconscious, wounded my arm. . . ."

I bent to examine his head.

"No never mind!" He pushed my arm away. "We must mount a rescue."

"Rescue for what?" Niniane came in from the forest, her basket on her arm.

"They have taken Julia and Jigahnsa," Emer cried.

"Conchobar!" I said. "We will speak to the king."

"His son, Maither. Finnchad."

I shook myself full awake. "His son, then. Bring my cloak."

We rode hard to Emain Macha. We raced into the great hall of the king, two healing women of almost forty years, pleading for our daughters' lives. Finnchad was all reason and quiet solicitude.

"I know that this separation will be difficult, but remember, such exchanges occur all the time. We raid the Welisc folk for slaves and they do the same. Neither side mistreats their captives. This you must know; is not your own mother-in-law one of our Welisc captives? Your daughters will serve their new village well and see a little of the world. And who knows, one day they may return to us."

Tahar stepped forward.

"I am Tahar, son of Rochad of Rigdonn. I am a warrior by training. Let me lead a party for their rescue. Once Ulster was the seat of great power, once the Royal Branch warriors were a name known to all the world. Let me return to us the warrior pride of Ulster!"

Already several men had stood, shouting their agreement, ready to accompany him, but the king gestured them to their seats.

"No such raid will go on while I am king. Shall we waste the resources of Ulster on two little girls, fourteen and ten? Was this how the Red Branch warriors achieved their fame and honor? Raids have occurred before and they will occur again. That is the way of our world."

He turned toward us.

"You are healing women; busy yourselves with your healing. Of that we always have need."

Something that had been asleep in me long and long awoke then. I drew myself up before him, took Emer's hand in mine.

"Your father was my friend; with him I have ridden to the country of the Other. The Hound was his right arm, the gate of Ulster. Rochad, father of my boy, Tahar, fought again and yet again for you when the Ulstermen were in their cursing. We three have served as your healers for all these many years. Never have we asked you for anything. This we ask, Finnchad, King of Ulster. Let my son lead the warriors of Ulster across the water."

"I will not hear of it," he said.

We turned to depart. At the door of his chamber, Emer turned.

"Has anyone ever bothered to tell you how utterly stupid you look in those silver horns?"

There was a shocked silence in the room, but I could see the snickering laughter on the faces of some of the men of Ulster.

"No?"

"Then let me be the first to tell you so."

We had made an enemy, but one without teeth or fangs.

We rode to Tracht Esi, the three of us. We sat beside the sea and looked across the water. At last I stood.

"It is time to return to this world," I said to Emer. I stood.

"What does she do?" asked Tahar.

"She will use the Bird-Sight. With it we will find our daughters."

Tahar nodded.

"This much I can do as well."

He stood and took my hand. Together we closed our eyes, together we raced across the water, up a long river that ran from the sea. Together we entered the village. They were tied side by side with the other captives in the village square, being examined for purchase. Jigahnsa was terrified. She clung to Julia's hand; her sobbing wrenched at my heart and I was glad that Emer could not see it.

"Hush now," Julia said quietly. "Look where Finnabair and Tahar have come for us."

"Tahar?" Jigahnsa said. "Where?"

"Right there at the shore."

Julia looked at me; her ancient grey eyes bored into mine.

"Again we cross the water, Maither. Tahar, my brother, I will care for Jigahnsa until you come."

The little girl inside her rose up then.

"Mama," she whispered. "I am afraid."

What gift could I give her to make her strong, to give her hope? I who had so little hope left. I cast about in my memory. Suddenly I knew.

"Julia, there is a story I must tell you for this journey. It was told to me by Flavi long ago."

She heard me out, her eyes wide.

"I will keep the Little Brother here beside us, for it seems that he, too, was a journeyer."

She was approached by a man who lifted her chin, looked at her teeth. He called to his wife who approached them. She examined both girls, pointed her hand at Julia. In perfect Welisc my little girl spoke.

"I am Julia; this is my sister Jigahnsa. We are sold as a pair."

The man leaned back laughing.

"Well, you are a bright and saucy one. Mother, meet a girl of Eriu who freely speaks our tongue."

"Did you see enough to know?"

"I saw the river that led from the sea and the village there beside it. I will find it. Will you trust me now?"

"You cannot go alone."

"I will not go alone. I am my father's son; I know how to drive a bargain."

He clasped me in his arms.

"You have surprised me, Maither. I did not know this Finnabair until today. My strong mother. This journeyer. Now I see why my father loved you so. Take care of Emer and Niniane. I promise that I will return."

. He turned back at the last moment.

"I remember that story, Maither. You told it to me, also, long ago. I wonder what became of his long journey."

I nodded, mute with hope and fear.

Six months passed before we heard or saw from Tahar, each day more terrible than the waiting for Rochad, the fear for both my children and for Emer's child a terrible crawling terror. Emer and I took to riding to Tracht Esi, watching out over the sea. Day after day and no boats came. We ceased to eat. Our skin stretched tight against our bones again; for the first time Niniane looked her age. I began to fear for her health.

"She cannot die before they return to us," I whispered to Emer in the darkness. We lay side by side, our hands clasped in wide-eyed wakefulness, as we now did almost every night. Near us, Niniane slept fitfully, her dreams punctuated by little moans, by tossing and turning.

"I am losing hope that they will ever return. Finnabair, you must use the Bird-Sight once again."

"Friend, I will try again at daybreak."

Niniane and Emer concealed themselves at the woods line with provisions. I wrapped myself in Cuchulainn's ancient cloak. I wished no one to see me on the river rock at Ferdiad's Ford. I waded out as I had done so long ago. At the pillar stone that flanked the rock, I saw his blood, still etched into the living rock.

"Nor wind nor water will wash you away," I whispered. "For we will remember."

I climbed up to the flat plate of the stone, stood in silence. I looked first to the east, across the water. I turned in my circle north, west, south.

No visions came to me, no sight of Julia and Jigahnsa. No view of Tahar.

What if all of them were gone? What if, in sending one to look for the others, we had lost them all?

I sat down on the rock.

"Rochad," I whispered. "I am alone in the dangerous world. I did not protect them well."

I sat there silent through the whole of the long day, willing the doors of sight to open. Toward dusk, I saw movement from away to the west, toward Connacht. I stood, faced west, opened the Bird-Sight. Nothing was there. But still I could see figures moving toward me in the distance. Not Bird-Sight then but humans, four of them.

I stood utterly still. I glanced towards the woods line; Niniane and Emer were still concealed.

I watched as the figures emerged from the blue light of evening, watched as they shaped themselves, two men, a young woman and a child. My heart began to trip and hammer.

"Please," I whispered. "Oh, please."

It was Mathramail's skinny blond height I recognized first. I gave a glad cry. They turned in my direction; Jigahnsa shrank toward Tahar, clinging to his hand. I remembered that they could not see me. I threw my hood back from my head.

"Emer," I cried. "Niniane. Run, oh run!"

29

If only you could have seen her. Blood of my blood!" she cried. "Bone of my bone! And everywhere her sword singing around her, her arms like the arms of a young warrior, the longsword splitting the air with sound. Never have I seen anything like it. Never." Tahar was standing before us, his arms swinging the imaginary sword.

Julia and Jigahnsa sat in the center of the circle, constantly in the arms of one of their mothers, their grandmother, every inch of them checked and rechecked, kissed and coddled.

"But Medb. You went to Medb."

"Well we knew that there would be no future with Finnchad the Horned."

"True enough," said Emer.

"He came first to me," said Mathramail. "But I am no warrior, as you know. The strategy of all of it, the force. It had to come from Medb and Ailill."

"And so it did," said Tahar. "All the warriors of Connacht, the boats, our stealth as we moved up the river in darkness. And Medb. She planned it to the last detail, backup upon backup and each of them to gather to us Julia and Jigahnsa. In the end we brought back every captive they had taken from Ulster and some few of our own. But she would have none but that Julia and Jigahnsa should be in her boat. Over and over she asked them if they had been hurt. Over and over she told them that she was sorry they had been afraid. Such a warrior as she has never lived."

"She is responsible for the death of your father and the death of the Hound," I said quietly.

"And she is our grandmother," said Tahar.

Julia spoke.

"And for returning us to you. Hear me, Maither. Medb is a warrior; that is all she is and all she knows. She has never taken your journeys, either of joy or of sorrow. She cannot love as you love. But this was the gift she could give you. This she said to me, 'Say to your maither that I return to her the child of her great love and the child of her Dog Warrior. Say to her that I would return to her all that I have taken were it in my power.' This is her apology, her plea for your forgiveness. What a warrior could do she did; she brought us back to you. That she did with all the strength that was in her."

"Your daughter is wise," said Niniane.

"What would you have me do, go to her? Make thanks to her for your return?"

The room was silent. I looked at all of them, one by one.

"I will not go alone," I said.

I had not been in Cruachan Ai for twenty years. My memories had colored it larger than it was, more imposing and bejeweled. They were at feasting when we came, all the warriors of Connacht gathered in the Great Hall, toasting their aging queen for her raid in Alba. She was standing before them, her cup raised, swinging the famous hair now woven through with grey.

I clung hard to Tahar's strong arm; my knees had gone to water. Julia held my right hand in her own. Behind me Emer came, Niniane on her left and Jigahnsa holding her hand. Mathramail preceded us. To the company, he cried aloud.

"I bring before you Finnabair, wife of Rochad of Rigdonn, and Emer, wife of Cuchulainn, Hound of Ulster."

The hall went silent, a complete and utter, breathing silence. We progressed up the long aisle between the tables of warriors in their clan plaid, women in their finest tunics.

We stood before the dais.

"Finnabair," my father cried, clapping his hands in delight. I had eyes for my mother only.

She lowered the cup to the table, pressed her hands hard against its edge. What happened next I still cannot relate. For the rest of my life, I will see it again and yet again.

She went down on one knee, lowered her head. When she raised it, her eyes were filled with unshed tears. In all my life, in all my life, I have never seen Medb of Connacht cry.

"Finnabair," she cried, her voice ringing throughout the room. "My daughter. Forgive me for the pain that I have brought on you and yours."

She remained on her knee, his face tilted toward mine, filled with hope and sorrow, with the long and twisted journey of our lives.

I lifted the cup from where she had placed it on the table. I raised it high. In the loudest voice I possessed I called my gratitude upon her. I called upon her my forgiveness and my blessing. I called my love upon Medb of Connacht.

"Blood of my blood," I cried. "Bone of my bone."

EPILOGUE

We returned to our healing work in Ulster. The memory of Rochad and the Hound drew us back to Emain Macha, to the rock in the river where so much joy and sorrow had transpired.

Julia apprenticed to the Druids, her spirit wisdom already older and wiser than mine, than many of theirs. Tahar chose to remain in Connacht, among the warriors who had stood behind him on his Welisc raid. He visited us often. When he was twenty-seven, having never married, he came to visit Emer and me, riding into the clearing where we were boiling herbs. He dismounted with the wide swinging stride that I remembered from his father, drew his arms around us both.

Jigahnsa emerged from the forest, seventeen and lovely, her gathering basket on her arm. Tahar had known her all his life; on that day, he saw her for the first time.

"Oh," he said. "Jigahnsa." It was enough and it was all. He stumbled forward to help her with her basket. After their marriage and departure to Connacht, Emer journeyed south to the Gardens of Lugh to see if she had any family there that she remembered. We packed her traveling bag with the skull of Cuchulainn. I cradled it gently in my hands, remembering the wild, red hair, the bulbous nose, the giant hands and wicked wit.

"Hello, old friend," I whispered. "I have missed you at the river."

Before she left, Emer and I walked hand in hand in the forest as we had done so many years in the Fid Duin.

"I do not know if we will meet again, friend."

She nodded. We had both lived too long and seen too much to give each other false assurance.

"And if this should be our last walk together, there is a story I must tell you for your journey," I said. "It was told to me by Flavi long ago; he would wish for you to carry it."

Niniane crossed the water in her eighty-fourth year. She was grinding herbs at her table when suddenly she stopped. "Finnabair," she said. Nothing more. She dropped to the floor, her grey curls still bobbing. I buried her next to Flavi; upon their rocks I had the stoneworker incise the *ogham* sticks that spoke for mother and for father.

I stayed alone in our hut then, doing the healing work of Ulster, the skull of Rochad my only company. I took to talking to him, to telling him the small details of my day. He had been gone for twenty-six years. I knew that I was too much alone, but I was not discontented.

I was in my fifty-third year when the Roman came. He was short and strong, a barrel-chested fellow, a centurion of much experience. Claudius, emperor of Rome, had invaded Alba. We had heard much of it here in Ulster—the horrors of the way Romans treated the women of the tribes, the way Claudius and his legions were systematically destroying the oak shrines of the Druids. Many of the priests of Alba had been murdered and those who could escape to us had done so. Hundreds were now among the ranks of Eriu. Julia had brought one or two to me for healing.

There had been whisperings that we would be invaded, fears that the Romans would come among us. We had heard that their name for our country was Hibernia, that they thought of us as barbarians. We hoped that they would believe that myth and stay away. And then came the centurion, leading a small exploratory force of Romans.

Their first encounter had been with the warriors of Ulster, who had been preparing for them for many months. Most of the Romans were dead; those who were not had been taken in among us as slaves. This one had been wounded in the arm. A Roman, he had been inclined to ignore it, but the wound had festered; it was full of pus and had begun to smell. Finnchad had sent him to me.

The Roman was as fearless as the leather vest he wore. Though he was not much taller than I, he was broad of chest with thickset legs and arms, made strong, I supposed, with fighting for Rome. He sat before me in silence, expecting, I surmised, painful barbarian medicine in a foreign tongue. I greeted him in his own tongue.

"*Quis es?*" I asked him.

He rocked back on the stool and his eyes grew wide.

"Graccus."

"*Salve,* Graccus."

"You are of Rome?" His tongue grew limber in the hearing of his own tongue.

"No, I am a healer of Hibernia."

"How have you learned the Roman tongue?"

"My husband's family is of Roman stock. From them have I learned your tongue. His mother was brought to Alba long ago by a centurion of Rome."

"By the very gods. I should never cease to be surprised by the world."

It all seemed to cheer him enormously and he smiled. His face, when he smiled, transformed. He became not a Roman, but a man. He reminded me of someone. I smiled in return.

"Where is your husband? Did I meet him in the fighting?"

I pointed to the skull on the shelf above my medicine table.

"Oh," he said. Then softly, "If you loved him, I am sorry."

"I did."

"Tell me your name, healer."

"I am Finnabair, daughter of . . . I am Finnabair."

"How lovely." His eyes watched mine intensely now.

I peered at the wound.

"Surely you are not a stupid man, are you? I had not heard that Romans were stupid."

His smile vanished. He looked both shocked and offended.

"I am not. Why do you ask this?"

"Because only a stupid man would let this wound become infected so. Only a stupid man would risk the gangrene that might cost him his arm."

"Or a man who is tired of life as a soldier."

"Ah, so you wish to die?"

He shrugged. "I wish to no longer be a soldier."

"Twice in my life I have wished to die," I said. Niniane's voice traveled to me down the years, saying the self-same words. I laughed and shook my head.

"It amuses you?"

"The way life circles amuses me."

He nodded. "Always there are surprises. Will I lose the arm?"

"Well, this infection could surprise you, Graccus. Infection travels as it will. You are strong and healthy; in you, the process would likely be slow. But it might travel to your heart, your head. Surely, you would lose your arm. But you might also lose your life. I will stop all of that."

He laughed and shook his head.

"And this amuses you?"

"You amuse me. No woman of Rome would ever speak

to a centurion so. But no woman of Rome would be a healer."

"The women of Eriu are different. We speak as we please. And we are healers, warriors, what we will."

"Well, I should not be surprised." He gestured toward the skull of Rochad. "I know of this custom with the skulls, that they contain the spirits of the dead, who stay beside you."

I watched his eyes.

"What say you of that custom?"

"I should think that it would comfort."

"It does so. But I am surprised to hear you say so. I am told that many of your people think us barbarians for our ways."

He shrugged.

"I have been posted in places of the world where none of the customs are Roman customs, where the women have not been as Roman women."

"Ah then, a man of the world."

He grinned and made a self-deprecating shrug.

I began to clean the wound, to slice away the infected skin. Graccus did not even seem to notice my ministrations.

"So now Rome will come to Hibernia, will invade us and force our women to be as Roman women. Is that the way?"

He tilted his head and looked at me for a while.

"I do not think that many men could force you, Finnabair. Such a woman as you would need to be won by a man of heart and mind."

A deep flush rose up my chest and burned at the edges of my hair. I had forgotten this heat, kept my head lowered until the warmth receded, swabbed at the wound. At last I looked up.

"Pretty words do little for one who has lived as long as I, Roman. They will not deter me from the truth."

"Very well. I will speak the truth to you, Finnabair, in truth because I think that your people shall never allow me to return to Alba."

"That is so; you are of Eire now, like it or no."

"Rome spreads itself thinner and thinner across the world. In this part of the world, there is much that we do not like. Across the water in the north, the Pictish people are crazy; they paint themselves blue." He gave a cursory glance to my tattoo. "Here, the Hibernian people are fierce warriors and secretive. Your terrain is horrible—forest and bog, lakes and mountains, always rain. Why must it always rain?" I shrugged in response; it was not a thing I often noticed. He continued. "When my expeditionary force does not return, Rome will send another. When that does not return, they will assume that the place is impenetrable, evil, perhaps replete with dark and barbarian magic."

I laughed aloud.

"Well this is good news indeed. I am one of a race of dark and rainy barbarians and that will save us."

He laughed aloud.

"So you see, a Roman has brought you good news."

"And a Roman who is glad that he will not be allowed to return to Rome."

His eyes widened.

"Are all of your healers wise, Finnabair?"

"I have lived long, Centurion, I have learned to watch and listen."

He nodded. "I, too, watch and listen. And I think that both of us have been alone for a long time. Perhaps too long, Finnabair."

"You are relentless, Roman."

"I am Roman."

I said nothing in response.

"Finnabair, will you permit me no avenue of conversation but politics?"

"So soon in my knowing of you? I will permit the truth."

He put his hand under my chin, held my eyes to his.

"Truth then. Yes, I should like to disappear here. No, I

do not ever wish to return to the armies of Rome. I have
served them well for more than thirty years and I am done
with war. I can build and carry as well as any, and can
share with the people of Eriu my Roman knowledge of
water and heat and roads. I should like to no longer be
alone. Perhaps I would not be too repulsive for a woman
of Eriu who might take me to husband. For I surmise that
here the women do the choosing."

"They do." My face grew far too warm cupped in the
large, rough hand. I stood to escape it, busied myself at
my herb shelf. "And there are many young, unmarried
women here among us who might one day choose you."

"I do not wish a young woman."

"Why ever not?"

"Because I have lived long. Because only a woman who
has also borne sorrow could understand a journeyer such
as I."

His gaze crept upward toward my journey mark.

"May I touch it?" he asked softly.

I blinked at my own foolishness, inclined my head anyway. He was beside me in a single catlike move. His body,
his leather tunic, smelled like a warm country. His fingers
found my face, touched warm and strong against my skin.
I sighed and closed my own eyes.

"It is cool, as water," he said.

I opened my eyes. His hazel eyes were locked on mine,
brown and green, replete with gentle sorrow.

"What is the cause of your sadness, Centurion?"

"It is a foolishness, healer, an incident so small in the
long and violent course of my life. A centurion is asked by
Rome to do many things that he cannot be proud of. It is
the lot of a warrior."

"My mother is a warrior," I said. "I know this to be
true."

"Your mother?"

"It is the Hibernian way. She is a fierce defender of her
people, of her grandchildren."

He shook his head.

"Such women as this." His hand caressed the journey mark again. My heart, so long quiescent, started up like a triphammer. I thought of Rochad and of Froech. For a moment I felt young, supple as a willow. His eyes never left mine. I cleared my throat.

"We were speaking of your sorrow."

"It happened more than a decade ago. Only one thing in all the services I have done for Rome. But I cannot shake it from my memory."

"Tell me then. A healer ministers to the spirit as well as the body."

He regarded me for a still moment. He took his hand from my face, returned to sit on the stool by my table. I felt almost bereft.

I sat down opposite him, began to wrap his cleaned wound with a fresh white linen.

"You will need to return in two days' time so that I may check the wound."

I finished winding the bandage around his arm. I moved to my basin and washed my hands twice, all the way to my elbows, as Flavius had taught me long ago. I began to prepare the salves that he would apply to it.

"So long? May I come sooner?"

"You may if it begins to smell."

At this he laughed aloud, smacking the tabletop.

"So you will see me for my stink, healer?"

I whirled to face him, my eyes wide. I braced my hands against my worktable.

He leapt up beside me, caught my upper arms in his hands.

"What is it? How have I offended?"

"No offense, Roman. It was a memory. From long ago."

"Then it would please me to hear it." He bent his head close to mine. "I think, Finnabair, that it would please me to hear all of your memories. Every one." He was earnest, the look on his face almost pleading in its hope.

"Why?"

"I do not know. Only that I know. I speak truth, healer. I promise you that."

A little silence spun between us. I looked at the skull of Rochad on its shelf. I thought of Froech. I knew what they would tell me. Do not dwell in loneliness; choose life.

I smiled at the Roman, a full and unstinting smile. His pupils widened.

"Let us begin with your memory, Graccus." I gestured to the table.

He nodded, cleared his throat. He released my arms reluctantly, returned to the stool.

"I was stationed in a place called Judea. Do you know of it?"

"I do not."

"It was the country of a people called the Jews."

"I do know of the Jews."

He shook his head.

"They are crazy. All of them. I am telling you." He shook his head. "They have too many rules, what they will eat, what they will not, days on which they will walk, days on which they will not move. They argue amongst themselves, Finnabair, the most contentious people I have ever known."

"You do not know the Hibernians yet."

At this he laughed aloud.

"You have wit, Finnabair."

"So I have been told, Graccus."

"At any rate, their great temple is in a city called Jerusalem. Do you know of it?"

"I do not."

"It is a most magnificent place—a building the size of a small city. But, oh, the temple priests. They put the senators of Rome to shame for debate and politics. Always, they are arguing the points of law, and then they involve Rome in their debates! Asking Rome to mediate, to impose our law, their laws. Some new prophet crops up among them every month. While I was there, there was a wild man who never washed. He lived in the desert and ate locusts. He was dirty; he stank and creatures lived inside his hair. But did they see him as a crazy man? As a man in need of a good Roman asylum? No, they thought him wise."

Again he let out a long, expelled breath.

"In my last months there, there was a rabbi . . ."

I shook my head.

"One of their teachers."

I gestured him to go ahead.

"From what I saw he was no threat to anyone, just a thin fellow with large dark eyes and curly hair. But they seemed to fear his teachings."

"What were those?"

"Well, for one thing, he actually told them to pay their Roman taxes." This made him laugh aloud. "Always a popular position. But there were other things. He preached a doctrine of forgiveness. He said that the law was less important than the people; if it came to a choice between the two, he broke the law. He consorted with tax collectors and prostitutes and the poor. He spoke of a time when there would be no armies and no war. As if that could ever happen.

"He did not endear himself to those priests. They held a trial and got Rome involved in the whole problem. Between Rome and those priests, they sentenced the poor fellow to death and crucified him."

He shook his head.

"But surely as a centurion of Rome, you became accustomed to such deaths. Why does this one upset you so?"

"Well, for one thing, they cannot find his body now. And the rumors are swirling around him—that he was the Messiah, come among them. That to know him is to put aside death."

" 'Messiah'?"

"A god man."

I gestured him to continue.

"Rome does not like Messiah rumors—it makes for difficult management of conquered peoples."

"But now you are no longer in Rome."

"No."

"So why does it worry you still?"

He eyes grew faraway and he looked off into the distance.

"Something happened when he was dying. There were three who were crucified together and we were given tours of duty to guard them, two centurions, four hours on, and then a change of guard. On my turn of duty, I gave all three of them a drink."

He shrugged.

"It was just a thing that we did. We soaked a sponge and gave them vinegar and water. That was all. It was customary."

"Then, what of it?"

"When I gave him his drink, he looked down at me. 'Graccus,' he said, 'my brother, I will remember this kindness. For it has brought me joy.' Joy, Finnabair. And he was dying in that awful way."

My hands had frozen in midair, the salves forgotten. I turned to face him.

"You see it, too, Finnabair. He could not have known my name. How did he know my name? And joy? He was dying."

"Oh, Graccus," I said. "Tell me the name of this rabbi of Judea. What was he called?"

He regarded me wide-eyed. "Why, Finnabair?"

"Only tell me. Quickly, Graccus."

"Well, we posted a sign above his head that read INRI. It meant, 'Behold, the King of the Jews.' But we meant it sarcastically. Sarcasm is a powerful tool of Rome; it reduces our enemies to objects of ridicule."

He looked ashamed.

"He should not have been ridiculed, the rabbi. Among his people he was called Yeshua ben Joseph."

My hand was shaking as I reached for his.

"Come with me, Graccus. There is a story I must tell you and it is a long and winding tale. And then, if you are up for a journey, we must take your tale to those I love. It is the ending to a story that was told us long ago."

"Will the journey be with you?" he asked. His great hand closed around mine tightly. It reminded me of someone, that great hand.

"It will," I said, directly.

His eyes locked onto mine. He smiled. "Then I will gladly journey."

We stood at the foot of the barrow of Niniane and Flavius. Graccus, having heard the story, held his hand against Flavi's stone, shook his head in wonder.

"I greet you, Elder Brother," he said in the Roman tongue.

"Flavi, Niniane," I said, "we bring to you the ending of the story."

And so we told it, Graccus and I. When we had finished, I opened what little voice I have to me. I sang to them the song of Little Brother.

It was a song of joy.

HISTORICAL BACKGROUND

The Tain is Ireland's *Iliad* and *Odyssey*, a great epic of battles, love, lust, betrayal, and magic. It contains hundreds of stories; the battle-epic itself is flanked by the *rimsceala*, the stories of what went before *The Tain* and what came after. It is supposedly true that Medb began the war because she wanted the brown bull in order to match her husband's hoard. This is entirely consistent with the character of Medb throughout *The Tain;* surely, we have all seen numerous leaders, even in our own time, who were more interested in sating their own desires than in ruling well.

If you wish to read *The Tain* and the *rimsceala* in actual translation, I strongly recommend Thomas Kinsella's superb translation *The Tain* and Randy Lee Eickhoff's lively rendition of the the epic, *The Raid*. Be prepared; *The Tain* is filled with what my students call "the begats"—long lists of every warrior called to battle, endless explanations of how this place or that in Ulster got its name from something that happened in the Tain.

In fact, in terms of actual geography, the action in *The Tain* ranges all over the northern half of Ireland, marching through the provinces of Ulster, Connacht, and Leinster, through what are now the counties of Roscommon, Meath, and West Meath, with the bulk of the action taking place in County Louth. But, because our story is not about armies on the march, but about individuals who are caught in wartime, I have confined most of the action of this book to a region which, on a modern map, includes Armagh (the site of the ancient center of Emain Macha) and modern Ardee, where the ford of the river is still called Ferdiad's Ford (Baile Atha Ferdia). Side trips in this story

take us to the mysterious forest of the Partraigi in far
northern Ulster (ancient site unspecified), Medb's stronghold of Cruachan Ai (now Rathcrogan in Co. Roscommon, Connacht), and lastly to an unnamed island off the
west coast of Connacht. Much of the action in *The Tain*
takes place at the fords of various rivers, fords being natural areas for defense, but also having some symbolic value
(as in crossing the water?) in a whole range of ancient
Irish stories. For our purposes, I have conflated multiple
fords in the epic to our one rock and our one river here in
the story.

Interestingly, more so even than geography, one of the
most detailed and fascinating aspects of the epic is the
writers' attention to what everyone—including the warriors—was wearing; it's like a best-dressed list of ancient
times and surely makes me understand why my ancestral
genes urge me toward the wearing of a wild variety of patterns, colors, and jewelry all at one time. For a writer of
historical fiction, these "red carpet" descriptions are little
diamonds, finds from which we can interpret and spin
whole incidents.

The Tain gives us two versions of what happened to
Finnabair. First it tells us that when seven hundred men
died fighting for loss of the right to bed her, she died of
shame. It does not tell us how this occurred, but says
that it occurred in the mountains and that to this day the
place is called Finnabair Slébe, Finnabair in the Mountains.

The second version of Finnabair's fate has far more in-
teresting potential for a writer of fiction. In the very last
verse of *The Tain* is a line that says, "Finnabair stayed
with Cuchulainn and the Connachtsmen returned to their
country."

Finnabair with Cuchulainn? The daughter of Medb of
Connacht? Why? How did she get there? What would she
do? Why would she stay?

Kinsella tells us that this is merely the storyteller's final flourish, which ignores Finnabair's earlier death and the fact that Cuchulainn has a beloved wife in Emer.

But what if Finnabair's earlier death is the flourish? These stories were written down by Christian monks hundreds of years after they occurred. The idea of a young woman who was offered like a prize cow to dozens of men and then had a good number of them die fighting for her would be at the very least foreign to the Christian monastic sensibility, and likely repugnant as well.

And what if Finnabair did not "stay with Cuchulainn" as a lover but as a friend and healer? She had, after all, been given in marriage to his friend and fellow-warrior Rochad mac Faitheman. What if love and purpose blossomed for Finnabair among her enemies?

I also know this; Irish women of the period of Medb were much like Irish-American women of today. They were not much for lying down to die of shame; they were much more likely to stand up and fight.

And so came Finnabair, staying with Cuchulainn, married to Rochad for good or ill, fighting for her own identity, for her own place in the history of *The Tain*. I admire her and love her deeply for standing up, for fighting back.

As for the Partraigi, *The Tain* does mention them, saying that they were dwellers in the Dark Forest, a tribe known as the People of the Stag. We know nothing further. There has been much recent speculation about the origins of humanity in North America, about the intersection of European peoples with North American aboriginal peoples. It has been my good fortune to learn and tell stories with tellers from the Abenaki, Seneca, Mohawk, Commanche, Dine, Hawaiian and Maori, and Irish nations (and of course with multiple American storytellers, all of us being 57-variety mutts). Based on those cross-cultural experiences, I decided to take the ancient journey both ways and create an anomalous, aboriginal, storytelling people of the forest in my Partraigi. I named their clan mother Jigahnsa in tribute to Jigonsaseh, the woman who spoke for the Peacemaker in Haudenosaunee (Iroquois) myth. As often happens to storytellers, I have fallen in love with the peaceful Partraigi and their stories and hope to go to live among them yet again in story.

Historically, *The Tain* takes place in a period of history that is rich with developments, not just in Ireland.

We know that *The Tain* takes places sometime around the time of Christ. A single historical reference tells us that Conchobar was king of Ulster in 30 B.C.; according to the *rimsceala*, he became king when he was only seven years old. We can assume that the incident with Deirdre takes place late in his reign, because he has her raised in the forest for almost two decades and then chases her all over Ireland and Scotland for several years. Also, he decides to keep her for himself when he is an adult king. Extrapolating a timeline from those slender clues, I have set this story of Finnabair to begin around A.D. 10 when Conchobar would be around fifty years old. At his death, it is hard to find which of his sons, if any, became king. With the death of the Hound, the power of Ulster declined. After Conchobar, most sources turn toward Meath and the kings who preceded the Fenian Cycle. For a storyteller, Finnchad in his Viking helmet is enough of a caricature to make him hard to resist.

You will note that I have called the Red Branch (Craobh Ruadh) warriors the Royal Branch (Craobh Rioga). Peter Beresford Ellis says that Royal Branch is more likely the true original name, with Red Branch being a historical spelling corruption (despite the red yew in the hall of Emain Macha). That makes sense to me so I have selected that convention.

In the larger world, much was going on at this time that would later have an impact on the history of Ireland. Julius Caesar invaded Britain in 55 B.C. and 54 B.C. Before and after those invasions, he fought the Gallic wars, which were the wars against the Celts of Gaul (France). Those Celtic peoples were killed, enslaved, Romanized, or driven across the water to Britain, Ireland, and Wales. Julius Caesar was assassinated in 44 B.C.

In Egypt, Marc Antony and Cleopatra were killed around 34 B.C. Almost forty years later, Jesus would have been about five years old when he encountered Flavi during his family's sojourn in Egypt.

The Emperor Claudius reinvaded England in A.D. 43, effectively destroying Celtic tribal culture there. It is true, however, that Rome never really colonized Scots or Irish territory, perhaps considering the terrain too rough or the people too crazy, or, in practical Roman fashion, seeing such an invasion as not being cost- effective. For this reason, Celtic culture survived and thrived in Ireland, even after the formal arrival of Christianity.

As those of you who have read my other books know, one of the aspects of history that I have been exploring, as I wend my way backward through time, is the way in which Christianity worked its way into the Celtic consciousness. It had a widespread foothold in Ireland by the time St. Patrick arrived in the fifth century (*I Am of Irelaunde*). How did it get there?

One of the strangest myths concerns Conall Cearnach, who took a stone to the forehead in our story. According to the myth, Conall was so distraught by the death of his friend the Hound that he left Ireland, went to fight among the Romans, was assigned to Judea, and was present at the crucifixion. A second myth concerns Conchobar mac Nessa, who took a brainball in the head at the end of *The Tain*. It didn't kill him, but he was required to live a sedate and quiet life. However, when Conall returned with the story of Christ, Conchobar became so upset by the method of his death that he hauled his sword from his scabbard and went crazy in the Great Hall, exploding the brainball and dying for his efforts. While these are entertaining stories, it is much more likely that Christianity came in story and rumor and borne in the ordinary stories of such travelers as Graccus the centurion.

Whatever the method of entry, for the Celtic, Christian belief was much more a matter of metaphysics than it was of rules and bureaucracy; Celtic Christianity was wonderfully different from the Roman version of Christian practice. (Read Peter Beresford Ellis, John O'Donohue, and Tim Cahill for detailed examples of early Celtic Christian practice.) How did it become that way? I believe that Christianity made its way into the Irish consciousness the way so many things have done—by the interweaving of the old with the new and by the encounters that we could all see and hear if we opened our ears and our eyes.

So, I am looking; I am listening. I hope that these stories help you to do the same.

Bail O Dhia ar an obair
Bless, O God, the work

Juilene Osborne-McKnight

ABOUT THE AUTHOR

Juilene Osborne-McKnight is an accomplished folklorist, storyteller, and teacher on Celtic culture and history. She lives in Pennsylvania. *Bright Sword of Ireland* is her third novel.